# PERFECT
# PARENTS

BOOKS BY L.G. DAVIS

*Liar Liar*

*The Stolen Breath*

*Don't Blink*

*The Midnight Wife*

*The Janitor's Wife*

# PERFECT PARENTS

## L.G. DAVIS

bookouture

Published by Bookouture in 2022

An imprint of Storyfire Ltd.
Carmelite House
50 Victoria Embankment
London EC4Y 0DZ

www.bookouture.com

ISBN: 978-1-80314-671-3
eBook ISBN: 978-1-80314-670-6

*This book is dedicated to my two children, Dara and Simon.*
*Thank you for decorating my life.*

# PROLOGUE

My car swerves into the street and I see the flames in the distance, licking at the sky and brightening the September night. I jump out and slam the door behind me, running toward the crackle and hiss of the fire. The air is filled with the smell of burned wood and charred leaves; thick gray smoke is rising into the night sky, and embers float in the air like fireflies.

As I get closer, waves of heat ripple across my skin and my vision starts to blur in the smoke. Squinting, I see her writhing on the ground, parts of her body and hair ablaze. With panic gripping my chest, I shrug off my long coat and throw it on top of her, hurriedly patting out the flames. The roof of the burning shed starts to collapse next to us, and I pull her up and tug her far away. When we are a good distance from the spreading fire, she collapses on the ground and I call 911.

"Send an ambulance right away," I plead and stumble through the address, coughing as the smoke stings my throat and chest.

"What's the emergency?" the female operator asks, her voice infuriatingly calm and robotic.

"There is a fire and a woman has been hurt." My voice is shaking. "Please hurry. It's bad." I pause and my heart breaks as I say the next words. "We also need the police."

As we wait for the ambulance, I look into the woman's tear-streaked, terrified face, pushing back her hair gently. She must have been so afraid. Looking up at the house, I see a figure staring out of the window and a shiver runs down my spine. I know who it is. I peel my gaze away and turn back to the woman on the ground, placing my hand on her shoulder.

"We'll get you to the hospital, and you'll be fine," I promise her, my voice cracking, my words hollow. She takes a few sharp breaths and, after a fraction of a second, her eyes widen and she begins to shake.

"I can't..." Her eyes begin to close and her breathing grows shallow. She's losing consciousness fast. I desperately try to think of any rudimentary first aid that might help her, as distant sirens fill me with relief.

When the fire truck and ambulance arrive, paramedics rush toward us and firefighters run to what's left of the shed. I sit on the ground, fighting back tears, and watch as they fight to save her life. But I know it could already be too late.

The sirens blare again, and two police cars approach. As soon as I tell them what I think happened, several officers run into the house with their guns drawn, leaving two behind to search the grounds.

"Over here! There's a body," one of the officers says to the other before dropping to the ground near the bushes on one side of the shed. "I'll check for a pulse."

My heart plummets and I run toward him. Collapsing

onto the ground, I see a pair of legs sticking out from under the bushes, and blood pooling beneath the body, dark and thick.

# CHAPTER 1

## PRESENT: 15 NOVEMBER 2018

Marcia Thorpe is sitting at a table by herself, leafing through the restaurant menu and unaware that I'm watching her. What if she's here to tell me they're not interested?

*No way.* Her body language is not that of someone who's about to deliver unpleasant news. She looks relaxed and confident—her posture perfect, long legs crossed under the table, chin tilted upward. As beautiful as she is with her ash-brown hair cut in a layered bob, large brown eyes, and porcelain skin, she also looks thin and delicate. I watch as she pushes her sunglasses up on her head. She's not eyeing the door, chewing her nails, or drinking endless cups of coffee to calm her nerves.

I swallow hard and try to breathe in deeply, but my throat sticks together and I can feel my forehead getting clammy with sweat. I can't go in there looking like a wreck, so I slip unnoticed into the restaurant and hurry to the ladies' room. Surrounded by pristine marble and glass, I splash cool water on my face and try to cover up the dark bags under my ash-gray eyes with my trusted concealer.

These telltale signs of stress, crying, and sleep deprivation have got to go.

I made Marcia the offer of a lifetime on November first, exactly two weeks ago, and I've been waiting with bated breath for an answer. I guess making me wait that long is to be expected; it's not a decision one takes lightly. But what Travis and Marcia Thorpe don't know is that while this is a difficult decision for me too, it is also something I need as much as they do, maybe more. I'd go as far as saying it's a matter of life and death for me, but I can't tell them that. Desperation repels.

After the creamy concealer has done its job and the mascara has thickened and lengthened my eyelashes, I sweep my bone-straight, blue-black hair into a ponytail at the nape of my neck. Hoping I'm now presentable enough, I step out of the ladies' room, dressed in an invisible cloak of false confidence. I'm good at that. It's my disguise, preventing people from seeing who I really am: an empty shell. A snail dried out by the sun until there's nothing left.

It can't be a good sign that Marcia's husband is not here, and the thought fills me with anxiety. Wouldn't they want to share the big news together? I've only met him once, when Marcia invited me to dinner at their home in Wellice, a seven-hour drive from Miami. She's the one I have spent the most time with, mostly online but also in person when I visited Wellice four months ago and when she came to Miami for a photo shoot. She is the face of MereLux & Co., a luxury jewelry multinational company owned by her family.

I walk over to the table and, when she sees me, her face lights up and she gets to her feet, but I notice a slight waver in her smile. Maybe she's wearing the same cloak of false confidence as I am. She looks different from the last time I saw her, too. She's lost a lot of weight in a short amount of time, and her tall frame is like a coatrack. Then again, as a model, maybe that's the look she's going for.

"Hi, Grace," she says, air-kissing me on both cheeks.

When she pulls away, I see it—the deep pain swirling in her eyes. I've seen it before, many times. And now it's up to me to make it melt away.

"Where's your husband?" I ask as I lower myself onto a padded chair.

Marcia sits back down. "Travis is upstairs; he had a call to make. He should be down shortly." She picks up the menu again. "While we wait for him, why don't you order yourself something to eat?"

"Nothing for me, thank you; I've already eaten." It's a lie, but until I know what Travis and Marcia have decided, I'll be too anxious to keep any food down.

"Okay," Marcia says. "How about some champagne?"

That's when I notice it: the chilling bottle of Dom Pérignon in a sweating silver bucket.

A pulse throbs at the base of my throat, followed by a thrill that surges through my body.

"Are we celebrating?" I ask, my voice wavering.

Marcia sets her palms flat on the table and leans forward. "Well, I was going to wait until Travis joins us, but I'm not a patient person."

"Have you decided?" I sit up straighter, put both my hands on my knees, and hold on to them.

"We *have* decided," she says with a soft smile. "Grace, we want you to be our surrogate."

Tears sting my eyes, and I lift the glass of water from the place setting in front of me, my hand shaking. It's really happening, and suddenly I'm not sure how to feel. Excited? Scared?

"What do you say?" She leans back and chews a corner of her lip. "Please don't say you changed your mind. Sorry we made you wait, but this is a big decision."

"No." I blink away my tears. "I didn't change my mind. I just... This is great news."

"That's absolutely wonderful." Marcia dabs at her eyes with a napkin before squeezing my hands tight. I can't tell if both our palms are sweating or just mine.

"I was so scared that you might decide it's not for you after all." She pauses. "Are you sure you want to do it for free? We have a huge budget set aside, you know."

I smile and nod. "I wouldn't have it any other way."

She studies my face for a few seconds, then she sweeps her hair aside. "I still don't really understand, Grace. It's so generous of you, but why would you want to do this for free for us... total strangers?"

"We're not strangers, Marcia," I say. "I like to think we're friends now."

"Friends," she repeats. "Yes, I like that, that's what we are. It's strange, but I feel like I have known you forever."

"Let me guess," a deep voice says from behind me. "You've already told her, haven't you?"

I turn to see Marcia's husband Travis arriving at our table in slacks and a black polo shirt. He's a handsome man in a rugged kind of way, with a chiseled jawline, denim-blue eyes, and sandy-blond hair that's the right kind of messy. I'd place him in his early forties, at least five years older than Marcia. When I met him for the first time, I was impressed by his kindness and humility, especially because even though he lives a wealthy lifestyle now, he wasn't ashamed of the fact that he grew up in a trailer park in Fort Lauderdale and how poor his family was. His humble demeanor made him relatable and easy to talk to.

Travis shakes my hand and kisses his wife on the lips before sitting down with his arm around her.

He turns to me again with a warm smile that crinkles the corners of his eyes. "Grace, it's really good to see you again and we are so grateful for your incredibly generous offer. You have no idea how much this means to Marcia and me. But I'm afraid I have to ask: why would you do this for us... for anyone?"

I guess I will have to get used to answering that question.

I shrug and return his smile. "I like making people happy."

"You're definitely succeeding at that." He folds his arms on the table. "Marcia mentioned that you haven't done this before."

I stiffen. "No, but I'm registered with several Florida-based surrogacy agencies."

"And they didn't find you a lucky couple?"

"There were a few interested people, but I'm picky. I wanted a couple I was drawn to." I rub my hands on my thighs. "Marcia and I have become close too, and it means a lot to me to be able to do this for friends."

"Friends," he says and the word hangs in the air between us. "I like that you see us in that light. We are so excited about this, and very grateful and honored that you chose us."

"We've wanted a baby for some time," Marcia adds, tears clinging to her eyelashes like dewdrops. "I feel like such a failure, but—"

"You don't have to feel that way." I reach a hand toward her across the table. "Asking for help is not a weakness."

"Thank you, Grace." Travis takes my hand in his. He

has soft hands for a man, softer than mine will ever be no matter how many creams I use.

"You're welcome. But I do think you should stop thanking me; we still have a long road ahead of us."

"But this is a huge first step," Travis says. "I just know it will go well."

"Honey," Marcia scolds, nudging him playfully in the side, "don't put pressure on her."

But that's exactly what he's doing. What if it doesn't work out? What if I give them hope and end up taking it away? No, I choose to believe that this was meant to be. It will happen. It has to.

"Let's believe everything will work out fine," I say to Travis.

"You are aware that this is going to be a traditional surrogacy, right?"

"Yes, Marcia and I talked about it."

She cried when she told me that, if we decided to do it, they would be using my eggs instead of hers. She will obtain a pre-birth parentage order that will allow her name to be on their child's birth certificate.

"And you don't want a family of your own?" Travis asks, gently.

"Of course. Of course I do. But not yet."

"I'm sure you realize how much you're sacrificing." He pauses. "This is your life and we don't want to disrupt it in any way."

I raise my gaze to his face again. I want him to believe every word I'm saying. "Yes, I'm well aware. I want to do this for you."

"I'm sorry to push you, Grace. It's just... This is a big deal for us."

When I look at Marcia, she's smiling widely with happy

tears coating her eyes. I wish I could pull her into a hug, suck up the joy she's exuding right now in the hope that it would melt away the darkness inside me.

"What are the next steps?" I ask her.

"We've already spoken to our lawyers and they're ready to draw up the papers. Of course, you will have to go through a few medical tests."

"I fully understand. I'm ready for it all."

"Good." She pulls the champagne bottle from the bucket and hands it to Travis, her eyes still on me. "Grace, you won't have to do this alone. We'll be by your side every step of the way."

The only thing left to do is to celebrate, and we do exactly that, with the entire bottle of champagne. Travis tries again to convince me to eat with them, but I decline.

"I'm meeting up with a friend. But I'm so happy we're going ahead, and whatever you need from me, just let me know."

Later, moments before stepping out the restaurant door, I look back at them and see Travis moving his chair closer to his wife, and drawing her in for a passionate kiss that ends with them smiling and gazing happily into each other's eyes, oblivious to the world around them.

I did that, I tell myself. I made them happy.


Half an hour later, my best friend Sydney Rivers is standing in front of me at our favorite steakhouse in downtown Miami, near my studio apartment. She's tall and slim, with a natural beauty that is admired by men and women alike. With her high cheekbones, long, slender neck, and golden-flecked brown eyes, she has a regal appearance wherever she goes.

"You look happy." She drops her cellphone into her crystal-beaded handbag.

Sydney is a handbag kind of girl, and when she's not selling houses, she's on the hunt for the next piece to add to her collection.

"Maybe that's because I *am* happy." I beam at her. I haven't said those words to anyone in quite some time.

The handle of her bag slides to the crook of her elbow as she gathers her dark-brown hair into a fluffy afro puff on top of her head with the help of an elastic band from around her wrist. "Did something amazing happen?"

"That's right," I say, as we walk into the restaurant. "I got some exciting news today."

We're seated at a table next to a wall with a colorful photo display of regular customers, including one of us.

"If anyone deserves good news, it's you, Grace Cooper," Sydney says. "Care to share it?"

"Let's order first."

I need a delay before I break the news to her. I know I might not get the reaction I'm hoping for. We make small talk until a waiter brings us our usual steak and fries, and Sydney watches me over her food as we eat in silence. I have a feeling she's nervous about what I'm about to say too, and that's why she's hesitant to bring it up again. Instead, she asks me how work is going. She's not happy when I tell her I took yet another day off, but she lets it slide.

Sydney talked her sister, Camille, into giving me a job at her flower shop, Dear Blooms. It's not my dream job, but it's something to keep me busy while I sort out my life.

"All right," she says finally. "Tell me the good news. What's going on with you?"

"I met up with the Thorpes."

"The Thorpes?" She raises an eyebrow. "The couple you told me about a while back?"

"Yep, the family I want to surrogate for." I'm not sure whether that's a verb, but if not, now it is, and I plan on using it.

Sydney drops her fork onto her plate. "You still want to be a surrogate? I thought it was a phase."

"It's not." My words come out sharper than I expected them to. "I'm serious about this, Sydney. They want me to give them a baby, and I agreed."

"Oh my God, Grace. Do you understand the implications this will have for your life?"

"Of course I do. I'm just going to have to put my life on hold for a little while, so I can make a nice couple happy."

"You don't even know them."

"I do! I feel like I know Marcia really well now. She's become a friend."

Sydney draws a hand across her eyes and down her face, and when she drops it, I see the concern blazing in her eyes. "I don't think you should do this. If you want to feel better about what happened, there are other ways."

"Not for me. You know what I went through, better than anyone." I pick up the napkin and twist it between my fingers. "You know how close I came—"

"But this is going too far. It's such an extreme way to make yourself feel better and, honestly, it might do the opposite."

"Look," I say, annoyance flaring up inside me. "I don't expect you to understand. This is probably strange to you, but I want to do it. You're my friend and I'm hoping you will support me. Nothing you say will change my mind."

She reaches across the table and rests a hand on my arm. "I'm trying, Grace. I'm trying to understand. If this is what you want, I don't have a choice, do I?" She pauses. "I just don't want you to make a mistake."

"I won't. I've made many mistakes in my life, and this is not one of them. It's hard, but it's one of my best decisions."

"Okay, so what happens next?" Sydney pushes away her food and folds her arms, her leg jiggling nervously.

"It means the papers will be drawn up and signed soon, and I'll go through some tests. After that, I'll get meds to help the eggs develop, then the egg retrieval procedure will start and—"

Her head snaps back and her eyebrows shoot up. "They will be using your eggs—?"

"Yes." I cut her off. "But it's not going to be my baby, not in the end. It will be theirs." I refuse to go down that rabbit hole.

"But it will be your DNA, Grace. How can you ignore that?"

"Please, Sydney, I'd appreciate it if you don't push me on this. I'll be making this couple's dream come true, and this is something I want to do. Let's just leave it at that."

"I know, but you have to understand that, as your friend, I just don't want you to end up regretting this. You're going to give up a child." She blinks back tears. "Grace, I have two kids. I can never imagine giving them up."

"Of course not, they're your children," I say. "The baby I'm going to carry won't be mine. It will be the Thorpes' kid."

"Okay." She sighs. "I'm just trying to save you from pain."

"I'm already in pain, Sydney. You know that." I bite down on my trembling lip. "You might think I'm only doing this for them, but they will be doing something for me too. I need this."

"How much?" She lobs the question at me like a tennis ball. "How much are they paying you for this?"

"Nothing," I say, looking down at my food. "I'm not doing this for money."

"You're kidding me, right?" Her voice is sharp now. "This is crazy, Grace. You'll be sacrificing so much for them and they're not even going to pay you?"

"No, they wanted to pay me a lot of money, but I told them I don't need... I don't want their money. Aside for the medical bills, of course. This is a gift and, honestly, it's as much of a gift to myself as it is to them."

Sydney shakes her head. "You might not want to hear this, but I'll say it, anyway: I think you're making a big mistake. You're going to regret this."

"Fine," I say, stubbornly. "I know in my heart that this is the right thing to do. I'm willing to pay the price."

# CHAPTER 2

Dr. Simon Kim, a top Miami OB/GYN, looks up from the papers on his desk and smiles. "Congratulations. You're going to be parents."

The doctor, who seems to be in his forties, is a man of average build, with a receding hairline and thick glasses. His voice is slow and steady, and he enunciates each word slowly and carefully without moving his lips much.

His dark gaze flits between Travis and Marcia, and I am ignored.

Marcia's hand flies to her mouth and she lets out a squeal of delight. "It worked?"

The doctor's smile widens. "It sure did. You're one of the lucky ones. The expected due date is the twenty-fifth of September."

My hand goes to my stomach, and I feel suddenly quite emotional. I keep telling myself I'm only the surrogate, but now that the pregnancy is a reality, I feel an unexpected connection to the baby growing inside me. I don't want to feel this way—it's going to make everything so much harder —but I can't help it. It's as if my maternal instincts are trying to take over my brain. But I can't let that happen, so I try to ignore my emotions and lock them deep within me.

When the doctor exits the room to offer us privacy, Travis jumps from his seat and strides over to the window, his hands clenching and unclenching, and the excitement that has been building up inside my chest turns icy cold. What if he regrets this? But when he turns around and walks back, the beaming smile on his face makes me release my breath. He pulls Marcia, who is weeping gently, from her chair and into his arms, holding her tight.

"I'm going to be a father," he says, looking at me over Marcia's shoulder. A tear trickles down his cheek.

Marcia breaks the embrace first and turns to me.

"Thank you so much, Grace," she says, her voice thick with tears. She wraps me in her arms and the scents of jasmine and sandalwood soothe me. For a small and frail woman, she's surprisingly strong. We cling to each other, crying and laughing at the same time.

It both comforts and terrifies me to know that this is really going to happen. What if I fail? Reports show that one in eight pregnancies end in miscarriage. I found out I was pregnant a week ago, but I kept it to myself and did several more tests to make sure. All of them were positive. When I told Marcia over the phone two days ago, she said they'd fly to Miami. They wanted to be present when the pregnancy was confirmed by a doctor. And now we know: it's really happening.

She finally lets go of me, and Travis takes her place and gives me a warm hug. "Thank you so much, Grace."

"We should celebrate," Marcia suggests. "Come to the hotel with us. Let's have lunch together."

"I'd love to, but I can't, I'm sorry. I have to go back to work."

Work. Every time I say the word, I think of the job I used to have, the one I lost. It's hard to believe that I was once the senior editor at *Living It*, a motivational magazine whose mission was to empower and inspire women in life and business. I had a great salary, a lavish townhouse, and a life I loved. Now I'm working at a job that doesn't light me up inside and only helps me pass the time. Being surrounded by flowers three days a week doesn't appeal to me.

My love for flowers has also been tainted by the anonymous bouquets of blood-red roses that I receive every few months. The last arrived two weeks ago with a note that read: *Thinking of you, Grace. I'm never far away*.

The person never leaves a name, but I know who it is, and I wish I could stop them. I wish I knew how they keep finding me.

"Is that a good idea?" Travis raises his eyebrows.

"What do you mean?" Marcia asks, frowning.

He puts an arm around her. "Work might be too stressful, especially with Grace being on her feet all day. She could take a break for a while and we can support her."

"I agree with Travis." Marcia puts her hand on my shoulder. "Let us support you financially during this time. You don't have to work at all."

"Really? I... I don't know what to say."

My instinct is to tell her that I love my job and want to continue working, but I'd be lying. The past few months have been hard, but I haven't given up my florist job because I didn't want to disappoint Sydney, and I do need the money. Plus, I'd had so much trouble holding down a job before that.

"You know what?" Travis says. "You don't have to give

us an answer now. Give it some thought and let us know what you decide. We'll do whatever you want."

Marcia grins at her husband, her face glowing with happiness as her eyes light up from within. The smile even makes her normally thin cheeks round and rosy like those of a little girl.

When the doctor returns to the room, he briefs me on everything I need to know as a newly pregnant woman. He tells me about the medications I should or should not take, the food I need to avoid and goes through all the important appointments I'm supposed to keep during the nine months of pregnancy. I'm familiar with everything he's telling me. I've googled it all and read lots of books about it. Marcia, on the other hand, is taking notes and occasionally looking up at the doctor as if she's in a lecture.

Finally, the three of us exit the sleek glass and steel building together into the cold winter air. The silence is instantly replaced by the sounds of a buzzing Miami city street, with car horns honking, cellphones ringing, and heels tapping against the sidewalk.

Marcia pulls me into another hug. "Thank you, so much. You have no idea how much this means to us." She repeats their offer to support me financially.

"I have an even better idea," Travis counters. "Move in with us. We have enough space."

Marcia glances in surprise at her husband before turning to smile at me. "That's a fantastic idea," she says. "You could stay in our guesthouse, and we'd get a chance to be a part of the pregnancy. And all your expenses would be paid, of course."

My mind flits back to those roses, and I realize that this could be an excellent opportunity to free myself from the past and go off-grid for a while. Perhaps this is exactly what

I need, and their offer is another sign that they're the perfect parents for the baby.

"That's... well, that's generous of you," I say, touched by their kindness.

"No, Grace, what you're doing for us is more generous than anything you could ever imagine." Marcia blinks away the moisture in her eyes. "It worked. Can you believe it?"

I shake my head and smile. "No, I can't. I'm so happy for you both."

"Let us know what you decide," Travis says, giving me one last hug as their cab pulls up and they step inside.

I remain standing in front of the building, tempted to put my hands on my belly again. A baby is growing inside me. Slowly, joy blooms inside my chest and spreads to my entire body. I haven't felt this content in a while. I just stand there grinning, and the people walking by glance at me suspiciously. But I don't care. Having a child gives me a renewed sense of purpose and a sense of self-worth, something I have been lacking these last few months and years. Until now, I've been going through the motions without feeling as though I was truly living. But now I'm doing something that matters, something that's bigger than just me. I feel like a bird with broken wings flying at last through a cloudless blue sky.

When I climb into a cab and lean my head back, tears finally come. I lied when I told Marcia and Travis I was going back to work. I've taken another day off. I didn't want them to worry, but I spent most of the morning on my knees in front of the toilet, retching. Hopefully, the morning sickness won't last for very long. Marcia and Travis's offer is a tempting one, particularly given how awful I've been feeling these past few weeks. And, if I don't work, I'll be able to focus entirely on the baby and make sure I have no stress that could negatively impact the pregnancy.

I can already see it in my mind, their happy faces as I hand them the baby and he or she grasps hold of their fingers and looks into their eyes. I hold on to that thought until I enter my apartment.

As usual, it's dark inside: I hardly open the blinds anymore. But not today. Today I let the light in and it floods the room, revealing the surrounding mess. The high ceilings, molding, and big windows would make my apartment look bigger than it is, but all the junk lying around makes it feel claustrophobic. There are fast-food cartons and old newspapers lying everywhere, clothes hanging from the backs of chairs. A bra on top of the TV.

Shame warms my cheeks. If it weren't for Sydney getting me the place for cheap, at least for now, I'd never have been able to afford to live in this part of town. But, instead of being grateful, I've turned it into a dumpster. Disgusted at myself, I throw open the windows, play a pop song from my feel-good playlist, and launch myself headfirst into scrubbing, dusting, and wiping every surface until it gleams.

It takes me over an hour before I see any progress, and I'm busy wiping the dishes in the kitchenette when the doorbell rings. I ignore it. If it's a delivery, they can leave it outside. I'm not expecting visitors. But it rings again, and again. Confused, I make my way to the door and pick up the receiver.

"Grace, it's me. Open up."

My heart sinks. It's Sydney. I haven't spoken to her for two days, not since I told her I was pregnant. She hung up and didn't answer when I called back. I can guess where this conversation will go and, frankly, I'm not in the mood for it.

The first thing she does when she comes upstairs is glance at my stomach, before even looking into my face.

"If you're here to judge me, don't. I can't afford to be stressed right now."

She closes the door and turns to me. "I'm here because I care about you."

I do know she cares about me. We've known each other since college, and she always had my back. She was by my side when my life was coming undone. She held me when I cried, was silent when I didn't want to speak, and listened when I was ready. She helped me piece my life back together and get used to my new normal. But I'm tired of constantly trying to convince her that what I'm doing is right for me, and nothing she can say or do will change my mind. It's too late now, anyway.

She looks around my apartment and raises her eyebrows. "Wow, it's clean around here. You must be feeling better."

"I feel great." I fold my arms across my chest.

"I'm glad to hear that. I mean it, Grace."

"But you still don't agree with what I'm doing."

"How could I? You're throwing your life away. Instead of starting over and giving yourself a chance, you're giving a chance to someone else. All because you want to get rid of your guilt. What happened is not your fault."

"We both know that's not true."

She takes a seat on the couch next to Barney, the one-eyed teddy bear I've had since I was a child. I sit next to her and put my hand on hers.

"I need to do this. I can't let them down. I've signed a contract now, anyway."

"Contracts are broken all the time, just like promises. It will be unpleasant, but—"

I snatch my hand away. "I can't believe you're telling me this right now. Especially since you know what happened."

"I'm sorry." Her eyes are damp, and we sit in silence for a few minutes before she speaks again. "Okay, if this is what you want, I'll do my best to support you. But I can't promise that I won't bring it up again. I'm your friend, and it's my responsibility to look out for you."

"I do appreciate you, but this is really important to me. I need you to respect my decision."

"I guess I don't have a choice, do I?" She pulls me close. "Promise me that after the baby comes, you will get your life together and focus on you."

I pull away from her and smile. "I can promise you that."

As I say the words to her, I make the same promise to myself. Once this is done, I'll have a clean slate to start over. I don't know whether I'll be happy—maybe I'll never really be happy again—but at least I'll be able to sleep better.

"Camille told me you didn't come to work this entire week," Sydney says finally.

I get to my feet and go to the small kitchen, only a few steps from the couch. "Do you want some tea?" I ask, my back turned to her.

"You won't get out of this conversation. Don't even try."

I turn around to face her. "I wasn't feeling well today. Morning sickness."

There's so much at stake for me right now. Going to a job I don't like and having to deal with customers who stress me out can't be good for me and the baby.

"You don't want this job, do you?" she asks. "I'm getting the feeling you want out."

"I'm sorry. I tried to like it, but it's not my thing. I wanted it to work out, but it's a stepping stone and nothing more. I did tell you it wouldn't be permanent."

"I know. I just wanted you to have something to do." She crosses her legs. "What are your plans? It will be hard for you to find a job while pregnant."

I pour myself a glass of lemon-flavored water and walk back to the couch. "Actually, I don't need to work, not right now. The Thorpes made me an offer."

"What kind of offer?"

"They want to contribute to my living expenses."

"They should; that's the least they can do. I still don't understand why you're doing it for free."

I take a sip of my water, ignoring her tone. "They offered me a place to stay... in Wellice."

"Excuse me? They want you to move?" Sydney's voice is louder now. "They're asking you to give up everything? Why not just mail you a check every month?"

"They want to be involved in this pregnancy as much as possible. I think it's a good idea; I'm thinking of accepting the offer. And I'm not really giving up much. I'll be moving out of here soon anyways since the rent is going to go up at renewal. This way, I won't need to look for a new place just yet. And if I'm gone for a while, maybe I'll stop getting those roses."

To be honest, the apartment also reminds me of the depression and loneliness that consumed me here, so I won't miss it all that much.

"That makes sense." Sydney presses her lips together. "But what if you don't get along with the Thorpes? You hardly know them and living with them for so long could be awkward. I think you should think it over for a while."

"You know what?" I say. "The pregnancy will bind me to them whether I live with them or not." I pause and place my hands on her shoulders. "Stop worrying so much. They're good people and I know the baby and I will be in safe hands."

# CHAPTER 3
## THURSDAY, 27 JUNE 2013

My phone beeps inside my bag for the third time, but I don't check to see who it is. Thirty more minutes and the brainstorming meeting with the *Living It* features team will be over. It's late June and the ideas for our ten-year anniversary November issue are flowing nicely. Next week we'll start the process of turning those ideas into a magazine in time to meet the deadlines set by the printer and the circulation department. The phone call will just have to wait; I can't allow anything to break the momentum. But when the phone vibrates again less than five minutes later, I take a peek and my sister Rachel's name flashes on the screen. Like her husband, Peter, she never calls me at work—not unless it's an emergency.

"Excuse me, guys. I need to take this." I take the call into the hallway.

"Rachel, are you okay? Is everything all right with the baby?" I press the phone harder against my ear, my eyes shut tight.

"No." The whispered word is barely audible, her voice smothered by tears. "I need you."

"Where are you?"

"Bathroom. At home."

"Okay. Hang in there. I'm on my way."

Maybe it's nothing. If it were something serious, she would have called 911, right? But she called me. It's the first time she's had a pregnancy go beyond twelve weeks. Surely fate wouldn't deal my sister another blow. Not after she's already lost three babies before she got a chance to hold them in her arms.

When I make it through the dead river of cars from my office in Brickell to their semi-detached home in Edgewater, she doesn't open the door so I use my spare key.

"Rachel, are you home?" I call, and when she doesn't respond, I run upstairs to the master bathroom, where she said she was. As soon as I enter the room, I skid to a halt in the doorway. My heart plummets at the sight of blood and I clutch my hand to my mouth.

"Not again," I whisper, and stumble back downstairs.

On my way out the front door, I catch sight of her neighbor Molly, staring at me from over the fence with a head full of curlers.

"Hi, Grace," she calls. I've been at Rachel's house often enough for everyone to know I'm her twin sister. "Is Rachel okay?" she asks, coming over to the fence.

"What did... what happened to her? Do you know?"

"There was an ambulance," she says. "They took her away. You don't know anything about it?"

I shake my head, my breath unsteady. "Do you know which hospital they took her to?"

"I'm sorry, I didn't speak to anyone. Peter wasn't home. I do pray that the baby is all right."

"Me too," I say, walking swiftly to my Toyota Prius. "I'll give him a call."

"You do that. Please tell Rachel we're here for her if she needs anything."

In the car, I dial Peter's phone number and he picks up on the second ring.

"Peter, what happened?" I ask.

"She's in hospital." There's a rush of breath before he continues, "The baby..." his voice drifts off before he can finish the sentence, but the pain between his words says enough.

"No, Peter." I swallow hard. "Please, tell me it's not—" He doesn't respond, not that I expect him to. "Which hospital? Where are you?"

"Dawson Hill Memorial," he says, and hangs up.

I arrive at the hospital forty minutes later. Shivering, I stumble out of the car and into the air-conditioned building. The spacious hospital has beige walls, white linoleum floors, and framed windows overlooking a parking lot. The smells of disinfectants and cleaning solutions are heavy in the air.

As soon as I arrive in the waiting room of the ER, I see Peter sitting in the corner, his eyes closed and his head tilted back.

"Peter?"

I touch his shoulder when he doesn't respond and he flinches and looks up at me with swollen, red-rimmed eyes.

My heart jumps to my throat. "Peter, what happened? Is the baby—?"

"Not good." He gets to his feet and goes to the window. His shoulders shake with sobs as he confirms my worst fears, that they have lost yet another unborn child.

"Oh, Peter, I'm so sorry." My eyes well up with tears as I go and pull him into my arms. His tears soak my shirt as he sobs into my shoulder, but I don't care.

Hugging him is like hugging a tree trunk. He is not only

several heads taller than me but also broad and muscular, exactly the kind of guy Rachel has always been attracted to. But I know that, underneath all the layers of muscle, Peter is a softy who draws kids to him like moths to a flame.

He pulls away and drops into one of the heavy plastic chairs that are bolted to the wall, his head in his hands. I sit down next to him, staring at my feet.

"How's Rachel?" It's a stupid question, but I need to know how badly she has taken this.

He raises his liquid blue eyes to me. "She's devastated."

"Do you think I can see her?"

"I don't think so. She asked me to leave, she wanted to be alone."

We remain in the waiting room for the next hour until we are given permission to see her. Rachel is lying in bed but, even though she's staring at us, she doesn't acknowledge us when we enter. She looks exhausted and gaunt, with dark rings around her gray eyes. Even though we have the same black hair, today hers seems dull and lifeless, and her skin is almost yellow as if she's jaundiced.

She finally fixes her gaze to the ceiling, and when I speak, she doesn't react at all. I don't understand how Rachel and Peter have handled it, how they could experience so much pain over and over again and still haven't stopped trying. They even picked out a name already. They always pick out a name.

After a while, Peter breaks down again and leaves the room so Rachel won't see him grieve.

I take my sister's hand in mine, my heart breaking. "Rachel, sweetie..." I search my mind for something else to say, but there's nothing. Sorry doesn't exactly cut it anymore.

The sound of her voice startles me. "I didn't... I didn't

think it would happen again." She moves her gaze from the ceiling to my face and her dry and colorless lips part. "I thought this was it."

She uses the same words every time she loses a baby. Each time she holds out hope, and every time she gets crushed in the end.

"I can't do this again," she says, her voice low and quiet, tightening her fingers around mine.

That is the first time on her long, painful quest to becoming a mother that she's admitted defeat. I move my forehead to hers and close my eyes, offering her comfort with my actions instead of my words. I don't trust myself to speak. I'm afraid that if I do, I will be unable to stop my tears.

"Grace, I need you to do something for me," she says.

I open my eyes and lift my head. "Anything."

She blows out a breath. "This may be too much to ask, but I really need you."

"I'm your sister," I assure her. "I will help in any way I can."

Since we were sixteen and our parents died in a car accident, Rachel has always been there for me. Now it's my turn to take care of her.

"Please have the baby for us, Grace," she says, her pain-filled eyes fixed on mine.

My body vibrates with shock as I walk into my living room and sit on the edge of my cream, three-seater leather couch, which I bought when I first started working at *Living It* magazine. It was a splurge, but it matches the elegant yet comfortable feel of my living room, with its hardwood floors and high-vaulted ceilings. A granite fireplace dominates one wall and is the focal point of the room, serving more of a decorative role than a functional one as it gives the place a cozy feel. On the creamy walls are framed black-and-white photos of friends and family, and Rachel smiles back at me from most of them. As my gaze moves to the colorful fish in the aquarium on one side of the living room, I think about her request.

If I do this for her, it will change both of our lives forever. Desperate to see the pain melt from her eyes, I surprised both of us by saying yes, immediately. But now doubt clouds my mind. Did I make the right decision? There are so many things to consider. Chad, my long-term boyfriend, is one of them, and he's on his way to see me right now. Over the phone, I told him about what happened to Rachel and Peter, but I didn't reveal the promise I made. Some things need to be said in person.

By the time Chad arrives, I'm a mess and he takes me into his arms to comfort me. It's not the first time, but I have lost a niece, and I can't stop thinking about the indescribable pain on Peter and Rachel's faces. I don't say much as he warms up some leftover pasta and puts on a comedy which I can't focus on, and after a while, I pick up the remote and switch off the TV.

"Hey," I say, turning to face him. "I need to talk to you about something. Rachel asked me to do something for her." I chew the inside of my cheek. "She asked me to be their surrogate."

"Their what?" He sweeps the dark, wavy hair from his forehead and narrows his eyes. "Did you say surrogate?"

"She's lost so many babies... she can't go through it again. So she wants me to carry a baby for them."

Chad picks up his glass of water and downs it in one go, then he just stares up at the ceiling.

"Say something, Chad. Please." I hold my breath and wait for him to speak. I have so many doubts now, and I need someone to assure me I made the right decision.

"What do you want me to say?" He picks up his glass again, lifting it all the way to his lips, only to realize it's empty. He lowers it onto the coffee table with a thud. "Tell me you're not going to do it."

I avert my gaze. "I—"

"Grace, you're not going to do it, are you?"

"My sister has suffered so much already. How could I say no?"

His eyes narrow. "You already agreed to do it? Without even talking to me."

"Yes. I did say yes." After the word has crossed my lips, I can't go back. "Rachel was so happy, so relieved. If you saw the look on her face—"

"What were you thinking, Grace?" he says through gritted teeth.

"I was thinking that Rachel was in pain. She lost a baby and she needs my help." Anger flares up inside my belly and pours out into my words. "I was hoping you would understand."

"I do understand. I understand that you want to make your sister feel better." He rakes a hand through his hair. "But this is a big deal. This will change your life." He grabs both my shoulders. "You're going to have a baby for somebody else, carry a real baby for nine months, then just give it away."

"Yes, that's what surrogacy is. But that's not what you're concerned about. Am I right? You're worried about us." I take his hand. "Baby, if I do this, it won't change our relationship."

Even as I say the words, I don't believe them. He gets off

the couch and walks to the window, and when he turns to face me, his expression is hard, emotionless.

"I love you," he says. "I want a future for us, but you have to admit that this will complicate things."

"I love you too. But I couldn't say no to her."

He comes back over, drops to his knees, and takes my hands again. "It can be undone. I'm sure she will understand if you change your mind. There are agencies out there that will help them connect with the right woman, someone who does this for a living."

"But no one would be as invested as I am in her happiness. I'm her sister."

I feel him pull away before he even withdraws his touch. "Don't do it, Grace. Don't do this to us."

"I'm sorry, but this is my decision. I understand that it will affect you, and that's why I will respect whatever decision you make after tonight." I close my eyes, feeling suddenly exhausted.

"You didn't even have enough time to think about it. You have no idea how you'll feel about this in the morning."

He has a point: the next morning, I wake up feeling scared and overwhelmed. But it's too late to back out. Rachel has called me several times from the hospital and sent endless messages to thank me. Even Peter has sent me a long email, telling me how happy I have made them. I can't let them down; Chad will just have to understand. While I'm brushing my teeth, another call comes in from Rachel.

"How are you feeling today?" I ask, studying my tired reflection in the bright gold-framed LED mirror. It's rectangular, and nearly fills an entire bathroom wall.

"I'm all right. I just wanted to say—"

"You don't need to," I cut her off. "No need to thank me again."

"I do. You don't understand. What you're doing for us means the world." Her voice trembles with each word. "You have no idea."

I put the call on speaker and sink onto the lip of the oval bathtub, digging my toes into the plush, white mat. "It's okay. I want to do this because I love you. We've always been there for each other. Why stop now?" I let out a long breath. "Whatever you need me to sign, I'm ready."

# CHAPTER 4
## PRESENT

On Tuesday, 2 April, as the plane rises higher in the skies above Miami International Airport, I close my eyes and lean back into the leather headrest. I used to be a fan of flying. I loved the anonymity of the airport, the steady sounds of engines, the clinking of items touching on a beverage cart, the click of seatbelts locking into place. I looked forward to the cocktail of perfumes and colognes mixed with fresh coffee and food served to passengers. Anything that had to do with flying used to give me a rush.

That was the Grace I used to be. Now a lot of things that used to appeal to me no longer have the same effect. I draw in a deep breath and wait for it to wash away some of the anxiety that has coursed through my veins for years. The baby I'm carrying is not only a new start for the Thorpes but also for me.

My eyes snap open when his face appears behind my eyelids. I can't think of him. Not now, not ever again. I grit my teeth, wishing I could keep the memories from following me to Wellice. I'm so tired of running from the past, and to grow a healthy baby I need to be in the right state of mind. I push my hand inside my handbag and touch the bottle of Xanax. I don't intend on taking any of the pills again, but it somehow makes me feel better knowing they're there.

Breathing deeply, I remind myself of how excited the Thorpes looked when they found out I was pregnant, almost three months ago. I can't let them down. I can't let myself down. I keep breathing slowly until my mind is clear, but dizziness takes the place of anxiety. One of the flight attendants brings me some water, and I take a couple of sips and imagine the stream flowing into my belly, where the baby is resting, protected until I bring it into the world.

During the first weeks of my pregnancy, Marcia and Travis traveled back and forth between Wellice and Miami in order to be present for every checkup. Although some of the appointments were mandatory, they insisted I see a doctor at least once a fortnight. I planned on moving to Wellice soon after I found out I was pregnant, but it was harder than I expected. It was not an easy task to leave everything I knew behind, even if it wasn't much.

"Are you okay?" the old lady next to me asks. "Your hands are shaking."

I glance at my hands and clasp them together. "I'm fine, thanks."

I try to force a smile, but it feels more like a grimace. The woman continues to stare at me curiously, as though she is expecting me to spill my secrets. Years ago, I used to be an outgoing person, someone who found it easy to strike up a conversation with a stranger. The skill had served me well in the magazine industry, but that person is long gone. Soon, the woman gets back to her *Miami Times*, and I pull out my phone and read a text from Sydney. She sent it shortly after she dropped me off at the airport, but I didn't get a chance to read it before now.

*Grace, I hope you find what you're looking for.*

She's still not on board with my decision, and when we were together we avoided the topic completely. But my growing belly is going to get hard to ignore. Maybe going away isn't such a bad thing.

I close my eyes again and squeeze them tight. Instead of thinking about the past, I force myself to focus on the future, visualizing myself giving birth to a healthy baby and handing it over to Marcia and Travis. Even though I've formed a friendship with Marcia, when the baby arrives, we'll all go our separate ways. It's better like that.

There are no major airports in Wellice, so Marcia will be picking me up from Tallahassee, which is only a thirty-minute drive to Wellice. I wanted to take the train, but they insisted I fly and, since they offered to pay for my ticket, I didn't argue. They've been so very generous, so attentive to everything and anything I might need.

Half an hour into our flight, a violent shake of the airplane sends my heart into my throat, but the pilot's voice fills the cabin to assure us that it is only minor turbulence. All is well, I tell myself and my baby. Life can't possibly throw any more pain my way. It will all be okay.

Of course, I knew from the start how desperate Marcia was to have a baby, but I had no idea until now just how excited she is. As I step out of her bronze Tesla, I'm met by the sight of a beautiful tree house with a river running past it. Hanging from a different branch of the same tree is a swing covered with ivy and pink flowers wrapped around it. There's even a pink trampoline in the grounds, ready for the new arrival. They seem to have two expectations, that the baby will be a girl and that it will come out of the womb already walking and ready to play. Aside from two old tool sheds, there are two other buildings on the property, and the large one, which I suspect is the main house, is painted a soft shade of pink.

"We had the house painted two weeks ago," Marcia says to me.

"I see," I say, my voice a touch too squeaky.

I should be excited that they're getting ready for the baby, but it's so much pressure. And even though I know the chances are slim, I can't stop worrying that something is going to go wrong. Maybe Sydney was right; maybe it wasn't a good idea for me to come to Wellice after all.

"It's so beautiful here," I say, because I can see Marcia is waiting for compliments.

"Thank you. I can't wait for the baby to live here. I do hope it's a girl," she says, smiling. "But, whatever we get, we'll be so happy and grateful." Marcia told me they don't want to know the gender: they want it to be a surprise. "Come on, let me show you the rest of the house. If you think this is beautiful, wait until you see what I have to show you."

A few moments later, we arrive at the porch and enter the house together, and I'm expecting to see more baby paraphernalia, but there's nothing. *Thank God.* The interior of the house hasn't changed much since the last time I visited. It's decorated with creams and whites, and expensive rugs cover the floors while Marcia's abstract paintings grace the walls. Aside from being a model, Marcia is also a talented artist, with some of her paintings hanging in galleries around the country. But, to be honest, the place looks more like a museum than a house. The living room alone is larger than the apartment I moved out of, and one entire wall is made of glass that overlooks the serene gardens with sweeping lawns, lush trees and bushes, and boxwood parterres surrounded by bougainvillea, periwinkles, coneflowers, and other flower types I don't recognize. A floor-to-ceiling bookcase covers the opposite wall. From what I can see, most titles are thriller and suspense, Marcia's favorite.

"Grace, you're here," Travis says, descending the stairs in khaki pants and a tan button-down shirt, his hair in its usual messy style. Padding across the wooden floor in bare feet, he comes over to give me a hug and smiles down at me, his blue eyes locking with mine. "How was your flight?"

"Oh, fine, thank you," I say, smiling, and take a step away from him. He's very kind, but he's one of those people who doesn't know how to respect personal space.

"That's wonderful." He bends to lift my luggage. "I'll take these to the guesthouse."

Marcia and I follow him through the main house and out into the backyard toward the guesthouse, and a fat ginger cat with a full, bushy tail follows behind us. She's beautiful, with orange fur, emerald eyes, and a pattern of white spots on the tips of her ears.

"Her name is Marigold." Marcia smiles. "We've had her for many years." She pulls a key from her pocket. "I hope you don't mind staying out here. We thought you'd want your privacy."

I appreciate that greatly, especially since I have no way of knowing when my next anxiety attack will hit. I wouldn't want them to be around when it happens. I haven't told them I suffer from anxiety, as I was afraid it would stop them from picking me to be their surrogate.

"Thank you so much," I say as she opens the door, leading us straight into a spacious living room.

My eyes land on a crisp white bassinet in a corner of the room. It has wheels and a small electronic pod attached to it, with various buttons on it. The main house has an adult feel to it, but this place is like a large nursery and even the air smells like baby powder. Stepping deeper into the living room, I take in everything—the rocking chair, the changing table leaning against one wall, the baby monitor on the mantle, everything a baby needs. Marcia did mention to me once that they plan to hire a live-in nanny, and I guess this is where she will be staying.

She takes my arm and gives it a gentle squeeze. "Let us give you a short tour."

I nod and allow her and Travis to lead the way down a short hallway and into the bedroom, which is primarily white, except for a gray carpet and pale-gray curtains. A cream and white bedspread covers a comfortable-looking double bed, which I can't wait to sink into after my short but still tiring journey. The bathroom has a similar color scheme: white walls, gray tiled floors, and two fluffy white towels hanging on a rack between the shower cubicle and the bath-tub. The rooms and decor are gorgeous and I'm honored that they went the extra mile to make me feel comfortable.

The next stop is the kitchen, and I also love that everything in it, from the cabinets and appliances to the counter-tops, is white and minimalist. The entire guesthouse is pristine and appears to have never been lived in. I feel myself instantly relax, but when we return to the living room, my gaze lands on a glass case with Barbies displayed inside it. There must be at least fifty to a hundred Barbies, all staring at me with their plastic eyes.

"Isn't it wonderful?" Marcia says, picking up a stuffed giraffe and hugging it to her body.

I cringe inwardly. "It's... it's so lovely."

*Liar.*

Despite the other rooms being beautiful, I'm now intimidated by this living room. I can't help but feel like *I'm* one of the Barbie dolls. Looking at them, I suddenly feel overwhelmingly claustrophobic. Trapped, even.

"We're glad you like it," Travis says, coming to stand next to Marcia as we move to the kitchen. "My wife spent weeks making it all comfortable for you. It's the least we can do after everything you're doing for us. Did I mention that she thinks the baby is going to be a girl?"

"I'm positive that it *is* a girl," Marcia says. "And this is going to be the perfect playhouse for our little princess."

"You know what, Grace?" Travis smiles, pulling his wife close. "I also hope it's a girl."

A little girl. Will she look like me? I imagine myself holding a smaller version of myself, and feel a sudden pang of sadness. *Don't do that*, I scold myself and clear my throat.

"What if it isn't a girl?" I ask, my voice husky.

"It doesn't matter. Girl or boy, it won't change how I'll feel." He rubs his beard. "We just want a baby." He kisses Marcia on her temple and she leans into him with a contented sigh.

I long for a love like theirs one day, but I can't allow myself to dwell on it. When Marcia moves away from him to look through the fridge and cupboards, Travis pulls me aside.

"We're so excited about this," he says in a low voice. "Please do everything you can to stay healthy, to keep the baby safe."

I glance over at Marcia. She looks so happy, and she has

put on a few much-needed pounds since the day they told me I would be their surrogate.

I give Travis a tight smile. More than most people, I know all too well that I can't give him any promises, not the kind he wants. Pregnancy does not come with a guaranteed baby at the end. What I do know is that I'll do everything in my power to protect this child.

"We'll have so much fun together," Marcia says, clasping her hands together. "I try to walk every day. How about you start joining me? It's the perfect way for you to stay healthy during the pregnancy, and we can do what we ladies do best, chat. We can start today after dinner if you're up to it. I could show you around the neighborhood." She pauses for breath. "I also don't want you to be bored during your time here, so I thought maybe whenever you have time, I can give you some painting lessons."

"I'd love that," I say. "All of it. The walks, and the painting lessons. I've always wanted to learn."

"Perfect. Then, my dear student, we shall start tomorrow."

As agreed, after dinner, before it gets dark, Marcia takes me on a walk. The tranquility of the neighborhood is a welcome change from busy Miami. The luxury houses are spaced far apart, giving it a village-like feel, and their perfectly manicured gardens are surrounded by large trees and tall hedges, shielding them from curious neighbors. Instead of cafés, restaurants, and shops, we pass a small park, a lush green golf course, and a tennis court.

Finally, we reach a small lake, where we sit on a crisp white wooden bench. Drawing in a long breath of the fresh air, wrapped in the scent of fresh grass and flowers, I gaze into the sunset that's slowly outlining the clouds like a paintbrush dipped in gold.

"Peaceful, isn't it?" Marcia takes my hand and holds it tight. "Grace, I know you said you're fine with doing this for us, but I realize how much you're putting on hold for us to become parents. I just want to reassure you that we'll take good care of you."

With a lump in my throat, I smile at her. "Thank you, Marcia. It's a pleasure to make this sacrifice for you. Can I be honest with you, though? Sometimes I do worry about something going wrong with the pregnancy and me not being able to make this happen."

"Everything will be just fine, Grace. I'm really happy you've moved in with us so we can be there for you. Whatever medical attention you need to make this journey easier for you, we'll make sure you have access to it." She looks me in the eye. "I don't want you to worry about a thing, okay?" She puts a hand on my shoulder. "Don't ever feel like you're alone in this. Whenever you need someone to talk to, or just a friend to watch a movie with, I'm here for you."

Feeling relieved and comforted, I smile back at her. I really could not have hoped for better parents for my baby, and I'm grateful that I can get to know them so well before the time comes.

# CHAPTER 5

I'm standing in the driveway of my townhouse, watching him through the windshield of his car. His eyes are vacant, like no one's been home inside his body for a while. But I can't look away. His eyes suddenly fill with rage as they turn toward me, and my scream almost chokes me and brings me back to consciousness.

I wake up in my new bed with a storm raging inside my body. The right side of my head is throbbing, the pain a knife slicing through my skull. The linen sheets stick to my skin, damp with sweat. I draw in a shaky breath, but it's not enough and I gulp in some more oxygen until I'm a little calmer.

That nightmare hasn't come back for close to six months now. I should have known that it would return, that it would follow me wherever I went, like he does. It was lying dormant deep within my subconscious, waiting to awaken and torment me when I least expected it. I jump out of bed and switch on the night light, but my sudden dizziness immediately reminds me I'm carrying a baby and should be more careful. Sometimes I forget, and that infuriates me. I should be careful; I should be aware of it every second of each day.

In the bathroom, after splashing water on my face, I sit down on the closed toilet and shut my eyes. I've been living with the Thorpes for two weeks now and honestly, I'm already dreading the next six months. Travis has been asking constant questions about whether I'm eating right and taking care of myself, or if I have any symptoms that need to be checked out, and it's starting to drive me insane. Marcia is easier, but on our daily walks I'm often able to tell that she's anxious, too, even though she tries to hide it.

I can't blame them. They've been trying to have a baby for the seven years of their marriage, and it's not their fault that I feel pressured. I chose to move in with them.

The sound of footsteps drifts through the slanted window, and the doorbell shrills as annoyance bubbles inside me. It's so early in the morning, and they claimed they wanted to give me the guesthouse to offer me privacy, but that's not what I've experienced so far. To be fair, Travis often comes over to fix things around the guesthouse, like the toilet he repaired yesterday because it was clogged, and the broken door handle last week. And Marcia simply cares about my well-being and reminds me to eat healthily. I can't possibly be mad at them for that, but they seem to be constantly there, fussing around me, and sometimes I just want to be left alone.

I pull myself off the toilet and cool my heated face again with water. If they see me even a little flustered, they'll start to worry. I press a fluffy towel to my face and toss it into the bathtub without folding it, creating a little imperfection. The over-the-top neatness of the place is getting on my nerves. Hands clenched at my sides, I make my way to the front door.

"Hello, Grace. Are you okay?" Marcia asks, as I open the door. It's 4 a.m., and I already saw her last night when we watched a movie together.

It's a cool April morning, and she's wearing a long dressing gown that's made of black expensive-looking silk and white lace around the collar and cuffs.

I force my face to smile, but my skin feels tight. "Yes, I'm fine. You're up early."

"So are you." She walks past me into the living room, holding two white mugs with golden rims. "I couldn't sleep so I was drinking tea on the porch, and I saw the light on in your bathroom. I thought I'd come and check to see if you were okay." She offers me one of the mugs. "I also brought you some warm milk to help you sleep."

I take the gold-rimmed mug and wrap my hands around it, warmth seeping into my palms as the scent of coconut wafts up to my nose. "That's kind of you."

Now that she's here, I no longer feel sleepy. It is thoughtful of her to come and check in on me, and last night we had such a good time together, talking about everything and nothing, even things that don't involve the baby.

As I curl my legs under me on the leather sofa, I ask her, "So how's work going?"

She lowers herself next to me, both hands around her mug. "There's not much to say, except that beginning next week, I'll be on extended leave and will only need to do the occasional photo shoot, but I refuse to travel." She takes a sip from her mug. "I want to be available to support you."

"Oh, that's very nice of you, and I appreciate the gesture, but I can take care of myself, you know. I know you love your work, Marcia. You shouldn't put it on hold because of me."

Marcia puts her mug on the side table and places her hand on my arm. "I know that. But I want to help you in any way I can. This is a big and scary step for most women, and I want to be here for you whenever you need me."

My stomach drops. She has been nothing but kind to me, and I have a feeling that she sometimes just craves some company. But even though she's my friend, the thought of her being around all the time for the next few months suffocates me. I'm not sure what I'm resisting, but sometimes I wonder if it's becoming a little painful for me to think of her preparing to be a mother, a mother to the child I'm carrying.

"Thank you for that," I say with as much kindness in my voice as I can muster. "I really appreciate it, but please don't feel obliged to babysit me."

Marcia chuckles. "On the contrary, I really want to do this." Her voice is filled with excitement. "I want to be as involved as possible in the process. I want my child to hear my voice even if it's second-hand, to already know me somehow." She sniffles and wipes her eye. "I've waited so long to be a mother."

"And you'll be an amazing one," I say, putting down my mug on the coffee table and leaning closer to her, an arm around her shoulders.

She scoots closer to me and lets me hug her. "I'm so happy I have you as a friend, Grace, and that you're the one bringing our baby into the world."

"So am I," I say, and I mean it.

"Good. Now, I better leave you to get some rest." She nods and picks up my mug. "You should drink this. It will help you relax."

I allow her to press the warm mug back into my hands,

but then I put it on the coffee table almost immediately, feeling light-headed again.

Marcia looks at me, worry clouding her eyes. "Are you all right? You don't look well. Should I call Dr. Miller?"

Not him again. They call their family doctor if I so much as cough in front of them.

"Nothing's wrong, I'm just a little tired. You're right, I should probably head back to bed."

"Good idea. I'll leave you to it."

"Drink the milk while it's still warm," she says before stepping out. "And remember, we're going shopping for the baby tomorrow. We need to buy a stroller, and Travis is coming. He'd like the baby to be there."

The baby is not even born yet, and it doesn't know what's going on outside my belly. The way both Marcia and Travis talk to it and insist on involving it in activities is a little bit annoying at times, but I know my hormones are just making me irritable.

"Hang in there," I whisper to myself as I close the door. "It'll be over before you know it."

I lean against the door and press the tips of my fingers against my eyes, desperate for my anxiety meds, but that's out of the question. I go straight to the bedroom, forgetting about the milk on the coffee table.

The ballerina clock ticks and ticks in the dark, but it doesn't succeed in lulling me to sleep. If Marcia had not shown up, I'd probably be sleeping by now. In need of a distraction, I pick up my phone and read the last message Sydney sent to me yesterday. We often connect through text or email, because it's hard to speak to her and not hear the note of disapproval in her voice.

*You okay over there? You've been quiet.*

My fingers fly over the screen as I type a reply.

*I'm fine.*

I hit send and get out of bed, suddenly feeling restless. As soon as my feet touch the ground, something furry brushes my leg and I jump.

"Hey, Marigold," I whisper. "Where did you come from?"

Since I arrived at the Thorpes', the cat has been keeping her distance from the guesthouse, only showing up occasionally and never staying more than a few minutes before she flees. I take careful steps toward her and she stares at me with narrowed eyes as I lower myself next to her, allowing her to sniff my hand.

*You can trust me, sweetie. I'm harmless.*

When she stays put, I place my hand on top of her. Her fur is soft and warm against my palm. I've never really been a cat person, but I do prefer some cats to others, and Marigold is one of the special ones.

"How did you get in?" I whisper, running my hand up and down her back. She purrs in response. I'm not sure how she could have come in, as all the windows and doors are closed and I don't have a cat flap in the front door. Perhaps she slipped in with Marcia without me noticing. Marigold turns onto her back and continues to purr, and I chuckle as I rub her belly.

"I don't mind you staying, but I think Marcia will be wondering where you are." When I move to pick her up to take her back to the main house, she shifts away from me.

"All right then, let me see what I can do." I send a quick text to Marcia, and she responds immediately.

*It's fine. She can spend the night with you. She's great company, I promise.*

"Looks like we're spending the night together," I tell Marigold as she finally lets me scoop her into my arms for a cuddle.

As soon as the sun comes up, I get a call from Sydney, a response to the text I sent her. She knows I was lying about being fine. I think of ignoring her call, but I'm also desperate to talk to someone outside of the Thorpe household.

"Hi," I say and brace myself for the "*I told you so.*"

"What happened?" she asks. "You're not okay, so don't even think about lying to me. I know you, Grace." The concern in her voice brings tears to my eyes.

"Look, I'm not in the mood for a lecture right now."

"You won't get one." She lets out a sigh. "I know I haven't been as supportive as I want to be, and I'm sorry. You're an adult and you have the right to make your own decisions." She pauses. "How are the future parents treating you?"

"Like a damn egg."

"Oh, no." Sydney chuckles, and it breaks the ice that's been standing between us for weeks now. "I'm sorry to hear that."

"Travis is constantly worrying, and they speak to the baby like it's already here." I lie back down on the bed with the phone to my ear. "Marcia is really sweet, but she can be a little overbearing too. She actually came over at four this morning. I went to the bathroom, and she saw the light on. She brought me some milk."

"That's a bit creepy."

"Maybe, but I also kind of understand them. They really want this child, and she just wants to be involved and make things easy for me."

"But they should also respect your privacy. That's why—"

"I know, I know. You already made it clear that you didn't think I should move in with them."

"I'm sorry." Sydney clears her throat. "Do you get out at all? I mean, doing things without them around?"

"Not really."

I haven't thought about going out much, since I have everything I need here and going out feels exhausting right now. Or maybe I'm really trying to avoid being stared at. Wellice is a small town, and people have different opinions when it comes to surrogacy. I don't want them to point fingers at me. The Thorpes are well known locally, and I'm willing to bet we are the talk of the town.

"Grace, you should get out. Being trapped on that property and being watched like a zoo animal can't be good for your mental health."

"Yeah, you're right. At least we're going out to shop for the baby later."

"You and the parents?"

"Yes. Travis wants the baby to be there, apparently."

"That's ridiculous. Why can't they go without you? You need to have time to yourself," she says. "I'm not saying you have to make new friends, but please get out there and have some alone time." Sydney takes a breath. "Okay, I'm done with the lecturing. I'm sorry you're going through a hard time."

"I hate to admit this to you, but I kind of regret coming here. But it's a little too late now."

I gave up everything in Miami. I don't have a job, an

apartment, or anything to go back to. Trying to build a new life in my current condition would be exhausting, and Marcia and Travis would be heartbroken if I left.

When I head to the living room after finishing my call with Sydney, I notice something strange. The mug of milk Marcia brought me last night is no longer on the coffee table where I left it.

# CHAPTER 6
## SATURDAY, 13 JULY 2013

My hands glide over my body, from my bust over the black satin ribbon around my waist, and down the skirt of the lavender cocktail dress. It's perfect. It arrived two hours ago, in a silver-lined box accompanied by a simple note from Chad.

*Get dressed and meet me at Gunther's Shack at seven. I can't wait to see you.*

We've been together for four years exactly. The last few months have been tough on us, but maybe tonight will help rekindle our spark. Since I told him I'm going to be a surrogate for Rachel, things had been strained, and in the last couple of weeks we haven't seen each other much at all. A week ago, he showed up at my door to apologize for not returning my calls and I told him that if we are going to stay together, he must accept my decision. He told me he loved me and that he isn't going anywhere. I said that I don't expect him to support me, but if he doesn't actively discourage me, I can live with that.

If only it was that simple. The pregnancy is the elephant in the room. Chad avoids the topic altogether, and when I bring it up, he brushes it off and changes the subject. But the papers are signed and Rachel, Peter, and I will start the process in less than a month. Chad doesn't know that yet, and I have a feeling he still hopes I will change my mind. Over the past week, I have been trying to gather up the courage to tell him, but I keep losing my nerve at the last second. Sooner or later, he will have to know, and I'm terrified of how he will react.

I leave the house at six thirty, taking a cab instead of driving because July has brought with it record rainfall this year and I get nervous driving in the rain after almost causing an accident last month.

Gunther's Shack is where Chad and I met for the first time. I'd gone there for dinner with friends and was carrying a passion fruit martini to my table when he bumped into me. The drink sloshed over the rim and spilled all over my blouse. He apologized, and insisted I give him my number, claiming he wanted to take me out for dinner to make it up to me. One week later, we went out on our first date.

I smile as I walk into the restaurant, gliding in my beautiful dress underneath the crystal chandeliers. My mouth parts a little when I spot him at a table planted right in the center of the restaurant. He looks distinguished and exudes self-confidence, which I have always found sexy in a man. Instead of it flopping over his forehead, his hair is swept back with gel, and even though he prefers a five o'clock shadow, he has gone for a clean-shaven look. The flickering candles on the table cast shadows that make his face look sculpted. A warm ripple surges through my veins, bringing my senses to life, and

I'm so focused on him that it takes me a moment to notice that the other tables in the restaurant are unoccupied. When I come close enough, he pushes back his chair and stands. A grin lights up his face the way the candles light up the table.

"Good evening, beautiful." He kisses me first on the forehead before his warm lips meet mine. "Happy anniversary to us." He picks up a bouquet of lilies and roses from the table and hands it to me.

"Thank you," I whisper, tears choking my throat. I never thought we'd get back to the way we were, but maybe this really is a new beginning. Our last two anniversaries were nothing special. We did what we normally did most days of the week—we ordered food and ate it in front of a movie. Tonight is different, and I'm so relieved.

"Someone made an effort." My eyes sweep the dining room. "Where is everybody?"

"Babe, forget everybody else. Tonight is about you and me." He pulls out a chair for me.

It doesn't surprise me that he reserved the entire restaurant. It's owned by a friend of his, an orthodontist like himself.

"Wow." I eye the champagne on the table. "This is really special."

"You are special." He sits down, then takes both my hands. "Tonight, I need us to remember what we have. I want us to talk about our future."

My mouth dries up, and I pull my hands from his. "Chad, we need to talk about something important." I hate bringing up the surrogacy in the middle of our romantic anniversary dinner, but if he wants to talk about our future, it's something we need to address.

"Let me say something first." He stands up again before

dropping to one knee, and I gasp when I see the black velvet box he pulls from his pocket.

"I want you, Grace," he says. "I want you forever."

Tears fill my eyes and drip down my cheeks, and I taste the salt at the corner of my lips.

The perfect words. The perfect man. The wrong time.

"You're asking me to marry you?" I stumble over my words.

"If you'll have me." He tilts his head to the side. "I'm not perfect, but we are good together. So, will you be my wife, Grace Cooper?"

He reaches for my hand again, and I find myself nodding. We kiss, we laugh, and we kiss some more. Then, out of nowhere, reality sets in and I ask him to sit.

"Chad, I want to marry you, but I also want to... I'm still going to be a surrogate for my sister. I signed the papers and—"

"Without telling me?" His voice is suddenly thick with anger.

"You never wanted to talk about it. You didn't want to be involved."

He shakes his head. "I don't understand why she can't find another surrogate. I'm sure there are enough of them out there to choose from. I sent you those websites."

"She wants *me* to do it for her, not some stranger. I'm her sister and I have made my decision." Since we're twins, and I'll be donating my eggs, the child will have a higher chance of actually looking like Rachel.

"But you don't have to support her that way. That's so drastic." He rubs the side of his face roughly. "And now you're about to get married. You need to focus on our future."

How did I miss it? I should have known the moment he dropped to one knee. The proposal came with a condition.

"That's why you proposed, isn't it? You want me to choose between you and my sister."

"No." He rubs his brow. "I proposed because I love you. I want to spend the rest of my life with you."

I'm too choked up to answer, so instead of gazing into his eyes, I watch raindrops sliding down the large window, blurring my view of the busy street outside. The waiter brings us ribeye steak, steamed asparagus, and roasted potatoes, and he places the plates in front of us with a flourish. We eat it in a silence that neither of us have the courage to fill with words. I had so much hope for tonight, but it's ended up being a disaster.

After dinner, Chad offers to drive me home, but I turn him down, and when he leaves, I walk outside in the rain for an hour, thoughts stumbling over each other in my mind, my hair and clothes soaking wet. What if Chad is right? What if I'm putting my life on hold and missing out on my chance at happiness? When my thoughts have tortured me enough, I take a cab to Rachel's house. She opens the door and sees me standing out there, my beautiful dress drenched, my makeup smudged by rainwater and tears.

I don't have to say a word; she already knows.

I try to apologize, to make her understand. I even show her the ring, but she shuts the door in my face. In one night, I have gained a fiancé and lost my sister.

I know that even if I change my mind and tell her I will go ahead with the surrogacy, she will never trust me again. I gave her hope, then I snatched it away to give it to somebody else. I betrayed the one person who means the world to me, my only family. Chad and I will get married, but the pain I caused Rachel will always stand between us.

The next morning, Chad calls me early.

"Good morning, fiancée." His voice is a deep, velvet murmur. "We're still getting married, right?"

"Yes." The word is like a hammer cracking my heart open and guilt burns the back of my throat, but it's not his fault that I chose him instead of my sister. "I can't wait to be your wife."

"Last night didn't go as well as I planned," Chad continues. "I want to make it up to you today. Let's have lunch to celebrate our engagement."

"I'm sorry, I can't. I have a terrible headache."

Thank God it's the weekend, and I don't have to go to the office. I have a few guest blog posts to review for a future feature, but it will be in the comfort of my own home.

I'm engaged to the man I love and I'm supposed to be the happiest girl in the world. But instead I feel empty, broken, and ashamed.

"Did you make a decision about the surrogacy?" Chad asks.

"I did, and you'll be happy to know I'm not going through with it."

As I listen to him telling me how pleased he is that I've come to my senses, I can't stop thinking about what the future holds for us. Every time we smile, every time we celebrate our love, I will be reminded of my sister's pain, of the dagger that I plunged into her heart.

Later down the line, when Chad and I have kids together, I'll be reminded of the fact that my sister couldn't have any. Or maybe fate will punish me by not giving me children of my own, so I can experience the same pain she did. For the rest of the day, I can't shake the feeling that, by betraying Rachel, I have cursed my future, and my happiness will always be tainted by her tears.

# CHAPTER 7
## PRESENT

I peel my eyes open and drag myself out of bed. Forget the nap. Sleep opens the door to nightmares, anyway. The claustrophobia of feeling trapped inside the guesthouse has reached a new high and I need to get out.

Even though in the fourth month of my pregnancy my bump is still quite small, I slide on a pair of maternity jeans and a striped black-and-white t-shirt—two pieces among the many clothes Marcia has filled up my closet with. She said she didn't want me to spend my own money on a baby that wasn't mine. I am grateful, but if I had been given the chance to choose my own clothes, I would've gone for bright colors to lift my mood. The clothes she picked are all shades of gray, black, and an occasional white.

Before stepping outside, I open the fridge and remove a bottle of the fresh watermelon juice I prepared in the morning. I pour myself a glass and take it with me outside, along with a book to read. Before I became pregnant, I hated watermelons. To me, they tasted like a sponge filled with sweet water. But, since falling pregnant, I have an intense craving for them and I can't seem to get enough. If I had a choice, I'd eat the fruit at every meal. Last night, Travis surprised me with the largest watermelon I'd ever seen, and he promised to bring more when I finish it.

Outside the guesthouse, the spring air feels warm against my skin, and a gentle breeze teases my hair. I walk along the flagstone path that cuts through the perfectly trimmed lawn, passing the tree house and Marcia's art studio, which looks as weathered as the tool shed a few steps away from it. She claims it inspires her more to paint there than in a perfect environment. I wish I could get a peek at some of the art pieces she's working on, but Travis said she's strict about anyone entering her studio. Even the painting lessons she gives me twice a week are held outside by the river.

"She's working on a painting for the nursery," he whispered to me once at dinner. "She won't let me see it until the baby comes."

I stroll past the shed and make my way toward a whitewashed vintage metal table with matching chairs covered by gray cushions. The garden furniture is positioned only a few steps from the edge of the river, underneath a large weeping willow. I put the juice on the table and flip my book open: *What to Expect When You're Expecting*, the most popular book out there when it comes to pregnancy. It was a gift from Marcia, one of two she bought. The second copy was for herself even though, once this is over, she's going to end up with two books. Whatever she gives me during this time, including the clothes, I'll leave behind.

A bright-green four-inch leaf detaches itself from a branch and falls on top of my head before sliding down my forehead and plopping between the pages of the book. I pick it up, hold it in the palm of my hand for a few seconds, then let it fall to the ground. I can't focus on the book, so I get to my feet and press my hands on my lower back, massaging away the constant ache. It refuses to budge, but that's okay. Being out here makes me feel better, and I close my eyes to enjoy the moment.

At first, I think it's the brush of the breeze across the nape of my neck, but it's not. It's the fine hairs rising, responding to a stare. I turn to see Travis standing at one of the windows of the main house, watching me. He gives me a wave and I hesitate before waving back, my jaw stiff.

Desperate to escape his stare, I kick off my sandals and walk away, nearing the edge of the river. The tickle of the grass on my bare feet is refreshing, like it used to be when I was a child visiting my grandparents' farm in Missouri. I throw a glance behind me at the house, and his eyes are still on me. I continue to walk along the edge, praying he won't come and join me. I spent most of yesterday evening with them after dinner and the only thing we talked about was the baby. Honestly, I'm desperate for a break, but I'm trying to be sensitive to the fact that it is their baby I'm carrying, and I came here so they could be a part of the journey.

I knew it would be hard, but not like this. Also, even though I hate to admit it to myself, talking about the baby with them is becoming increasingly difficult. Despite trying hard to disconnect myself emotionally from the life growing inside me, some days it feels impossible.

When I'm a safe distance away and can no longer see his face clearly through the window, the tension in my shoulders and back melts away. I shut my eyes and inhale the scent of wildflowers. Then I take a step toward the water, sliding my feet into the liquid. The initial shock of cold makes me gasp, but it's not long until I start enjoying the gentle waves dancing over my feet. I don't even mind the touch of the slimy rocks underfoot. The buzzing insects and the birdsong make me feel like I'm far away, in a place where I don't have to worry about a thing.

Less than ten minutes later, a twig snaps behind me and I spin around to find Marcia standing there. She must have been working in her studio and saw me walk by through the small window.

"Hi, Grace," she says, coming to stand next to me. "It's such a lovely day. Would you like to come into the house for some smoothies? I made them fresh, and they're packed with nutrients for you and the baby."

The smoothies. Even though she means well and only wants me and the baby to get all the vitamins we need, she makes combinations I can't stand and just the thought of drinking them makes me want to throw up. Her spinach smoothies are the worst.

"No, that's all right. I already had one not long ago, avocado and peaches."

Shortly before I arrived, Marcia brought a blender to my kitchen along with a recipe book for pregnancy green smoothies, and showed me how to make them.

"Great. Then why don't we go shopping for the baby?"

I want to say no, and I know I should since last time we went shopping it was exhausting. Marcia and Travis couldn't decide on what kind of stroller to buy. In the end, they purchased two oversized strollers, an adorable white one for Marcia and the baby's outings, and a black-and-white high-tech one for Travis. Who buys two strollers for a baby?

But why should I care? It's not my baby, and it's not my money. What does annoy me is that both strollers are inside the guesthouse living room, along with everything else they keep buying.

Marcia pushes her hands into the pockets of her jeans.

"After the shopping, I'll get out of your hair and you can have a little time to yourself in town. I've noticed that you hardly go out of the house and I don't want you to feel like you're in prison." She gives me a wink. "I'm sure a couple of hours away from us would be refreshing, don't you think?"

I'm relieved at her perceptiveness, but I wouldn't want her to feel like I resent them. I open my mouth to speak, but she holds up her hand. "You don't have to feel bad about it. I completely understand."

"All right, if you insist. I'll take the car so I can drive myself back."

Marcia and Travis have given me a Volvo XC40 that I can use when I'm staying with them. Travis mentioned that the main reason for giving me access to a vehicle is so I can be mobile on the off-chance I need to get to the hospital in an emergency. I doubt very much that he wants me to be driving around town for the hell of it.

Marcia picks up a shiny, black pebble and tosses it into the water. "You should definitely do that. It's time you gave it a test drive."

"Where are you two going?" Travis asks a little later, when we're about to get into our cars. He looks clean and fresh in a white polo shirt and dark denims.

"Shopping for the baby," Marcia says, opening her car door. "Want to join us?"

"I wish I could. But I have a class with the high school kids today."

"I see," Marcia says brightly.

Travis and Marcia met when he was hired to shoot for a campaign for MereLux, one that Marcia was spearheading, long before she started modeling for the brand. She said it was love at first sight, and after they got married, Travis took her last name instead of the other way around. Marcia felt that he was spending too much time away from home for photo shoots, so he gave his fashion photography career up for her. With the Thorpe fortune supporting him, he doesn't need to work but he spends his time giving photography lessons to the locals and tourists.

"Be careful out there," he says to me. "You're carrying precious cargo."

The shopping trip is a grueling experience, with Marcia agonizing over every little item, and by the time we're done, I'm desperate to get away from her and be alone for a while. I've never enjoyed shopping in places like this; I find the big, crowded stores and the harsh lighting stressful, and it always makes my anxiety rise. I wait until she's stuffing the bags into the trunk before saying goodbye.

"Enjoy your alone time." She pulls me into a hug. "I'll see you later at the house."

When she gets into the car, it feels like some of the chains around me break away. I wander around town for a bit, popping in and out of smaller, quieter shops and searching for a unique handbag for Sydney. In a store selling recycled products, I come across a tote made from computer keyboard keys. I search inside for a price tag and find none.

"How much is this?" I ask the woman behind the counter. Despite the heat, she's wearing a neon green knitted hat with a matching sweater.

A flash of humor crosses her face. "Whatever you think it's worth."

I frown. "I—what do you mean?"

"I'm terrible at math, so I let the customer decide."

"Nancy, stop teasing the customers." An elderly man

with a full gray beard emerges from a door behind the counter. "What my daughter is trying to say is, we're a donation-only shop. Our products are made from junk found around town. Junk is free, so we don't charge for raw materials. All you pay for is the work put into the product, and you get to decide what that's worth. Call it a donation. Half of what we earn goes toward several charities in town."

"I can't do that." I look down at the beautiful bag and smile at the woman. "I'm not good at math either. Please help me out."

"Then have it for free," the man says. "You'll still be helping our little corner of the earth stay clean. Tourists do it all the time."

"That's kind, but I won't take it for free." Touched by what they're doing, I hand him forty-five dollars, all the money I have in my purse. "I wish I could give you more, but this is all I have."

"This is too much," he says, counting the money, and he tries to give me back twenty dollars. I refuse, and walk out of the store with the promise to return again in the future. I continue my walk down Main Street, and when I come across the Wellice-based MereLux boutique, I decide not to enter and say hello. I spend enough time around the Thorpes and their possessions. Today is my day off.

I only stop walking when my legs start to ache, and the straps of my sandals cut into my skin. I need to sit somewhere, to give my feet a rest. The first time I visited Wellice, Marcia took me to Clayton's Coffee Lounge, a small café nestled between the post office and an ice cream shop.

"It's not the food that draws people to it," Marcia had said. "Although it is really good here. It's like the kitchen of Wellice, where residents gather to catch up on each other's lives. Come on, let me show you what I mean."

The place is packed, but it does feel good to be surrounded by life. I look around for a free table with no luck. I'm about to turn away when, over the sounds of laughter, cutlery clinking, and the rock music, someone speaks to me.

"Why don't you join me? This is a table for two and I'm by myself."

The woman is at the table closest to the door wearing a loose lavender blouse and dark pants. Her red hair, streaked with gray and frizzy, is secured with a chocolate-brown scrunchie. Her blue eyes are warm but sad, and there are dark bags under them, like her lower eyelids are ice cream melting in the heat. Despite the kind offer, her lips don't look like they've been touched by a smile for a long time. In front of the empty chair is a full cup of coffee that someone left behind. She stretches out a hand and pulls it toward her.

"That's kind of you. Thank you."

I take a seat and order a salad and a glass of fresh orange juice, and I eat my food while she stares at me from across the table, occasionally taking a sip of her coffee. I'm not sure what to say, and the food has trouble getting down my throat. I don't like people watching me when I'm eating.

"I'm new in town," I offer, finally. I might as well try to strike up a conversation; the silence is unbearable.

"Yes, I've heard about you," she says. "You're the young lady helping out the Thorpes, aren't you?"

"It's not a big deal." I stab a lettuce leaf and bring it to my lips.

"It sure is. Not many people would be willing to do what you're doing for strangers."

I shrug. "They're not strangers, not really. I'm a friend of the family."

"It must still be hard." She lifts the cup of coffee to her cracked lips.

"You mean being a surrogate? Well, it's—"

"I mean doing something good for people who don't deserve it." She drains her cup of coffee and lowers it back to the table.

"Why do you say that?" I ask, frowning.

"I'm sorry." She waves her hand dismissively. "Ignore me. I have a habit of saying everything I'm thinking. I better get out of here." She gives me a small smile and gets to her feet, grabbing her battered leather purse. "It was nice to meet you."

She rushes off before I have a chance to speak.

# CHAPTER 8

It's a few minutes after seven on a balmy June morning, two months after I moved in with the Thorpes. I'm resting in my living room, sipping my tea, when I hear a commotion outside, and then a chair scraping across the wooden floor of the porch. Stepping outside the door, I find a woman sitting in a rocking chair on the porch. She must be in her mid-fifties with a stylish updo, large pearls around her neck, and an expensive-looking cream blouse and black skirt, and she's smoking a long, thin cigarette.

When she sees me, she exhales the smoke and stands up, drops her cigarette in a nearby ashtray, then walks toward me, her arm outstretched. Her nails are painted a deep red, the same color as her lipstick. "I assume you are Grace."

"Yes, hello," I say, taking her hand in mine, and she gives it a firm shake. "I don't think we've met."

She removes her glasses and cleans them with a red silk cloth, a faint smile on her lips. "I'm Agnes. I've heard a lot about you."

I'm about to respond when I spy Marcia walking toward

us, her cheeks flushed red. She's wearing a white silk bathrobe and her damp hair is combed back. She must have just stepped out of the shower.

"Mom, what are you doing over here so early?" she asks. "It's important that Grace gets as much sleep as possible."

Agnes is the woman who tightly holds the reins of the MereLux brand. Her husband, Marcia's father, died five years ago, and she took over and drove the business to greater heights of success. I saw photos of her online, but she looked much younger and more heavily made up.

Agnes smiles at her daughter. "I just wanted to introduce myself to our new guest, and to have a quick word with her."

Marcia's shoulders stiffen. "About what, Mom?"

"Why, about the child she's carrying, of course."

"I don't think that's a good idea right now," Marcia says, her voice terse and her face tight.

Agnes pushes her glasses against her face and moves to the edge of the porch before looking back at me. "It was nice meeting you, Grace. Maybe we can talk some other time then."

She takes out her cigarette from the ashtray and walks down the pathway back to the house.

With a frustrated sigh, Marcia grabs my hand and pulls me inside, where she drops onto the couch, her eyes apologetic. "I'm sorry about my mother disturbing you like that. She can be quite intrusive sometimes." She attempts to sweep her hair from her eyes, but it swings right back into place. "I had no idea she was coming over here. I was going to warn you about her before breakfast. I guess she beat me to it."

"Don't worry about it. I was already awake and she seemed nice." I rub the back of my neck. "She said she wanted to talk to me about the baby. Do you know what she meant?"

"Yes. I'm afraid she's not on board with the surrogacy." Marcia's lips are pursed as she taps her foot in a fast rhythm. She doesn't even look at me as she speaks. "She thinks we gave up too easily... you know, trying to have a child on our own."

"I'm really sorry to hear that, Marcia. I'm sure it would have been nice to have your mother's support." I give her a quick hug because she looks so sad. "Maybe she'll come around once the baby is born."

Marcia scoffs and breaks our embrace. "Honestly, I don't think that will ever happen. She tried so hard to talk me out of doing this, but it's my life, not hers. She has always been controlling. That's just how she is, I guess. Some things never change."

That must be where Marcia gets it. But I am surprised and sad to hear that her mother doesn't want the baby. It would have been nice if she were excited to be a grandmother.

Marcia rubs her forehead in a circular motion. "Don't worry about her. I'll make sure she doesn't bother you."

"Thanks. Does she live close by?"

"No. She lives here, with us. She was on a long vacation in Turkey with a friend when you arrived. Now she's back to remind me of the huge mistake she thinks I'm making." She pauses. "Well, the second mistake."

"What was the first?" I ask, not sure if I really want to know the answer.

Marcia turns to me with a somber expression on her face. "She thinks I married the wrong man."

"She doesn't like Travis?" I frown.

"Oh, she likes Travis all right... as a person. She just thinks he married me for my money, even though he didn't know about it until after we were engaged. It's hard sometimes," she says, biting her lip. "Trying to put out fires between Travis and my mother can be exhausting. When I first introduced them, I thought they got along fine. I don't know where all the animosity suddenly came from." She rests her hand on my belly and blows out a breath. "I thought this baby would bring us all together. Now I don't think that's ever going to happen. Too much damage has been done."

Just what I need, to get entangled in a family feud. I know that no family is perfect, and I feel sorry for Marcia, but I just feel the stress will be too much for me.

"Marcia, I've been thinking," I say and take a few seconds to draw her attention back to me. "You've been so kind to me, and I understand that you want to take care of me during this time, but I don't think this arrangement is really working for me."

"Do you mean staying here, or are you talking about being our surrogate?" she asks slowly.

"Staying here. I'm thinking maybe it wasn't such a good idea."

A frown sweeps across her face. "What do you mean by that? I thought we were getting along really well. If you ask me, I think it's the perfect arrangement. We're like one happy family."

"I don't mean it like that," I say. "Staying here is great. What I mean is that I need my personal space." I place my hands on both knees and squeeze out my frustration. "I think it's best for me to stay somewhere else until the baby comes. I could get a room at the same hotel I stayed at when I first came—"

"Nonsense," she snaps. "I will not have you staying in that cheap hotel. What will people think of us?"

"They might not think anything at all." I pause. "I just need my space. The thing is, you and Travis are constantly watching me, and it's making me nervous."

Sometimes the truth is the only way out of a bad situation. Except she doesn't know the whole truth about why I'm doing this in the first place. Would she feel betrayed if she knew how I manipulated my way into their lives? Would it even matter? They want a baby and I'll give them one. That's what counts in the end, right?

Marcia gets up and comes to stand in front of me.

"I'm sorry if you've been feeling suffocated, Grace. We don't mean to make you feel that way. We're just so excited about the baby and sometimes we get a little carried away." Her brown eyes well up and she blinks back the tears. "You have no idea how it feels to watch your stomach growing, knowing that you're carrying our baby. I can't carry my own child, but when you involve me it makes some of the pain go away. Please don't cut us out. I'll try harder. I'll have a word with Travis. We'll give you the space you need. You don't need to move out."

I want to continue to fight for my freedom, but the broken look on her face and the tears on her cheeks make me swallow my words. I don't want to hurt her or rob her of this opportunity. I'm here to make her pain go away, not make it worse. I make a spur-of-the-moment decision I might end up regretting and reach out to hug her. "I'm sorry, I do want you to be on this journey with me. I want you and Travis to be involved."

I know how much it will hurt her if I leave, and I can't do that to her.

"You mean you're not leaving us? You're staying till the end?"

I pull away to look into her eyes. "Until the end of this journey, but the beginning of another chapter for you and your baby."

She's crying now. "You're such a wonderful person, Grace. I'll never forget this."

Once her crying subsides, I'm the first to pull away.

"Marcia, if I'm staying here, some things need to change. I'd prefer to prepare my own meals here, in the guesthouse, if that's okay. We can't let that beautiful kitchen go to waste."

Now that I know Marcia's mother will be living here, I will do whatever it takes to keep a distance from her, so I'm not causing any friction or feeling any further stress. Sitting at the dining table sharing a meal with her when it's clear she doesn't want me there would be torture.

"Done." Marcia smiles. "But I will buy all the groceries for you. I'll make sure the kitchen is fully stocked every week with healthy food for you and the baby. I'll have Beatrice restock it tomorrow. And she'll continue cleaning up this place for you every day."

Beatrice is the housekeeper, but I hardly see her as she usually cleans the guesthouse when I'm not indoors, either out for a walk in the garden or sitting by the river. She does seem very friendly and made me promise to let her know if I need anything at all.

"Sure. I don't mind that. You can buy the groceries, and Beatrice can clean."

I'd prefer to do my own cleaning, but if I say that it will lead to a fight I won't win. Marcia will not want me to strain myself when they have someone who's paid to do the work.

"One more thing," she says. "We would love it if you

would have at least one meal a week with us. Would that be okay?"

"I can do that." If I have the other days to myself, I can cope with one meal with them.

"Great." Marcia squeezes my hand. "I want you to be happy, Grace. Only then can you bring a bundle of joy into the world."

She moves her hand to my stomach again and caresses it: another thing I can't stand. Both Travis and Marcia seem to think it's okay to touch me anytime they feel like it, no permission needed. While Marcia's hand is still on my belly, the baby kicks and she squeals. I almost feel guilty for wanting to keep her at a distance, but if I'm going to keep my sanity, boundaries need to be set.

After she has talked to the baby and rubbed my belly some more, I tell her I need to take a shower before breakfast. I watch her through the window as she makes her way back to the main house, but, at the last second, she turns and walks toward her studio. She pulls a key from her pocket and lets herself in.

Before jumping into the shower, I grab my calendar from the nightstand and cross out today's date. I'm acting like a prisoner in a jail cell, counting down the days until I'm free. I know I'm doing the right thing. But sometimes it feels like I'm serving time for what I did, rather than countering all the pain I caused.

# CHAPTER 9

In the morning, Travis is standing on the doorstep holding two bags of groceries. "These are for you," he says with a faint smile on his face. "Beatrice wanted to bring them over, but I thought it would be a good excuse to come and see the baby... and see how you're doing. Marcia told me you got a visit from Agnes yesterday."

"I did," I say, reaching out to grab the bags. "Thank you so much for these."

"No, no," he says. "They're heavy. I don't want you to strain yourself. Let me bring them inside for you."

"Thank you." I step back and give him space to pass.

I follow him into the kitchen and watch him place the bags on the countertop. I can't help but notice the way he's looking at me, his eyes filled with curiosity.

"What did Agnes want to talk to you about?" He dips his head to the side, his gaze holding mine. "I hope she didn't upset you in any way."

I turn around and open a cabinet to put things away. "She just wanted to introduce herself." I really don't want to discuss their family issues. Whatever is going on between them has nothing to do with me.

"You don't have to do that," he says, and I hear a bag opening. "I don't mind putting away the groceries for you."

"That's all right, Mr. Thorpe," a voice says behind us. "I'll handle it. It's my job, after all."

Turning around, we see Beatrice standing in the doorway with a bucket filled with cleaning supplies. She has sallow, wrinkled skin and close-set, raven-colored eyes that are magnified by her glasses, making her look a bit like an owl. Her surprisingly lustrous gray hair is always worn in a long braid down her back, and she's dressed in her usual attire, a light-blue dress, complete with her white apron.

"Very well," Travis says. "I'll leave it in your hands then."

He strides out of the kitchen and disappears through the door, and as soon as he's gone, I let out a deep breath.

"Thought you might want him out of your hair," Beatrice says when we're alone. "What they don't understand is that smothering you is not going to help get the baby here any faster or healthier. If anything, it'll make you miserable and that could affect the little one."

"Thank you for rescuing me, Beatrice. I think I needed that." I open a bag and begin to put things away.

"I can help you with that, Miss Cooper."

"Oh, don't worry about it. I'm perfectly capable of doing things around the house. And please, call me Grace." I reach for an onion and she stops me by placing her hand over mine.

"It doesn't matter how you feel, Grace. This is my job. Back in the day, pregnant women worked until their waters broke. I did the same while pregnant with my daughter. But this is Marcia's house, and she told me not to let you lift a finger, so that's what I'll do." She lets go of my hand again.

"No one will know if you don't tell them. I'll go crazy if I do nothing around here." I lift a handful of oranges and hand them over to her with a grin.

She just laughs, then side by side we put the groceries away. I soon realize that Beatrice doesn't much care for idle chit-chat, so, while we work, I just listen to the sound of her humming. Finally, I get a break from talking about the baby.

We're done after a few minutes and I go to take a luke-warm bath while Beatrice cleans the kitchen. After I finish, I head back to the kitchen and find her standing by the window, looking out. Travis is out there, standing in the garden, holding a cellphone to his ear. The kitchen smells fresh and the counters are clear and glinting, and I walk over to Beatrice and place my hand on her back. "Is everything all right?"

Startled, she turns around and flashes me a smile. "Yes, of course, everything is fine. I was just waiting to ask if I could do anything else for you. Even though it's a little early for lunch, I can prepare it for you and you can heat it up later."

"That's very kind of you, but I'll fix myself some food later. Thanks for everything."

"It's no bother. If you need anything, just let me know. I am at your disposal."

After glancing out the window once more, she wipes her hands on a kitchen towel and leaves the room.

Still standing in the kitchen, I peer outside as well, wondering why Beatrice seemed so interested in watching Travis, and why, earlier, she had not acknowledged that this is his home too.

# CHAPTER 10

The woman with the red hair and sad eyes is back. I've been coming to the café often in the last two weeks, hoping to see her again, and today she's finally here. I've spent a lot of time thinking about what she said to me, her words haunting my quiet moments. Why did she have to say those things about the Thorpes? What did she mean?

She's sitting alone in a darker part of the café. Her posture is slumped forward as if the whole world is pressing down on her shoulders, her hand wrapped around a single cup of coffee while another cup sits in front of the empty seat across from her. I left the house early, before Marcia, Travis, or Agnes got in my way, and the café is mostly empty.

It's been a week since I spoke to Marcia about wanting more space, and I do have a bit more freedom now, but not much. The one thing that has changed is that she and Travis now knock before coming into the guesthouse, instead of just walking in. Regardless, I try to get out as much as I can, even though I know Travis doesn't approve. He hasn't said it in words, but I can tell it annoys him when he asks me where I've been or where I'm going. A slight twitch of the lips as he attempts to smile, the barely audible sharp intake of breath. I try to remind myself that he's just worried about the baby, and he wants me to be where they can keep an eye on me. I don't need anyone's permission to be free to do what I want, but it does make me feel better that Marcia is okay with it at least.

The one positive thing is that Agnes barely says a word to me other than the simplest of pleasantries. Whenever we cross paths in the yard, she often looks like she wants to say something, but then she never does.

"This one's on the house," says Clayton, the café owner, sliding a glass of orange juice in front of me at the counter. "Freshly pressed and ready to be enjoyed."

"You don't have to do that," I say, smiling up at him.

His olive-black eyes twinkle and he flings a dish towel over his broad shoulder. "I know that. But I want to."

Clayton is another reason I come back to the café. He's over six feet with close-cropped caramel hair, tanned skin, and a wide smile. But it's not his good looks that keep me returning. Last time, when the woman with the red hair left abruptly, he came and sat with me. He said he recognized me from the first time I visited Wellice to meet Marcia, and I was surprised to find that he even knew me by name. But it's easy to be famous in a small town, and, as I suspected, the surrogacy is a hot topic among the locals. I've heard the whispers on the street. But, unlike the others, Clayton doesn't look at me like I'm an alien, and I like to think we have struck up a friendship.

"Thank you for the drink," I say to him and look back at the woman, watching her watching me.

I look away and notice the café filling up fast with

stressed-looking people in suits and teenagers staring at their phones.

"Take a seat," Clayton says. "I need to take a few orders, then I'll come and join you in a bit. Is there anything else I can bring you?"

"Not right now." I make my way to a table that still gives me a great view of the woman.

"Curious about her, are you?" Clayton asks, startling me. I didn't notice him following me to the table.

I raise an eyebrow. "Who do you mean?"

"Cora Lane," he says. His grin reveals a slightly crooked tooth that enhances his looks rather than taking away from them. "She's a regular. Comes at least twice a week. She always orders two cups of coffee, but never drinks them both."

"Why does she do that?"

"She used to come here with her daughter." Clayton's expression grows serious, and he lowers his voice. "Now that her daughter is no longer here, she continues to show up. I think she orders the other coffee for her."

Sadness sweeps over me as I watch Cora staring into her coffee cup.

"What happened to her daughter?"

"She was hit by a car; it was all over the papers."

"Oh wow, that's so sad." I lean in closer. "Last time, she made a weird comment to me. She said it must be strange for me to be doing something good for people who do not deserve it."

Clayton frowns and looks in Cora's direction. "She said that?"

I nod. "I asked her what she meant, but she stood up and left, as though she had said too much and needed to get away before she could say more."

"I might have an idea why she made that comment," he says. "But before I tell you more, I have more coffee addicts to feed. I'll be right back."

As he slides back into the role of barista, I'm tempted to speak to Cora again. She looks so sad, so lonely. Before I change my mind, I pull myself to my feet and the baby gives me a kick, as if to say it's a bad idea. Cora doesn't see me coming, and I can see that she's staring at something on the table. The moment she senses my presence, she jumps, and a photo falls to the floor. She doesn't need to tell me it's her daughter; the woman in the picture is a younger version of her. By the time I pick up the photo and hand it back to her, I've already memorized the moss-green dress, the bright-blue eyes, the thick, russet curls.

"What do you want?" she snaps, placing it face down next to the other cup of coffee and looking up at me.

"Hello again." I smile. "I was wondering if I can treat you to something... a donut maybe?"

"You're very kind to offer, but no, thank you." Her lips curl into a slow smile that soon disappears. "I won't let you spend their money on me."

"The Thorpes' money?" I ask.

I'm not invited, but I still take a seat, and she grabs the photo from the table and shoves it into her battered leather purse.

"You don't like the Thorpes much, do you? May I ask why?"

"You may not," she says sharply, then gives me an apologetic smile. "I'm sorry, I don't mean to be rude. I just don't like talking about them." She reaches out and taps my hand before getting up. "Have a good day."

With that, she gets up and leaves the café, and, still holding on to my unanswered questions, I return to my own table. Cora has made me even more curious about the Thorpes. But why do I care so much? I'm only here for a while. All I need to know is that they will be good parents to the child growing inside me, a child they want more than anything in the world. Nothing else should matter.

"Don't take it personally," Clayton says to me a few minutes later when I tell him what happened. "Cora may seem a bit cold at times, but beneath her grief she's a kind and generous woman who has helped a lot of people in this town, including me. She's just in pain. Sometimes it's hard to let go."

I look at him curiously, noticing the way his voice dropped to almost a hush when he said those last words. Has he lost someone he loves, too?

"You say it like you know from experience," I say, inviting him to share.

Each time I come to the café, our conversation revolves around the town, its people, and sometimes the weather. He has never said anything about himself, and I didn't want to be curious. But now I am.

He forces a smile that immediately crumbles. "My wife. She died two years ago... cancer."

"Oh, I'm so sorry, Clayton." Without thinking, I reach for his hand and give it a brief squeeze.

"Life goes on. At least I still have my daughter." A genuine smile warms up his face again. "Heidi. She's five."

My mother died when I was much older than Heidi, and the pain still stabs my gut. I guess grief never disappears, it just tucks itself away until a memory awakens it. I give him time with his thoughts and wait for him to speak. He tells me that it was a week after his wife's death that he moved back to Wellice from DC, where he worked as an intellectual property lawyer.

"You're a lawyer? I had no idea."

"Hard to imagine, huh?" He glances down at his rock and roll t-shirt. "Gone are the days of stifling suits and ties. I do miss the job, but not a life on the treadmill."

"Do you see yourself doing it again?"

He shrugs. "I don't know. Maybe. Maybe not. Right now, this is where we belong. This is where we heal." He rubs his eyes. "As I was saying, I think I know why Cora made that weird comment to you, about you doing something for people who don't deserve it."

"Why do you think she said it?"

I want him to go on telling me about himself, but he clearly doesn't want to speak about it anymore.

"Her daughter, Daisy Lane, used to work for the Thorpes. Most people do in this town. They own many of the businesses here. She was a salesperson in the boutique here in town."

"Isn't them giving her daughter a job reason enough for her to like the Thorpes?"

"At the time of her death, a little over a year ago, she was no longer employed there. She'd been fired."

"Oh," I say. "So, her mother is angry with them about that?"

"I guess so."

I pick at my fingernails. "Do you know why her daughter was fired?"

"Apparently Marcia Thorpe had a falling out with her." Clayton pauses. "You know what, let's not gossip, there's enough of that in this town. I should give you a tour sometime; I'm getting the feeling this is the only place you come to."

A blush creeps into my cheeks. "That's because this is the only place where I have a friend."

"Well, you're welcome here anytime." He smiles.

"Thanks, Clayton. And I'll take you up on your offer for a tour one of these days."

"Do that. For what it's worth," he continues, "I think what you're doing for the Thorpes is incredible. It doesn't matter what anyone else thinks."

I remain at the café for another half an hour before heading out. In my hand is a note with Clayton's number.

Back at the Thorpes, I hurry down the path between the main house and the guesthouse before anyone tries to speak to me. I'm about to unlock the door when I notice a piece of paper at my feet, lying flat on the doorstep. A hand-written note.

When I read the words, my body goes rigid.

*You're making a big mistake. This won't end well.*

My throat tightens as I look around, but I don't see anyone. I pick up the note with trembling hands. My temples are pounding with rage as I march into my bedroom. Then I stop suddenly in shock at the scene in front of me.

The mattress is stripped of its sheets, which are lying in a crumpled mess at the foot of the bed. I made the bed before I left the house. I always do.

# CHAPTER 11

I'm inside the dark closet, surrounded by the smells of the new clothes and shoes I haven't worn yet and my own sweat. My legs are outstretched, my belly nestled between my thighs, the June heat causing sweat to glue my skin to the wooden floor. This is what I was terrified of: the panic attacks, never knowing when they will hit, doing everything to keep them away. There was a knock on the door thirty minutes ago, and now all my senses are on full alert. I was sleeping, and when I finally got up to check, there was nobody there. At first, I thought I imagined it, but then I remembered the note I found on the doorstep two days ago.

*You're making a big mistake. This won't end well.*

The words repeat themselves over and over inside my head as I wrap my arms around my upper body. A trickle of dread touches my spine, sending a chill spreading through my entire body. What if someone wants to drive me to the edge of madness, forcing my body to sabotage the birth of the child I promised to bring into this world?

I can't stop thinking about Agnes, how opposed she is to the pregnancy. How far would she go to protect her daughter from something she thinks will harm her? I didn't confront her about the note and the unmade bed, even though I'm sure it was her trying to drive me away. I decided the best revenge would be to do nothing, ignoring her, pretending her games don't faze me. But here I am—inside a closet in the middle of the night, afraid of an old woman.

I don't want to mention it to Marcia or Travis, because it might only make them even more protective and worried about me. And I don't have any evidence to prove it *is* Agnes. Marcia would never believe that her mother would threaten me like that. So, I'll have to find a way to handle her on my own without upsetting Marcia. I'm strong enough.

*And yet you're hiding inside the closet?*

I force myself to step out of my hiding place, resisting the urge to switch on the lights. I sit on the bed and wedge my shaking hands between my knees. The darkness is softened by silver moonlight filtering in through the slits in the curtains. I need to pull myself together. The longer I sit here, the more I obsess over whether that knock on the door really happened or if it's something my imagination cooked up. I need to speak to someone who might be able to calm me down.

Sydney. I pick up the phone from the nightstand and switch on the screen, watching the green light chase away some of the darkness. She doesn't pick up but, as soon as I hang up, she calls back.

"Hey, stranger," she says.

"Sorry it's been a while," I say, resting a hand on my damp forehead.

She pauses, then asks, "How's the baby?"

I dip my head to one side. It's not like her to ask about anything relating to my pregnancy.

"Fine, I think." I put a hand on my belly for a few seconds before moving it away again.

"I'm happy to hear that." I can hear the falsehood behind her cheeriness, but it's okay, she's trying.

"We don't have to talk about the baby," I say.

"Grace, are you okay?" she asks. "You sound strange."

"Not really." I press my lips together to keep the tears at bay.

"Did something happen?"

"I had a panic attack."

Sydney knows all about them. For a while, I called her every time I had one. They had been happening less and less over the years, but when they do happen, they are rough.

"Did something trigger it?"

"I thought I heard knocking. When I went to check, there was no one there."

"Are you sure?"

"No." I close my eyes and focus on the thick darkness behind my eyelids. "I'm not sure. Maybe it was a dream."

"Did you try your breathing exercises?"

"I did, and it helped a bit." I scrunch up my face in embarrassment. "I was inside the closet."

"That bad, huh?" Concern drips from Sydney's voice. "Thunderstorm or hurricane?"

"Thunderstorm." I smile in spite of myself. "I called you before it got worse."

"That's good. But you need to see a doctor. Your blood pressure must be sky high and that's not good... for you or the baby." Knowing that she's trying to support me means a lot, and my desire to open up grows.

"I will, but I think it's also important for me to deal with the root cause."

"Are the Thorpes still treating you like an egg?"

"Kind of. I didn't tell you this, but Marcia's mother is living here now too, at the house with Marcia and Travis. When I moved here, she was on a trip to Turkey."

"Is she nice? Is she excited about the baby?"

"Quite the opposite. Marcia said she's totally against it. I haven't really spoken to her much."

Sydney goes quiet again. Will she side with Agnes or change the subject?

"I can only imagine how that might give you even more anxiety," she says, to my surprise.

"I think she's trying to drive me away." I lie down on my side, holding my bump.

"What? What is she doing?"

"You know what, I don't want to get into it." Telling her about everything that has been happening will work me up even more. "It's hard living with someone who disapproves, that's all."

"Maybe you should come back home," Sydney says, the same thing she proposed last time we talked.

"You know I can't do that."

I don't even have a home. Back in Miami, I would be a pregnant, homeless, jobless woman. Sydney, who has put my few belongings for storage in their attic, would let me stay with her, but I don't know if I could cope with her constant disapproval.

"Grace, you're unhappy over there, and it sounds like they're treating you like crap. You need to take care of yourself right now, not just the baby. Your mental health is important too."

"I'll be back home before long, and it's not that bad. I'm fine, really. It's just one of those nights."

"It doesn't sound like you're fine." I can almost see her worried expression. "Grace, I understand that you agreed to this arrangement, and you don't want to break a promise, but you being unhappy doesn't help anyone."

"Don't worry about me. I'll handle it."

"Fine. Then you need to talk to that old lady. Whatever she's doing, she needs to stop."

I let out a bitter laugh. "She doesn't speak to me. Most of the time, she pretty much pretends I don't exist."

Our conversation peters out after that. There's only one thing Sydney wants to say to me, and she knows I won't listen. Unable to sleep, I go to the living room and switch on the TV. I don't care if Marcia sees the light. If she wants to come to the guesthouse, let her; I'm too tired to care.

I thought coming to Wellice would help me be more at peace, but instead the stress here is wreaking havoc with my body and mind. My eyes are heavy and sore from lack of sleep and my head feels like a brick. There's nothing worth watching, so I stop at the news channel and mute the TV.

The words on the screen tell me the news segment is about Julia Williams, a woman in Corlake, a nearby town, who was found dead in a lake close to where she lived. That was about seven months ago, and the marks around her neck suggest she may have been murdered.

I'd already heard the story making the rounds at Clayton's Coffee Lounge.

Bad news is not something I can handle right now. I flick off the TV and push myself to my swollen feet, and that's when I notice the open window. The opening is only a few inches wide, but I'm certain I checked every window before I went to bed. I push back the curtains and peer through the glass. I'm sure someone is out there, watching me. Is it Agnes?

I remain standing at the window. I won't let her or anyone else intimidate me, not after I've come this far. I'm not going anywhere, and neither is the baby.

# CHAPTER 12

Two days after hiding in the closet like a coward, I leave the house at six before Marcia or Travis come to check up on me. I need to have some space, and Agnes needs to stay the hell away from me. I get into the car, toss my purse onto the passenger's seat, and start the engine, and when the car slides out of the driveway, I clench the steering wheel tight.

*Don't look up at the windows. Don't look.*

I'd bet good money one of them is watching.

My hope is to catch Clayton before the customers arrive at the café. Although it officially opens at seven, he mentioned he's often there around six to get things ready for the day. But I arrive at twenty minutes past six to find the door locked, and the "closed" sign up. I place my hands on both sides of my face and peer through the glass door. There's no movement inside, but I guess I shouldn't be surprised. Wellice is a laid-back town and most posted business hours are only a formality; they can change at the drop of a hat. I guess in a small town, anything goes.

Maybe the café is opening its doors later today, and Clayton doesn't feel the need to come in early. Random working hours must have been quite an adjustment for him after his career as a lawyer. Or maybe that's what he had been looking for, a more relaxed environment, a place to start over after the death of his wife.

To kill time, I take a stroll to the Fairy Botanical Garden, a five-minute walk from the coffee shop. I'm already drained and feel heavy from lack of sleep, but instead of resting on one of the benches, I follow the meandering walkways toward the fishpond in the center of the garden. It's surrounded by blue and white hydrangeas and lavender, and a fairy statue is standing proudly in its center, carrying an overflowing pail of water. Being in the garden is like being transported into a magical, mystical realm, a place I would have loved as a child. When I think about my child someday coming here, running among the flowers and playing at the edge of the pond, it makes my heart happy.

I grit my teeth and shut my eyes, forcing my mind to stop thinking of the child as mine, even by mistake. When I open them, I ignore the tightening of my throat and focus on my surroundings.

The only other people in the garden with me are two men tending to nearby plants, gardening tools and bags of potting soil at their feet. They wave and I wave back before turning away. I focus on the water, watching colorful fish swimming back and forth, free and unburdened by life's troubles. I had an aquarium as a child in my bedroom and in every place I've lived as an adult, some smaller than others. I gave my last one to Sydney for safekeeping before I moved to Wellice, and she promised to give it back when I found my new home.

Where will that be? Will I even return to Miami after this, or go somewhere else? Everything is up in the air right now and thinking about the future uses up too much energy. The little energy I have must be spent on making it through the present. Right now, my future is limited to the time when the baby is born.

The ringing of my phone in my purse pulls me from the hypnotic state I have sunken into, and I stare at the screen and groan. It's Marcia, probably wanting to check up on me because they saw me drive away this morning. My finger hovers over the pick-up button, but I shake my head and put the phone away. The ringing continues for a while and finally dies before, a few seconds later, it starts all over again.

"For God's sake," I mutter, my jaw tightening. "Why can't they leave me alone for just a couple of hours?"

I know Marcia tries to give me space, but sometimes she's so intrusive and her constant fretting is bad for my own anxiety. When the ringing continues, I close my eyes, counting the seconds until it stops again. The harsh sound finally dies and is replaced by the hiss of a sprinkler in the distance, and the hum of bees and rustling of leaves in the trees above. I glance back at the gardeners. Only one is left, and he's on his knees, a hand holding one of the white flowers sprouting from a bush. His mouth is moving, as if he's talking to it, and a smile ruffles the corners of my lips. It's nice to see someone enjoying their job. I draw in a deep breath, enjoying the invigorating, sweet scent of flowers.

Ten minutes later, I turn to walk back to the blossom-covered front gate. I'm not sure whether it's the pregnancy hormones or just everything in general, but my eyes brim with tears. This is not at all how I thought things would be. I swipe at the tears with the heels of my hands and swallow the lump lodged in my throat. When I pass the church, my phone trills again. It continues to ring until I reach the café, which is open now, but I'm no longer in the mood to go inside. Instead, I get back to my car and slam the door shut, and twenty minutes later I'm back. As soon as I step out of the car, Travis bursts out from the house and, when he nears me, I notice the deep frown on his brow.

"Grace, you had us worried. Where did you go so early? And why didn't you answer Marcia's calls? I thought—"

"I went to the botanical garden. I needed some fresh air." My voice is hard, daring him to question my decision to exercise my freedom of movement.

"You should have told us. You can't just leave like that without letting us know."

"Oh, Grace, thank God you're all right." Marcia runs out of the house and puts her arms around me. She's still wearing her white silk pajamas and the material feels cool and smooth against my palms as I press my hands to her back.

"Marcia, I'm fine. I didn't mean to worry you. I just went for a walk."

Marcia pulls away and grips my hands. "That's okay," she says. "Please don't think we're trying to control you. You know I don't mind you going out. I was just so worried that something had happened, and you'd gone to the hospital without telling us. And you've got to be careful, going out alone around here. Did you hear about the woman who was found stabbed in Tallahassee? I know it happened a long time ago, but it's believed to be murder and they haven't caught the person who did it. Another woman was also—"

"We'd appreciate it if you don't do that again, please," Travis interrupts, his voice gentle. "You just need to let us know where you're going, so we don't worry about our baby." Arm outstretched, he moves closer, and places a hand on my belly, but I move away and cover my stomach with both hands as the maternal instincts I'd been ignoring push their way to the surface, forcing me to honor my desire to be possessive of the baby even for a second, especially now that I'm annoyed with them.

"With all due respect, Travis, I don't need permission to go out. That wasn't part of the deal, and I can take care of myself."

I may be pregnant with their child, but they don't own me. I should have made that clear from the start instead of following their unspoken rules.

"Of course you can," Marcia says quickly. "You can have all the freedom you like. What Travis is trying to say is we want to make sure you're safe. That's all."

"Marcia, do you mind if we talk?" I ask her, my cheeks burning. "In private?"

"Sure. What about?" She glances at Travis and begins to bite her nails.

"It's important. Do you mind if we go to the guesthouse?" Without waiting for her reply, I start walking and she comes after me. Before we reach the guesthouse, Marcia overtakes me and unlocks the door herself with the key she carries around with her.

"It must be something serious," she says, when we enter the living room.

"It is." I sit and watch her do the same. "Marcia, I've been meaning to bring this to your attention for a while, but—"

Her body tenses next to me. "Is the baby okay?"

"The baby is fine," I say. At least I hope it is. Yesterday, the doctor came over to check up on me and have dinner with them. He said my blood pressure was quite low, and suggested I take it slow, rest, and make sure to stay hydrated.

"Okay." She clears her throat. "Then what's bothering you?"

"Your mother," I say. "I want to talk to you about your mother."

"What about her?" Her tone is guarded, and she shifts a few inches away from me.

"I think she is doing things to scare me."

"Scare you?" I'm looking straight ahead, so I can't see Marcia's face as it starts to crumble, but I can feel her gaze. "I'm not sure I follow."

"I just... I'm getting the feeling she wants me to leave." I can't stop thinking about the note I found on the doorstep, and the state of my bedroom.

"That's ridiculous, Grace." Marcia rubs her hands up and down her thighs, then brings them to rest in her lap.

"You yourself told me she doesn't want this child in her family."

Silence falls and stretches on. Then she speaks, her voice almost a whisper. "What did she do?"

"A few days ago, I found a threatening note on the doorstep. Marcia, I think it was her who put it there."

Marcia says nothing as I tell her the words that were written on it, words I have repeated over and over inside my head. I would have shown her the note, but I have no idea where it is. I thought I had put it in the drawer of my bedside table, but I can't find it.

"I'm sorry, Grace. Finding that note must have been scary for you. And you're right, my mother doesn't want the baby. She thinks I'll regret having a child that's biologically Travis's and not mine. She would have preferred for us to keep trying to conceive or even adopt." She pauses. "She gets upset sometimes. But she's harmless really. I'll have a word with her."

"Thank you."

Marcia gets up from the couch and goes to the window to stare out at the main house. But I'm not done yet.

"We spoke about my need for privacy last time, but I still don't get the feeling that I have it."

"What do you mean?"

"You and Travis come to the guesthouse whenever you want. Travis, especially."

They no longer walk in when I'm at home, but I still feel uncomfortable with them invading my personal space when I'm out. When a tenant rents a place, the landlord can't just walk in without telling them.

"Actually, I don't." Her voice is firm now. "Are you saying you don't want us to come here anymore? It *is* our house, and we're getting this space ready for the baby."

Annoyance tickles the back of my throat.

"That's not what I'm saying. I'd just like to be notified if someone is coming here, even when I'm not in."

"I understand," she says in a strained voice. To my surprise, she reaches into her pocket. "Here's the spare key. From now on, we'll respect your privacy and, if you're not home, we won't enter. I'll speak to Travis and my mom."

She places the piece of metal into the palm of my hand, and I wrap my fingers around it.

"Thank you," I say.

"You're welcome." She pushes both hands into the pockets of her jeans. "But please, Grace, don't shut us out completely."

"I won't." I pause. "Another thing. I want to go away for a while. For a few days, a weekend maybe."

Her eyes widen. "You're leaving? Where are you going?"

"I'm not leaving town; I'll stay in a hotel for a few days."

Spending time around them has drained me, and I need

a chance to replenish my energy, even if I have to spend some of my dwindling savings to get what I want.

"But you'll be all alone. What if something happens to the baby?"

"You worry too much. Nothing will happen. And if something *does* happen, I'll call you and nine-one-one."

She breathes out, and her bangs lift before falling again to shroud her eyes. "Fine, but you're not going to stay in some cheap hotel. I'll choose the hotel—and I'll make sure you get all the pampering you need, too."

She still doesn't get it. I only want to be alone, to get the chance to pull myself together and brace myself for what the future holds.

"Thank you. I appreciate that."

"Good. I'll go back to the house to make some calls and arrange for you to go away for the weekend. I will miss our walks, but I fully respect that you need your space." She fidgets with her hands. "Do you think we can at least have another movie night before you leave?"

"Sure. How about at eight?"

"Great." She nods and heads to her studio first. The sound of the fragile door slamming shut is so loud it reaches me. I won't be surprised if she has damaged it.

# CHAPTER 13

The following morning, a loud knock on the door vibrates through the guesthouse. I zip up my small suitcase and hurry to the door. Agnes is standing on the doorstep, dressed for business as usual, in a navy pinstriped suit this time and matching velvet pumps. She runs her business from the house and only goes into the main office two or three times a week. Every other day, her assistant shows up to help her.

"I hope I'm not bothering you," she says. Her expression is not exactly unfriendly, but it's also not warm or welcoming. It seems like she's making a lot of effort to be cordial and polite.

"It's okay," I say, making an effort as well. "Can I help you with something?"

She takes a step forward, and her cigarette-tainted breath makes me want to gag. "I wanted to finish that conversation we started when we first met."

"Sure, come on in," I say, opening the door wider.

"I'm sure Marcia or Travis told you that I don't approve of the surrogacy," she says as we enter the living room. "It's not that I have anything against you, because I don't." She pauses, trying to find the right words to say. "I actually commend you for being a surrogate, but I just don't agree with you doing it for my daughter. Marcia deserves to have her own child."

"And she will." I place my hands on my belly. "This is her child."

A corner of Agnes's cheek twitches, but she doesn't smile. "We both know that's not true. It's not her egg, which means, it's not her baby... not biologically." She sighs. "It's also not fair to that child, coming into this world and not knowing that the woman raising her is not her biological mother."

"I understand, Mrs. Thorpe." I try to make my voice sound calm and assertive. "But what matters most is that the child is loved by his or her parents, regardless of who gave birth to them."

For a moment, we stare at each other in silence, and the air between us feels heavy. Then Agnes lets out a hoarse smoker's cough and, stepping forward, takes my hand.

"I know my daughter. Every time she looks into the face of that child, she'll see you, not herself. Can you imagine how painful that will be for her? And what if one day you decide you want the child back? What will that do to her?" Her bony hand squeezes mine. "Grace, please help me stop her from inflicting this pain on herself and the child. Cancel the contract and walk away."

I pull my hand from hers and step back. "I can't do that," I say, my words catching in my throat. "And I'll never ask for the child back. I wouldn't do that to Marcia."

A hint of anger appears in her eyes, then disappears a second later. "I know that you care about Marcia, and you don't want to hurt her either." Her lips form a thin line. "So,

I want to make you an offer, Grace, and I hope you will consider it."

I don't say anything, just sit down and wait for her to continue.

"I'll give you twenty-five thousand dollars if you cancel the contract and leave with your baby."

I gasp. "What? That's an absurd offer. How could you—?"

"Because it's the right thing to do. I'm offering you money to walk away. I'm even willing to provide child support."

I must admit that her offer is slightly tempting, given my current financial situation, but I don't even blink before rejecting it.

"You're forgetting one important thing. Even though the baby is not biologically Marcia's, it's Travis's. I can't take it away from its father without reason."

Silence falls between us, then she speaks again. "What if I offer you more money to disappear, where neither Travis nor Marcia could find you? You can use it to create a new life for yourself."

My eyes widen. I can't believe she's actually serious about this. "Absolutely not." I shake my head. "The answer is no. Thank you, but I will not take your money, Mrs. Thorpe. I'm sure you already know that Marcia and Travis are not paying me to do this. That's because this is not about the money. I just want to do a good thing for a couple who are desperate to have a child. And if you love your daughter, you will be happy for her, otherwise you risk destroying your relationship."

Agnes deflates like a hot air balloon, her shoulders hunching forward. But she catches herself and stands tall again, a smile on her face. "Don't answer now. Think about it and let me know your decision." She turns around and walks out the door.

When there's a knock on the door again ten minutes later, I know it's Marcia.

"I'm so sorry." She puts an arm around my shoulders. "Are you okay? I saw my mother walk out of here a few minutes ago."

I nod. "I'm fine. Marcia, I hope you don't mind, but I should finish packing."

The longer she stays, the more I might be tempted to tell her about the offer her mother just made me, but I know she'd be devastated, and I care about her too much to put her through that. Even after the baby is born and I'm gone, her mother will stay with her for the rest of her life, and this could destroy them.

She smiles at me. "Of course. I'll leave you to it."

Fifteen minutes later when I open the door to leave for the hotel, I bump into Travis, who was about to knock on my door. I can see Marcia hovering not too far away.

"Marcia told me you're going away for a few days," he says. "Grace, I don't think it's a good idea. You came here so we could be on this journey with you, so we can help."

"Yes, that's right." I close the door behind me and wheel my suitcase to the car. "But I need some space. I talked to Marcia about it; I'm sure she'll explain everything to you."

Before he can respond, Marcia joins us.

"Like I told you, Grace needs some time away," she says to her husband. "The hotel is often fully booked in June, but I was able to get her a nice and comfortable room. A bit of peace and quiet will do her and the baby good, Travis. She'll be well taken care of."

Travis shakes his head and walks away without another word, and Marcia engulfs me in a hug. "Try to get some rest. Everything will be all right, you'll see." She presses her cheek to mine, and for a moment I'm reminded that, even though things are hard, we are in this together; we both want the same thing.

"Should I drive you?" she asks, pulling away.

"No, it's okay. I'll drive myself." I glance at my suitcase.

"Don't even think about it. That suitcase is way too heavy for you to carry." She picks it up and hauls it into the trunk. "They're expecting you at the Sawyer Hotel, and I've booked some treatments for you in the spa."

I smile at her gratefully. I do appreciate her going the extra mile to make sure I'm comfortable there. She's trying, and honestly, after losing so many babies, I understand why she's holding on to this one with both hands.

"Marcia," I say gently, "I can't wait to give you this baby."

Sudden tears come to her eyes, preventing her from speaking. It's fine. I already know what she wants to say.

"I should go. I'll see you on Sunday."

"Make it Monday. That way you'll have a few more hours to yourself."

She walks back into the house just as Beatrice walks out with a garbage bag and smiles at me. I know Beatrice is approaching retirement age, and she often looks frail and tired. But when she cleans, she works quickly, efficiently, and leaves every room spotless. Once a day, she still comes to clean up the guesthouse even though I always tidy up after myself, and we share some pleasant, if brief, conversations. We discuss the weather, the town, and the news in general. She tells me about her daughter, Daphne, and granddaughter, Maggie, who works at the bank in town. We also talk about the garden, which she loves tending; two days ago, she showed up with a herb-filled pot for the guesthouse kitchen. What we talk about is often mundane, but it's always a relief not to talk about the baby.

As Beatrice dumps the bag, we wave goodbye to each other and I get into the car, looking forward to a few days without the Thorpes. As I open the car window and the morning breeze floats in, the baby kicks and I allow myself to secretly relish the swell of excitement, to pretend for a moment that I'm pregnant with a baby that I will get to keep, that we will always be as connected as we are in this moment. But then I pull myself back to the present fast, detaching myself from the impossible dream.

After driving for a few minutes along a street lined with tall, leafy trees, I peer into the rearview mirror and spot a red Jeep Grand Cherokee that looks just like Travis's. My throat tightens. It can't be. The car draws nearer, and I exhale. It's a woman I don't know behind the wheel.

Twenty minutes later, I arrive at the hotel and check in. The hotel manager, who introduces herself as Rayna Drews, insists on escorting me personally to my room, a luxury suite with all the amenities I could have imagined. It's nice to have a break from the Barbie dolls and the piles of baby things.

"Miss Cooper, we hope you'll enjoy your stay with us. If you need anything, do not hesitate to let us know."

Before the manager leaves, she reminds me of the spa treatments Marcia has booked for me, including a mud bath. I'm guessing the Thorpes are paying them quite a bit of money to give me such special treatment. Left alone, I lie on my bed, stretch out my arms and enjoy the delicious silence. After a few minutes, I get up again and open the windows, and a strange feeling comes over me when I don't see Marcia, Travis, or Agnes. I'm free.

Sydney keeps asking why I don't just leave if I feel so

stifled, and I have considered it sometimes. But deep down I still carry the heavy anxiety that what happened with Rachel's pregnancies could happen to mine, so I'm also very grateful for the close attention and medical support the Thorpes are giving me.

Before settling in, I call Clayton.

"What a lovely surprise," he says. "I never thought you'd call."

"Well, someone told me to call them when I have time. And, as it turns out, that's all I have for the next three days."

"Why three days?"

"I'm not staying with the Thorpes right now. I've moved into the Sawyer Hotel for the weekend. Well, they checked me into the hotel." I lean into the mountain of cushions.

"Sounds like fun. In that case, I have a proposal to make. Let me take you to dinner tomorrow night. My mother would be happy to have Heidi all to herself. I could propose lunch, but you should experience Wellice by night. I can pick you up at seven."

"Sounds great. Let's do it." I pause. "A quick warning though: after nine p.m., I'm usually knocked out and ready for bed. Making a baby takes quite a lot of energy."

When he laughs, a warm, pleasant sensation unfurls inside my belly, and I try to pretend it's not there.

"Okay," he says. "I promise to bring you back to the hotel by nine p.m., at the latest."

"Then it's a date," I blurt out, before smacking my forehead. "I mean, I'll see you tomorrow."

It's not a date. Just two friends meeting up to eat food. Nothing more.

"It's a date," he says with a chuckle, and we hang up.

I'm unpacking my things when I come across an old photo, tucked away in one of the side pockets of my suitcase. When I pull it out and stare at it, my good mood evaporates and my eyes blur with tears. Unable to deal with the emotions, I push the photo back in its place and change my mind about unpacking. Instead, I leave the suite and go out for a walk in the hotel garden, opting for a bench in front of the fountain. Wherever I go, I tend to gravitate toward water, searching for the kind of peace only it can give.

The baby is the light at the end of the tunnel, for both me and the Thorpes. I have to believe that nothing will go wrong.

# CHAPTER 14
## SATURDAY, 12 JULY 2014

The phone rings and when I see who the caller is, my fingers tighten around the device and my body tenses up. The last time I talked to Rachel on the phone was last July, the day after I made the decision not to be their surrogate, the day I lost her. Before that, we used to speak at least once a day. Now we never call, we just email or text no more than once a month, mainly me. I tried calling her several times, but she never answered except to send me a text saying, *What do you want?*

I want my sister back and a chance to fix what I broke. Unfortunately, wanting something too badly is almost a guarantee that you won't get it. I curl up in bed, still holding the ringing phone in a vice grip. The desire to hear my sister's voice after so many months comes hand in hand with crippling anxiety. With so much pain hanging between us, how will we even start the conversation? I have lost count of how many of my apologies went ignored. The endless texts, the long emails, all unanswered and left to go stale. When we communicated, I would always say, "How are you doing? I hope you're okay."

The answer was always the same, two simple words: *I'm fine*. I know it's a lie. I understand her pain and bitterness and why she hates me. I chose a man over her, letting her down when she needed me most. The decision I made to cancel the arrangement I had come to with Rachel and Peter had more to do with me than with Chad. It stemmed from the fear of letting Rachel down; I know that now. If it didn't work for Rachel so many times over, why would it work for me? What if I couldn't conceive or carry the baby to term? What if, instead of joy, I brought her even more pain?

I chose to chicken out so I wouldn't end up hurting her, but I did anyway, and now I have another chance to make things right. If I must apologize a thousand times, so be it. I take a deep breath and press the button.

"I'm really sorry," I say, before she has a chance to speak. "I'm sorry that I hurt you like that. I feel terrible." As tears spring to my eyes, I yank a tissue from a box on my nightstand. "I shouldn't have listened to Chad."

I don't tell her that things with Chad are complicated now, that our relationship is broken. It all started two months ago, after he let it slip that he really *did* propose to test if I loved him enough to choose him over Rachel. One truth followed another, and eventually he admitted he isn't ready to get married anytime soon; he wants the day to be extravagant and to save up for a while longer. We are still together, but the sting of betrayal runs deep.

I was so stupid; I should have known what he was doing. He has never admitted it to me, but I get the impression that he's jealous of my relationship with Rachel. When he became a part of my life, my sister and I were inseparable. We are twins, after all. It was always us against the world. And, as an only child, he finds it hard to understand the bond we shared.

Sometimes, I ask myself if Chad had not proposed that day, would I have gone through with the surrogacy, or would I have ended up still disappointing Rachel?

The silence on the other end stretches and thickens. Clearly, Rachel has not forgiven me, but then why did she reach out? She coughs and goes silent again for a few seconds before finally speaking.

"I'm not calling to talk about that. I don't... I don't want to discuss it. I have some good news." Her tone has transformed from somber to light and excited. Rachel has always been that way. When she's deeply hurt, she ignores the pain rather than talking about it. I'm the opposite; it tortures me so much more to hold it in.

"Tell me." I crumple the tissue in my hand and force a smile. "I'd love to hear the good news." I try to lighten my voice, but it feels false.

"I'm pregnant," she squeals. "The due date is next March. It will be a spring baby."

There it is again, the familiar excitement in her voice, the hope that comes with every new pregnancy, like the past never happened. I want to be happy for her, but her words settle in my stomach like a stone sinking to the bottom of the ocean. After what happened last time, the doctors told her that another pregnancy would probably end in a miscarriage, and she should perhaps consider other options. But Rachel is never one to quit, even when things get hard.

"I'm so happy for you, Rachel," I say with tears in my eyes, both of joy and dread. "That's really... wow. That *is* great news." Even though I'm nervous about this baby not making it either, I have another chance to support her and I will.

"Do you mean it?" she asks. "You're really happy for me?"

"Of course I am," I reply. "How can you even ask that?"

"Thank you." She giggles. "You know what, Grace? I have a good feeling that this is it. I think this time it will work."

I silently pray that she's right.

"Peter must be so happy," I say.

"Very happy. He feels the same way I do. We *will* get to meet this baby."

Peter shares the same kind of enthusiasm and hope as his wife, more focused on the good rather than the bad, the present rather than the past, living life forward instead of in rewind. Who am I to doubt them?

"Let's meet for lunch tomorrow, so I can tell you all about it. I'll bring the ultrasound photo."

"Yes, that would be really nice." I bite back tears.

We talk about the baby for an hour and when doubts and fears arise in me, I push them down. I'm putting my sister first this time, the most important person to me. I lift my left hand and the diamond engagement ring glints at me, reminding me of what I did, urging me to make things right.

After Rachel's call, I meet Chad for breakfast, like I do every Saturday morning. As soon as I enter the restaurant, his creased brow, rigid posture, and narrowed eyes warn me that something is wrong.

"Is everything all right?" I ask, bending to kiss him on the lips, but he turns to give me his cheek instead.

"I tried calling you several times," he says, dropping into his chair. "You didn't pick up."

"My sister called me." I can't hide the smile that creeps up on my face.

He visibly stiffens. "Rachel?"

"Obviously Rachel; I only have one sister," I say sharply and pick up the menu even though I already know what I'm having. "Should we order?"

"What did she want?" Chad asks.

I lower the menu. "She's pregnant again."

"I thought you two didn't speak anymore." His mouth stretches into a tight-lipped smile.

"We made up. She reached out to me."

"Well, since you have her back, I guess you don't need me anymore. You'll continue to put that woman first." His fists clench on the table.

"What are you saying, Chad? She's my sister. I haven't spoken to her on the phone in a year. Can't you try to be happy for me?"

He scoffs. "I want to, but I can't. Now that Rachel is back in your life, you'll no longer have time for us, again. And when she loses her baby, and we both know she will, you'll be the one at her side for weeks on end. You'll put our relationship and your life on hold, just as you always do." He shakes his head. "I'm sorry, Grace, but I can't do this anymore."

"How dare you?" I snap, my temples throbbing with rage. "I never thought you could be this cruel. How could you say those things?"

"No," he retorts. "You're cruel to yourself to let her back into your life after she's ignored you for a year. The world always has to revolve around her. I'm sick of it."

"You know what, Chad?" I push my chair back and shoot to my feet. "I have bad news for you. Rachel will never go away. When she needs me, I will be there for her, and I won't let you or anyone else make me feel guilty for that."

"So what are you saying, Grace? That you're choosing her instead of me?"

"I guess I am." I pause. "I don't think I want this anymore. You're not the person I thought you were." I start to walk away from the table when he calls my name.

I spin around, tears coating my eyes. "What?" I shout. I don't care that people are watching, that I'm embarrassing him.

"In that case, can I have my ring back?" His face shows no expression whatsoever, his eyes calm and cold, and it frightens me.

"Of course," I say, sliding it off my finger. I return to the table and drop it into his cup of coffee.

"You'll never be happy without me, I promise you that," he says. "And I just know that once you walk out that door, you'll regret doing this, and you'll come groveling back to me." He fishes the ring from the coffee and holds it up to the light. "You'll beg me to put this ring back on your finger."

"No, Chad," I reply. "I won't do that, and I'll be just fine without you." Then I turn and walk out.

The next morning, I find him sitting on my front step with a bouquet of red roses and an apology. He says he made a mistake and begs me to give us another chance, but I don't. Before he gets back into his car, he swears that he will never let me go. He will always be waiting for me to realize that he's the only one for me.

# CHAPTER 15
## PRESENT

"Clayton tells me you're from Miami," Nina Price says, putting a slice of buttered whole wheat bread on my plate, next to the cold meats. She looks nothing like her son. While he's on the darker side, she has pale-blonde hair, pale skin, with a spattering of freckles, and clear-blue eyes. It's my last day away from the Thorpes, and Clayton talked me into having breakfast at his place with his mother and daughter. He said it was Nina's idea to invite me over.

Clayton's Coffee Lounge used to be hers, and she named it after her only child. When he returned to town, she handed the reins over to him, a way to keep him busy for a while so he wouldn't dwell on the loss of his wife and lose himself in his grief.

"Yes, I am," I reply. "Miami is my hometown... or city, actually."

Nina takes a seat. "Can you believe I've never been to a big city before? Not even when Clayton lived in Washington, DC. They terrify me! Too many people, too much traffic."

"I totally get you," I say.

"Mom, did I tell you that Grace was a magazine editor?" Clayton asks while cutting Heidi's sausages into smaller pieces.

"Well, that's fancy. What made you quit all that and come here to...?" Her voice drifts off and she looks down at her food. It's as if she's realized the answer and knows her question may be more personal than she meant it to be.

"It doesn't matter why Grace left her job, Mom," Clayton cuts in. "She chose to do something nice for some-body. Isn't that all that matters?"

They have no idea that I left the job long before I decided to become a surrogate.

"Of course." Red spots appear on Nina's cheeks. "I'm sorry if I made you uncomfortable, Grace. It's a little hard to know what to say."

"You didn't make me feel uncomfortable." I stab a baby tomato with my fork and bring it to my lips. "It's quite refreshing for someone to talk about it in front of me. Most people around here discuss it behind my back."

"See, Clayton." Nina throws her son a look. "She doesn't mind talking about it."

It looks like Clayton had warned her beforehand against bringing up the topic. But how could she not? It's not as if I can hide my pregnancy.

"Is the baby's daddy in Miami?" Heidi asks.

The fork that was on its way to my lips freezes in midair. Maybe it wasn't a good idea to bring up the topic in front of Clayton's daughter.

"Heidi," Clayton scolds, then looks at me. "I'm so sorry."

"It's fine." I wait until I've finished chewing before I address her question. "Actually, the father of the baby is right here in Wellice."

"Is he your husband?" she asks, her head tipped to the side, and her big, brown eyes bright.

Clayton closes his eyes and pinches the bridge of his nose. When he attempts to speak, I hold up a hand to stop him. Heidi deserves to know the truth, at least some version of it. I raise both my eyebrows at him, asking for permission without words, and he shrugs and leans back in his chair.

"You know what?" I fill Heidi's glass with more apple juice mixed with water. "I want to tell you a little secret. The baby inside my tummy is not mine."

Heidi's eyes widen with curiosity. "Somebody else's baby is in your tummy? That's funny."

"A little, but it's also exciting."

Heidi glances at her father. "I don't understand."

"Sweetheart," Clayton interjects. "Grace is a nice person. She's so nice that she wants to give a baby to someone who doesn't already have one."

"Like a gift?"

"Exactly like that." I smile at Clayton, thanking him for helping me out. "I love making people happy."

"Okay," Heidi says. "When I get big, I want to do that. I'm going to give someone a baby."

The silence that falls over the table is palpable, and no one knows how to break it. Finally, Nina stands up from the table. "I think we're done here. Come on, marshmallow. Let me drive you to school." She gives me a wink.

"It was nice meeting you, Heidi," I say to the little girl. "Hopefully I'll see you again sometime."

"I want to see the baby when it comes out." Heidi bounces up and down.

"I'm pretty sure you will."

Satisfied by my answer, she slides off her chair, kisses her father, then comes to stand next to me, putting both hands over my stomach. "Nice to meet you, baby. I'll see you around." We all laugh, then Nina tells Heidi to go put on her shoes. Before she follows her granddaughter out of the kitchen, she looks at me.

"Only a special person can do what you're doing, Grace," she says. "I'm happy to have met someone like you."

I nod, not trusting myself to speak. The tears are too close. When Nina and Heidi leave the house, Clayton and I remain at the table, finishing up our food. He has the day off and is in no rush to go anywhere.

"I'm sorry if that conversation made you uncomfortable." He raises his cup of coffee to his lips.

"It didn't, Clayton. You have a lovely family. Your daughter is so sweet."

It pains me to know that Heidi will never get to know her mother's love. Being a single parent must be so hard for Clayton, but he told me that if his mother was able to do it, so can he.

"Thank you," Clayton says. "Heidi went through a rough time, but coming here has done her good."

"Are you planning on staying for a while?"

"I don't plan on doing anything right now. I choose to focus on the present until it feels right to think about the future again." He pauses. "But you're leaving soon, aren't you? When are you due?"

"September twenty-fifth. Three more months left, then it will all be over."

"Will you go back to Miami, to the magazine world?"

"I don't have plans for either, but I guess I should start thinking about that. Three months is not exactly long."

Once the baby arrives, I'll no longer have a home to go to.

"Don't pressure yourself," Clayton says. "Anyway, it was nice to spend time with you this weekend."

"Yes, it was. Thank you for showing me around, I had so much fun."

Clayton did not show me anything I haven't already seen, but it was nice seeing the town he grew up in through his eyes.

"Maybe we can do it again sometime," he suggests.

"I'd like that. But it all depends on how much energy I have on a particular day. I get drained so easily now." Even though the short tour we went on the day after I arrived at the hotel was fun, I was so exhausted by the end that I almost fell asleep during dinner.

"Not a problem. We can do lazy things. I promise not to take you on exhausting walks anymore."

I laugh. "I'd appreciate that."

Clayton stands up from his chair and clears the table, and I get to my feet as well. "Let me help."

"No. Sit and relax. I've got this."

I watch as he moves easily around the kitchen, doing the dishes and putting away the breakfast items. At one point, he turns around and catches me staring, and our eyes lock for a long time. I'm the first to look away.

"Look, I should head back to the hotel to pack. I'm expected to check out by twelve."

"Yeah, I'll drive you back."

"Are you sure? I can take a cab."

"That's not going to happen. I brought you here and I will take you back." He folds the black-and-white checkered dish towel in his hands and hangs it over the oven rail.

Inside his SUV, we don't speak much, but it isn't uncomfortable and when he pulls up at the hotel entrance, he turns to me. "Don't let them get to you. And if you need a friend, you know where to find me. You have my number."

"Why are you being so kind to me, Clayton?"

He shrugs and his mouth quirks up at the corners. "I don't know. I guess I like you a little."

I want to tell him I like him too, but I can't. I wouldn't want to give him the wrong impression. My life is way too complicated for anything more than friendship.

"Thank you again for breakfast and everything else. I'll see you around."

He chuckles. "You certainly will."

Back in my hotel room, I switch on my phone. I had it switched off because I didn't want my time with Clayton and his family to be disturbed by Marcia's endless calls. She has called me five times and left a voice message.

"Hi, Grace. I'm calling to let you know that you no longer have to worry about my mother. I'll explain more when we speak."

I finish packing swiftly, and when I go downstairs to check out and leave, I'm surprised to find Marcia and Agnes in the lobby. Marcia runs over to give me a hug and puts her hand on my stomach. "I'm so happy to see you both."

"You too, Marcia. But you didn't have to come and get me," I say. "I have the car, remember?"

"Oh, yes, I know." Marcia glances in her mother's direction, then back at me. "I was calling to let you know that my mother is moving in here until the baby is born." She leans closer to me and whispers, "I don't want her upsetting you any longer."

"She's going to stay in this hotel?" I peer over her shoulder at Agnes, who's talking to two of the hotel employees. "You don't have to do that, Marcia. It's still a while until the baby comes."

"If you're worried about us spending money, don't be. This hotel belongs to us. My aunt is the hotel manager; my mother's maiden name is Sawyer."

"I had no idea." Maybe I shouldn't be surprised. Clayton did tell me that they own a lot of businesses in town.

"It's not a big deal. What's important is that my mother will be out of your hair. You don't have to feel bad; she was happy to move out. She will only be coming to the house once a week for dinner."

I'm about to respond when Agnes approaches us.

"I'll go speak to my aunt for a bit," Marcia says and walks away. "I'll be right back."

"Grace," Agnes says in a formal tone, "I hope you enjoyed your stay here. Marcia likely told you that they asked me to move in here for a while as they don't trust me around you. I'm convinced it was Travis's idea." She pauses as if trying to regain control of her emotions. "While I would prefer to be in my own home, I hope that with me out of the house, you will take the time to think about my offer."

I'm about to reject her again when she holds up a hand. "Don't say anything yet. I'll stop by the house soon and we can discuss it then. I should go up to my room." She gives me a nod and walks toward the elevator, followed by a porter carrying two large designer suitcases.

"I'll help her settle in. See you at the house?" Marcia calls as she runs after them on her six-inch heels.

"Yeah," I say, still dumbfounded by Agnes's inability to take no for an answer. "See you later."

On my way back to the house, I feel more prepared for what will come next. Not having Agnes around lifts some of the weight I've been carrying. When I get there, Travis comes out to greet me with an awkward hug. "I'm glad you're back."

"Thanks." I pull away and smile back at him.

"How's my baby?" I can't help flinching a little when he lays his hands on my belly.

"Fine. The baby is fine."

"That's great." He steps away and stares at me. "Grace, I want to apologize for the other day. The way I reacted to you going away."

"That's okay."

He pushes his hands into his pockets. "I hope that taking time away did you good. I heard you made some new friends in town."

I narrow my eyes at him. "I... Yes, I did."

"It's okay. You don't have to feel awkward about it. It's not as if you're dating someone." He laughs like it's a funny joke, but his eyes are tense.

"Not right now, no." What is he getting at?

He lets out an audible sigh. "Thank God. We wouldn't want any complications now, would we?" He pauses. "I need to edit some photos, but first, let me help you take your bags to the guesthouse."

After he puts my luggage inside and leaves me, an uneasy feeling rises in my stomach. How does he know that I didn't spend the time alone?

# CHAPTER 16

I switch off the lights in the house and check that the windows and doors are locked. If I don't, I won't be able to fall asleep. I feel heavier today, depleted of energy, ready for the baby to arrive. The weight of exhaustion pushes me down onto the bed and deeper into the mattress, and I rub my temples, but the pounding in my head continues to taunt me. I refuse to take meds, but maybe sleep will help. That is, of course, if I'm able to relax enough to drift off.

I stare into the semidarkness, watching the August moonlight making the curtains glow. The soft light helps my eyes adjust to the dark, but I don't want them to. I'm about to close my eyes, to force them to obey me, when a ball of pain explodes in my abdomen. It resembles the menstrual cramps I suffered from as a teenager, only worse. So much worse. The painful sensation moves like a wave from the top to the bottom of my belly.

My hands hold on to my stomach, and I do my best to breathe through my mouth. When the cramp goes away, only to return moments later, fear grips me. My heart is thudding, sweat sliding its way down my forehead to my pillow. I turn to lie on my other side, praying out loud that the pain means nothing. The stress of the past few weeks must have taken its toll, and my body is rebelling against me. Once I get some rest, I'll be fine. But the pain doesn't let go. Every time I think it's gone, it rears its ugly head again. I want to move, but it feels like I'm chained to the bed.

I've read many books on labor contractions. This feels like one. Something warm spreads underneath me and my mind instantly knows what it is. More tears flood my eyes. It can't be, it's a month and a half too early. My body has to be playing tricks on me. Gritting my teeth, I stretch out my hand toward the nightstand and fumble around for my phone. The tips of my fingers come into contact with it, but they push it farther away from me until it thuds to the floor. I groan and try to get out of bed, to pick up the phone, to call for help. When I stand up, my head starts spinning and my body sways from side to side. I bend my knees slightly, but before I can reach the phone with my hand, another cramp cuts through me like a knife.

A scream pushes its way up my throat and pours from my lips. Dropping to my knees, I squeeze my eyes shut, waiting for this wave to pass. When it finally does, I find the phone and call 911, hands trembling. But when an operator picks up, I don't have the strength to speak. The words coming from my lips are a jumbled mess. More pain strikes, and another scream escapes. The phone slips from my hand and hits the floor for a second time. I can hear the muffled voice of the person on the other side, but I cannot respond.

"Help," I whimper, one arm around my belly, the other gripping the frame of the bed. As I sink deeper into the dark waters of agony, the voice from the phone becomes faint until I no longer hear it through the rush in my ears.

When I get another reprieve, I drag myself back onto

the bed and lie in a fetal position, gasping for air. I don't even react when I hear a sound in the house, growing louder by the second. Footsteps are making their way to my room, and someone is calling my name. I'm unable to answer them. It hurts too much to do anything.

But it's okay. I recognize the voice: it's Marcia. The door creaks open.

"Oh my God." Marcia rushes to the bed. "It's too early. The baby can't come now."

I've reached the point where I don't care if the baby comes early. I just want to be free from the pain.

"Help me," I whisper again. She cannot help on her own, she's not a doctor. She needs to call the ambulance. My eyes drift shut again, and oblivion starts to pull me under. All I can see behind my eyelids are little dots now.

"I need to take you to the hospital." Marcia's voice is squeaky with panic. "Breathe," she begs. "Just breathe." Her footsteps move around the room, and she starts talking, maybe to someone on the phone. She's panting as though she shares the pain I'm in.

"Hang in there," she soothes, finally coming back to my bedside. "The ambulance will be here soon." Instead of answering, I start to cry. Marcia does everything to comfort me. She wipes away the tears, rubs my back, tries to make me comfortable on the bed. But she fails. If anything, I'm feeling worse. I need her to be here, and I need her to leave me alone. Sometimes her touch is comforting. Sometimes it hurts. Her hands leave my body, and I listen to her walk away from the bed. There's a rush of water in the bathroom, then a cool cloth touches my forehead.

It doesn't help. The only thing that will help is if the baby leaves my body. I really think that, if it doesn't, I might die. Marcia goes away again, and when she returns, her voice is accompanied by many others. The paramedics are here. They will help.

More pain strikes. I'm certain the baby is pushing itself out, tearing through my body. Then there's nothing, no more pain, just a ringing in my ears. The baby must be out, but I can't hear it crying. A few seconds go by, or maybe it's minutes, I cannot tell. I'm still too weak to open my eyes, but my ears are alert to the conversations, the desperation in Marcia's voice.

"My baby," she cries. "What's wrong with her?"

"We're so sorry, Mrs. Thorpe," someone says to Marcia, a male voice I know quite well. It's him. "There's nothing we can do. The baby was not meant to be born."

As fear rages through me, my throat closes, and more tears push their way through my closed eyelids. The baby didn't make it. I failed Marcia, I failed Travis, I failed myself. I made a promise I couldn't keep, again. Sobs rock my body like earthquake tremors.

"It's okay," someone whispers, a different man this time. A hand is placed on my forehead, and my damp hair is pushed from my face. "It's okay, Grace. You're having a bad dream, that's all."

I open my damp eyes, expecting to see Marcia, the paramedics, and him. But none of them are in the room. It was just a dream.

All that pain, that excruciating pain... somehow none of it was real. The only person here with me is Travis, sitting in the armchair next to my bed.

"What...?" My voice drifts off as I search my abdomen for the baby, making sure it's still inside, safe and sound. Nothing seems to have changed.

"You had a nightmare, I think." He continues to stroke my forehead.

I move my head away a few inches, as it slowly dawns on me that this is wrong. Travis is not supposed to be here, invading my personal space. Not after the discussion I had with Marcia.

"I heard you screaming," he says. "I came to make sure everything was okay."

He heard me screaming? He must have been really close; I'm pretty sure he would not have heard a sound if he were in the main house. Or was I that loud?

"I couldn't sleep," he adds. "I was out for a walk."

I blink, my head groggy. "What time is it?"

"A little after midnight."

"Thank you for checking up on me," I say. "I'm fine now."

I hope he will take the hint and leave the guesthouse.

"Are you sure?" His face is creased with worry.

"Yes, I'm fine. You can go home and sleep."

He shakes his head. "I don't mind staying. I can sleep on the couch in the living room, in case you have another nightmare."

"No, you don't have to do that."

"All right then. We'll see you in the morning. If you need anything, call us." He still keeps his hand on my forehead, his palm moving against my skin. I'm about to move away from him when a sound catches my attention. It's coming from the living room.

"Someone is in the house," I whisper.

His hand still on me, Travis turns to stare at the door just as it's pushed open, and Marcia enters the doorway. He snatches his hand away, and in a few words, he explains to his wife what happened. Her eyes grow wide with worry, and she rushes to my bedside like she had in my dream.

I spend the next several minutes trying to reassure her

that the baby and I are fine and there's no reason to worry, but she insists that, in the morning, I must see Dr. Miller. I don't object; it will put my mind at ease too.

Once Travis and Marcia leave, I can't stop thinking about the voice in my dream, the one that belonged to the man I can never get away from. The man who will continue to haunt me for the rest of my life.

# CHAPTER 17

Two days after our visit to Dr. Miller, Marcia knocks on my guesthouse door carrying a fancy-looking flat square box with a silver bow on top.

"What's that?" I ask when I let her in, and she hands it to me.

"Just something to cheer you up after your awful nightmare the other night. I could tell how shaken you were by it." She chews a corner of her nail. "It's also an apology of sorts."

My hand runs over the box's velvety surface. "For what?"

"You told me you wanted your space, but I know Travis is still checking up on you and the baby a lot." She pauses. "Please don't hold it against him, Grace. He's just so protective because after so many losses, he gets worried. He really wants everything to be all right, and so do I." She rubs her hands together in excitement. "Go on, open your present."

As we sit on the couch, I carefully open the box to reveal teal-colored stretchy fabric folded inside.

"That's your yoga outfit," Marcia chirps before I have the chance to figure out what it is. She takes out the tissue paper and lays it on my lap. "I thought maybe you should do something that helps you unwind. Yoga is one of the best exercises you can do for your body and your mind, and it's a good activity for pregnant women."

I lift the tank top from the box; beneath it are matching leggings. "I'm not very good at yoga," I admit. "I'm a little lacking in the flexibility department."

"Oh, sweetie, you don't have to go it alone, and you can start as a beginner. I've signed you up for prenatal yoga in town; there's a class tomorrow."

"Tomorrow?" I stare at the box of yoga clothes with dread. "I'm not sure if that's a good idea."

Since the nightmare, I haven't trusted myself to do much outside the guesthouse, afraid I would go into labor at any moment, even though Dr. Miller assured us the baby was fine, and he didn't expect it to arrive before its due date. I'm constantly thinking about the baby's movements, worrying that I'll miss a change in them that would alert me to something going wrong.

"Why not?" Marcia asks. "It's the perfect opportunity for you to go out and have some time alone. It will be good for you."

As I gaze into my friend's kind eyes, I feel guilty for dismissing her. She's just trying to help, but I'm not sure how I feel about going to a yoga class, particularly since tomorrow, 10 August—my birthday—is a difficult day for me.

"Okay, I'll try it," I say, eventually.

After the class, I think I'll give Clayton a surprise visit at the café so we can have lunch together. I haven't seen him since the day I joined them for breakfast at his house, but he calls almost every day to check up on me.

"Fabulous." Marcia's face lights up as she gets to her feet. "I think you're going to love it."

When she leaves, I look down at the outfit again, hoping I won't end up embarrassing myself in front of a bunch of strangers.

The pair of teal yoga leggings and matching top Marcia bought me are easy to spot among the darker shades in the drawer. I'm still a little nervous about the class, but being surrounded by people who are going through the same thing and getting the opportunity to ask them some questions doesn't sound like such a bad idea. I get dressed quickly and eat a bowl of fruit for breakfast. It's 11 a.m. when I step out the door.

"You should really start letting me drive you," Marcia says, coming to greet me when I'm about to get into my car.

"Oh, that's okay. I'm not sick, just pregnant."

"But you're getting so big, Grace. I want you and the baby to be safe."

"You worry too much." I chuckle. "I'm a good driver, pregnant or not. The baby and I will be fine." One of my fears is going into labor while in traffic, but she doesn't need to know that.

"You're right, I'm being silly. You're perfectly capable of driving yourself. I have a photo shoot to get to anyway. Have fun."

I give her a smile and get into the car, adjusting the seat to make space for my growing belly.

When I arrive at the studio, I grab my purse and water

bottle and waddle to the door. I turn the handle, but it doesn't move. I glance at my watch, then at the laminated piece of paper on the door. The session is supposed to start in five minutes. How in the world do these people stay in business? After ten minutes of waiting, I call the yoga instructor, but I only get voicemail. Shaking my head, I return to my car. I'll wait another twenty minutes, and if no one shows up, I'm gone.

Fifteen minutes later, I spot another pregnant woman making her way toward the studio, a water bottle in her hand. She's average height, with curly brown hair that's only a few shades darker than her skin. When she comes to a halt in front of the door, I get out of the car to join her.

"Hi," she says, stretching out her slender hand. "You must be my newest student. I'm Andrea."

"Hi, Andrea." I shake her hand. "I'm Grace. Nice to meet you."

"I'm sorry to be a little late," she says, digging into her purse.

A little. That's an understatement, but I let it go. When we enter the yoga studio, Andrea tells me that she used to be a dancer, but when she got pregnant, she started doing yoga at home. She liked it so much she wondered if there were other people out there who might enjoy it.

"So, I turned my dance studio into a yoga studio instead."

I'm not sure how I feel about her not being a professional yoga instructor. Then again, I'm not really here for the physical benefits that yoga promises. I just want to be around other pregnant women, to ask them my burning questions and see if they share the same fears that keep me awake at night.

"Where are the others?" I ask as Andrea makes her way around the room, opening windows and laying out mats.

"They'll get here when they get here. I don't stress about time. Pregnant women already have a lot going on."

"True," I say, taking in my surroundings. There are mirrors on almost every wall and a sparkling chandelier hangs from the center of the ceiling. There's not much else in the place, and I appreciate the sense of space.

"This is a nice place," I say.

"I'm glad you like it." Andrea stops what she's doing to observe me. "How far along are you?"

"Six weeks and four days to go, but it feels like ten weeks," I say with a laugh.

"You can say that again. I'm five months pregnant and sometimes I wonder how I'm going to make it to nine."

"Have you been in this town for long?" I ask.

"Not really. I'm not originally from Wellice. I came here on vacation and met my husband. I'm originally from Philadelphia. I was a professional ballerina, but I gave it all up for love."

As we chat, two ladies enter the studio, and ten minutes later, three more women arrive.

Andrea rubs her hands together. "Everyone's here. Shall we get started?"

I nod, but I'm not able to focus on anything she shows us in the class, as the other ladies are distracting me with furtive looks in my direction. They know who I am. Everyone here probably does, and they obviously don't approve of what I'm doing. I came here hoping to bond with them, but my instinct tells me it's better to keep my distance.

The moves are hard and last too long. I'm the only one using the wall for balance in order to do the warrior pose.

Sweat drips into my eyes and my body begs me to stop torturing it, but I refuse to be the first person to quit. Instead of focusing on what I'm doing, my eyes keep going to the clock on the wall behind Andrea. The class seems to go on forever before she claps her hands. "Well done, ladies. That's it for today. See you next Saturday."

I wipe the sweat from my brow and murmur, "Thank God."

I pick up my bottle and take a slug of water, and the other ladies reach into their bags. They place containers of cut-up vegetables and other healthy snacks on a long glass table against one wall.

"Would you like to join us?" Andrea asks. I shake my head. I'm hungry, but I can't eat their food when I brought nothing. "I didn't know—"

"That's all right," she says, nudging me toward the table. "We usually use this time to get to know each other better. The food isn't what's important."

On our way to the table, I catch a whisper floating in the air. One single word. Thorpe. I want to leave before the gossip continues, but Andrea is so kind to me. I don't mind getting to know her. She picks up one of the Tupperware containers filled with carrot sticks and celery. "Have some."

"Thanks." I reach for a carrot.

"I hope you enjoyed the class," she says.

"I did." I bite on the sweet carrot. "It was... interesting."

If there's one thing I know for sure, it's that I won't be returning.

"Don't mind what other people say," she says, leaning in. "Not many people understand what you're doing."

"You're right about that."

"I struggled to conceive," she goes on to say. "We tried everything, and even considered adoption. But shortly before we started the process, we got our little surprise. Twins."

"You're pregnant with twins?"

"No, this is our third child. We have twin boys, three years old. This time, it will be a girl. How about yours?" she asks, then catches herself. "I mean, do you know what the Thorpes are expecting?"

"They don't want to know. They want it to be a surprise." I pause. "Speaking of pregnancy, do you get nightmares?"

"You mean the scary dreams that feel so real they freak you out?"

"Exactly those." I laugh. "I've been having so many of them."

"That's no surprise. Pregnant women are known to have vivid dreams."

"So it's normal?"

"It is, don't worry about it. Pregnancy comes with a lot of struggles, but it's a beautiful thing too. Maybe I'll even want more kids after this." She touches my arm. "Grace, I hope you will come again next week."

"I'm not quite sure whether I'll be available next Saturday, but I'll try." I want to leave it at that, but she's been so kind to me. She deserves honesty. "Andrea, the truth is, I don't think I will come. I don't feel like I'm welcome here."

"I'm sorry to hear that. It's not often that you see someone doing what you're doing. I don't think you should take it personally." She shrugs. "What matters is that you're doing something amazing. I'm so happy for Marcia. She really wants a child of her own."

"You guys know each other?"

"Yes. She was one of the first people to welcome me into

town when I arrived six years ago. It's hard to find your place in this community when you're a newcomer."

"I totally agree." I lift my hand and put it on my stomach, only to drop it again. Lately, each time I touch my stomach in Marcia's presence she throws me a strange look. I understand. She doesn't want me to bond with the child. So now I'm training myself not to touch my belly unless I have to.

Andrea takes a swig from her water bottle. "How many children of your own do you have?" she asks.

"This is my first pregnancy."

The moment the words leave my lips, I cringe. Whatever I tell Andrea could make it back to Marcia, and she might not find it amusing that I'm discussing the surrogacy with anyone. It's best for me to end the discussion right now.

"I'm sorry, I should leave. I have somewhere to be."

She squeezes my arm. "I understand."

I thank her for the carrots and her time and hurry out the door and, inside the car, I rest my head against the steering wheel as my tears start to surface. I jump when someone knocks on my window.

"Clayton?" I ask when our eyes meet. Embarrassed, I wipe away the tears and roll down the window. "What are you doing here?"

"I wanted to surprise you," he says. "You said you were coming here, so I thought I'd drop by." He frowns. "Looks like you need a friend." He points to the passenger seat. "May I come in?"

"Sure," I say, and I pick up my purse to make space for him. When I tell him that I felt like an outcast in yoga class, he listens, his eyes sympathetic and gentle, and he hands me a tissue to blow my nose.

"Come here," he says, opening his arms, and I lean into him.

As I squeeze my eyes shut, I try to forget the memories that this day will always bring back, the events that left me with an aching heart and a biting guilt that consumes me every day. A constant reminder of what I did.

# CHAPTER 18
## FRIDAY, 13 MARCH 2015

Peter calls when I'm packing for my trip to Seattle to attend a two-day meeting with Jaden, Inc., a cosmetics firm, and a leading magazine advertiser. I spent the last night polishing up my presentation slides and my eyes are heavy with sleep. The magazine industry is cut-throat and high-paying advertisers are tough to get. If we don't bring our A-game, Jaden, Inc. will simply throw their money at our competitors.

"Is everything okay, Peter?" I ask, dropping a tube of toothpaste into my cosmetics bag. At first, I only hear breathing on the other end, but then it's followed by laughter. "She's in labor, Grace. Rachel is in labor. The baby is coming."

"Oh, my God. That's wonderful, Peter." A rollercoaster of emotions overtakes me, a plunge into dread followed by quickly mounting excitement.

Fear has plagued me throughout Rachel's pregnancy. Every day I have been waiting for the call that will tell me the baby did not make it, that something went wrong. But nine months have flown by, and my fears have not materialized. At her most recent prenatal checkup, Rachel's

OB/GYN assured her the baby looked healthy and there was no cause for concern. Now the day has finally come, the day I will get to meet my niece. Peter and Rachel's dream of becoming parents is on the verge of coming true.

I intend to be a hands-on aunt, stepping in anytime they need me. I'm already so in love with my niece, and I know I will treat her like my own child.

"Oh, Peter, I'm so happy for you. For both of you." I join in his laughter.

When he confirms which hospital Rachel is in, I say excitedly, "I'm on my way. Tell Rachel I'll see her soon."

As soon as I hang up, I call Roman Wyatt, my boss and the owner of *Living It* magazine.

"What do you mean, you're not attending the meeting?" His voice crackles like lightning. "You know this meeting is make or break, right?"

"I do, Roman, but there's been a family emergency. I'm sorry. I'll send my updated slides to the team. Addison should be able to present."

Addison Smith is the assistant editor, and we've worked on the presentation together. It shouldn't be hard for her to slip into my shoes. With her astounding presentation skills, she'll blow them out of the water.

"You've got to be kidding me," he huffs. "Grace, the advertisers expect you to lead the meeting. Your flight leaves in two hours and I expect you to be on it."

"I'm sorry, Roman. I won't be on that flight. My sister is in labor, and I need to be with her."

"That's the big emergency? You want to skip the meeting because your sister is in labor? I don't believe this." His voice rises to a crescendo. "You can't skip an important meeting because your sister is giving birth. If it were you in labor, that would be another story."

I want to explain to him how much the birth means to my family, and how long my sister and her husband have been yearning for a baby, but I doubt that he will understand. Roman is a workaholic who only cares about his company and doesn't understand how anyone would put their personal life first.

"Let me be perfectly clear, Grace," he continues. "If you don't show up to that meeting, you're out."

My mouth drops open. "Are you seriously threatening to fire me for this?"

"It's not a threat. This is my magazine. I can do whatever the hell I want."

"Fine, Roman. Go ahead. I work harder than anybody in your company. See if you can manage without me."

I am the backbone of his magazine, the first person to enter the building every morning and the last to leave. I hold his business together, and he knows it. So honestly, I don't think he will really fire me. He has made these kinds of threats many times before when he wasn't getting what he wanted. He hangs up before I can say anything else, and at first, I stand there fuming, but my anger is soon washed away by the rush of excitement bubbling up inside me. Rachel is finally going to be a mother.

When I call Addison to explain the situation, she's fully supportive and assures me she will gladly take the reins. I drive like a maniac through the congested streets of Miami, and at every traffic light, my blood pressure rises as I urge the lights to change. By the time I arrive at the hospital, I'm sweating so much my blouse clings to my back.

As I walk through the rotating doors of the building, I transfer the large card I bought on the way from my right hand to my left because my palm is suddenly sweaty. I finally make it to the fifth floor, where the maternity unit is located.

When the elevator doors slide open, I find Peter standing there, a huge grin on his face. He looks tired, but, more than that, he looks happy. I give him a hug and hold him tight.

"How's she doing?" I ask.

"Everything is going really well." He wipes the sweat from his brow, and I notice a slight tremble in his hand.

"Can I go in and see her?"

"Sure. I'm just going to get myself a coffee before I go back."

"Peter, if you're tired, we can take turns being in the room with her. That way she'll never be alone."

"I'd appreciate that. Thank you."

"You don't have to thank me," I say. "We're family."

He tells me Rachel's room number and goes to get his coffee, and I enter the room to find my sister lying in a hospital bed, her face marked by both pain and happiness. I place the card on the windowsill and go to hug her, tears streaming down both of our faces.

"I can't believe this is happening," she says. "Emma is coming. I'm going to be a mother."

She stiffens in my arms. A contraction must have snuck up on her, and a loud gasp confirms it. She relaxes again, and I gaze into her face.

"You're going to be the best mother in the whole world." I kiss her forehead and place a hand on each side of her face. "And I promise to be the best aunty. Emma won't even know who her real mother is."

We both laugh before Rachel succumbs to another contraction.

"Is the nursery ready?" I ask, to distract her from the pain.

"It's perfect." She closes her eyes and smiles. "My daughter will love it."

Every time Rachel becomes pregnant, she and Peter build a brand-new nursery for the baby. They return or sell most of the items that belonged to the baby they lost and go on another shopping spree for the new arrival. Every pregnancy is a fresh start for them, and they never want to be reminded of what they lost. The only thing that is never ready is the crib, except this time.

When Peter returns, I excuse myself to give them their moment together. "I'll be outside, but I'll come in from time to time to see how you're doing."

Rachel smiles and squeezes my hand. "I forgive you, Grace."

I nod, blinking away the tears. I have been waiting so long to hear those words, but now that she has said them, I still don't feel relief. She may have forgiven me, but I will never forgive myself. The guilt will always remain with me. I kiss her on the cheek and hurry to the bathroom, where I grip the edge of the sink and cry. When the tears finally stop, I wash my face and go to the waiting room—only two doors from Rachel's room—and listen, wincing each time she screams. I feel her pain, but I do my best to focus on the good that will come out of her torture. An hour later, Peter comes out of the room, his face rumpled, his hair sticking out in all directions.

"Do you mind taking over?" he asks. "I need to use the bathroom."

"Of course," I say and stand up.

I go in to find that Rachel is so exhausted she can't speak to me anymore. Her hand falls limp in mine, but I hold onto her as she pushes through every contraction, and I listen to the midwife telling her she's almost there. I tell her she's doing great, but she doesn't believe me.

"Shut up, Grace," she yells at one point, and I don't hold it against her.

When Peter returns, I allow him to take his place next to his wife, and I pace the hallway outside. It seems like hours pass until, finally, Rachel stops screaming. Did the baby come? Then the screaming starts again, louder, sharper. The pain becomes too much for me to bear, so I return to the waiting room. I can still hear her, but the sounds are muffled.

Peter and I continue to take turns to be with her for six more hours. She's in so much pain, but she won't take any drugs for it because she thinks it would harm the baby. I wish I had a remote control with a button that could fast-forward time.

Two more hours later, Peter comes out to tell me she's fully dilated, and the baby will arrive soon. He hurries away to get her some iced water and, back at Rachel's side, I silently urge him to come back quickly. I don't want him to miss the most important moment in his life.

"Peter," Rachel whispers, her voice weak. "Where?"

"He'll be here soon," I say. "He's just getting you some water."

"You need to push again, love," the midwife urges. "Give it everything you've got."

She tries, then drops back onto the cushions.

"Again," the woman says. "I can see your baby. Give it one last big push."

"I am," Rachel snaps, her eyes bloodshot, her face red. She bares her teeth and gets ready to push again, her shoulders lifting from the bed before they drop back down. "I can't," she cries.

"You can!" I urge her. "You can do this, Rachel. You're almost there."

*Please, Peter, hurry*, I think. *Come and see your child come into the world.*

The doctor, nurses and midwife keep begging her to keep going. She tries hard, but the baby still doesn't come. Suddenly, her eyes bulge out of her face, her teeth chatter, and a thick vein pops out of her forehead. Then she collapses back onto the pillows and, immediately, I can see that something is very wrong.

"What's wrong? What's happening to my sister?"

"You have to leave," the doctor orders. Within seconds, the room is packed with medical personnel, and I'm ushered out. In the hallway, I bump into Peter, who's running back to Rachel's room, clutching a paper cup.

"Why are you not with her?" he asks, then his eyes light up. "Is the baby here?"

I slump against the wall. "Peter, something's wrong."

"What do you mean, something's wrong?" He drops the cup and rushes to Rachel's birthing room, but he's also told to stay out.

"What the hell happened, Grace?" He's talking to me, but his eyes are still fixed on the door.

"I don't know. She just started shaking. She couldn't... She can't push anymore."

His hands in his hair, he sinks to the floor. It feels like hours before someone comes out to speak to us.

"I'm so sorry," the doctor, a kind-looking woman with short brown hair says. "We did everything we could."

"The baby didn't make it?" I whisper, my throat thick with tears.

"My wife... How's my wife?" Peter asks, scrambling to his feet and holding onto the wall as if his legs can barely keep him upright.

"Neither of them made it. I'm so sorry."

Desperate for answers, Peter reaches for the doctor's arm. "But how...? What happened?"

"While we were trying to deliver the baby, your wife's blood pressure dropped drastically. We tried to stabilize it, but it was too late. She suffered a stroke. We attempted to save the baby by performing an emergency C-section, but the baby's heart had stopped beating."

"No, no, no," Peter howls and claps his hand over his mouth as he collapses to his knees then curls forward, his head in his hands.

Despite my desire to reach out to him and comfort him, I am paralyzed, and all I can do is clutch my chest and let out a choked sob. I feel like a nail has been driven through my heart.

It is hard to comprehend how such a thing could happen. Although Rachel had failed pregnancies in the past, she was healthy and had no complaints. She ate healthily and was in shape. She did everything right.

But I didn't.

If I had done it for her, if I had agreed to carry her child, maybe she would still be alive.

The stroke didn't kill her; I did.

# CHAPTER 19
## PRESENT

When I returned to the guesthouse after my yoga class, Marcia caught me crying and insisted on knowing what was wrong. So I caved and told her it's my birthday, and knowing that my twin sister is not here to celebrate it with me breaks my heart.

I didn't tell her how Rachel's death happened and my role in it, of course. Seeing me so upset, she immediately insisted I dine with them, not wanting me to be alone. I accepted only when she promised not to make a big deal out of my birthday. I don't want any singing or cake, because I don't deserve to be celebrated.

I wouldn't have come if I'd known Agnes was going to be joining us, too.

The way she's staring at me now, almost unblinkingly, sets my teeth on edge. I just know that when she gets the chance, she'll try again to dissuade me from giving the baby to Marcia and Travis, and I already feel exhausted even before the conversation.

Feeling both uncomfortable and emotional, I glance

down at the dry steak on my plate, wishing I were home and in my bed. I need to get out of here as soon as possible.

"Mom, how have you been at the hotel?" Marcia asks in an attempt to lighten the mood. "I hope you're allowing them to pamper you."

Even though she's smiling, Marcia looks tired and somewhat pale, as if she's also having a low day. It took her twenty minutes to come downstairs after we were seated, her eyes drowsy from a late-afternoon nap.

Agnes takes a drink of wine and picks up her knife and fork. "Let's just say, I'm much more appreciated over there than in this place."

"Come on, Mom," Marcia says. "Don't say that. That's not fair."

Agnes slices through her meat with such force that the knife scrapes the glamorous gold and white porcelain plate. "What do you want me to say, darling? You kicked me out of my own home, and you expect everything to be hunky-dory?"

As if in slow motion, Marcia's shoulders collapse, then she swallows her food and says, "We didn't kick you out, Mom. We only wanted to do what's right, considering the circumstances. And, if I remember correctly, you were quite happy to agree to the arrangement."

Agnes's upper lip curls upward and her nostrils flare. "That's because I don't approve of what you're doing. That baby—"

Travis drops his cutlery onto the plate and glares at his mother-in-law. "This is not the place, Agnes. You're going too far."

"You don't have the right to silence me," Agnes replies. "I have the right to say whatever I want in my own home.

You impregnated a stranger and you expect me to be okay with it? That won't happen."

"Grace is our surrogate," Marcia shoots back, her hands clasped together on the table, veins showing through her translucent skin. "Whether you like it or not, the baby growing inside Grace is my child and your grandchild."

"You know that's not true, darling. Whether *you* like it or not, it will never be your child either."

"That's enough, Agnes. This has to stop." Travis's fist lands on the table, shaking the plates and making juice and wine spill onto the tablecloth, staining it a dark burgundy.

Beatrice appears from the kitchen and, after a brief sympathetic smile in my direction, she starts to dab away the mess—a useless effort, but she does her best. After she's finished, she bends down to whisper something to Marcia, who whispers back and nods, and Beatrice disappears back into the kitchen. Seconds later, the kitchen back door clicks shut. It's probably Beatrice going out for some fresh air, escaping the war zone. Who can blame her?

"I think I should call it a night," I whisper to Marcia.

"You're not going anywhere." She doesn't bother to lower her voice. The words are meant for me, but her eyes are on her mother's face. "You're doing a wonderful thing for us, and because of that, I consider you to be a part of this family, not a stranger. Everyone else has to learn to live with it."

"A member of the family." Agnes's mouth twitches in amusement. "You're living in a dream world, my child."

"I stopped being a child many years ago, Mom. Maybe it's time you accepted that as well."

"I've had enough of this disrespect." Agnes tries to get to her feet with grace, but she sways from too much wine. "I'll be in the library. When you're done with your dinner, take me back to my hotel."

She grabs a napkin, presses it to her lips, and drops it on the table. It lands in her unfinished food and starts soaking up the brown sauce around her half-eaten steak.

We watch in silence as she walks unsteadily out of the room.

"I'm so sorry, Grace." Travis pats my hand. "Please don't let her words get to you."

I nod and slide my hand away from under his.

Marcia's eyes are filled with tears as she looks at me. "I shouldn't have invited her," she says. "I should have known this would happen. I hoped maybe she had come to her senses."

"Your mother will never change," Travis says in a tone that could cut through steel. "We both know that."

"I'm sorry," I say and push back my chair. The conversation is in danger of escalating into an argument that I don't want to be a part of. "I feel a bit dizzy. I'll go out for some air."

Travis jumps to his feet as well. "Do you need anything?"

"No, thank you," I say over my shoulder. "I just need a moment. I'll be right back."

Neither of them say another word to me as I exit the dining room and step onto the terrace outside the living room. Leaning against the wall, I close my eyes and count to fifty to calm myself down. The moment I open my eyes again, I hear footsteps behind me. I turn, expecting to see Marcia or Travis, but it's Agnes with a glass of water in her hand.

"Marcia came to have a word with me and she said

you're feeling a little under the weather. I hope I didn't upset you. Here, have a drink."

"Thank you." I take the glass from her hands and take a sip, just enough to moisten my lips.

Silence stretches between us, and it feels like something's hanging in the air, words waiting to be spoken. Neither of us speaks for nearly a minute before Agnes takes a deep breath. "I'm sorry I spoiled the dinner this evening. But you must understand that I'm a mother, and I just want my daughter to be happy." She glances at my stomach. "I just don't think this is the right way to go about it. This arrangement was doomed from the outset." She pauses, then closes the two glass doors. "Have you thought about my offer? Twenty-five thousand dollars. That's the average payment for surrogates, but you get to keep the child… your child. You can go somewhere where Travis won't find you."

"It isn't my child, Mrs. Thorpe. The baby belongs to Marcia and Travis." I pull back a strand of hair that has fallen out of my ponytail and meet her gaze. "I have thought about your offer, and I have decided not to accept it."

"Why not?" Her gaze is steely and unwavering. "Many people would jump at the chance to have this kind of money."

"I'm not one of them." I take another drink of water, trying to calm my accelerated heart rate. "I want nothing more than to give this child to its rightful parents. I intend to keep my promise."

I take a step toward the door, but she grabs my wrist and pulls me back. "How about if I sweeten the offer?" she asks, her voice tinged with desperation. "Thirty thousand dollars in cash, and I'll pay for the child's education."

I swallow hard, trying to push back the emotion that's threatening to choke me. "Thank you, Mrs. Thorpe," I say in a firm voice and untangle my hand from her grasp. "But I'm not interested."

"You're making a mistake that you will live to regret," she says. Her face is red, her top lip curled in a sneer as she pushes past me and steps into the house, leaving me outside.

I'm sick of her trying to intimidate me into giving her what she wants. Marcia is my friend, and I'll never betray her. I will give her the baby she longs for, and if that means standing up to her mother, so be it. To regain my composure, I sit in one of the chairs at the round table, and Travis joins me less than five minutes later, lowering himself into the chair next to me.

"Grace? Are you okay?"

"Yes... I think so." I give him a weak smile. "It's just been a long day."

"Agnes was out here just now; she said something to upset you again, didn't she?"

When I don't respond, he wraps an arm around my shoulders and I immediately feel some of the tension leaving my body. "Don't let her poisonous words get to you. She likes to get her way, but the best course of action is to ignore her. I'm talking from experience."

I chuckle and at the same time I move forward a few inches so his arm slips off my shoulders. "I guess I have no choice but to do just that, but I think I may need to attend more yoga classes to help me stay calm."

"Yoga?" Travis's eyes widen in surprise. "You shouldn't do that. All those complicated stretches could harm the baby."

"It's quite the opposite, actually," I say, trying to keep a straight face. "If done properly, prenatal yoga can actually benefit the baby. The class I attended today—"

"You practiced yoga today?" His expression tightens into a frown.

"I did, and even though it was challenging to get into some of the positions, I felt more relaxed afterwards."

"Grace," he says, his frown deepening, "I'm sorry, but I don't want you to do any more yoga, not when you're pregnant with our child. It's too much of a risk." He stands up as he says this and I can't help but feel like a little girl who's been scolded by a parent, and it infuriates me.

"I'm sorry, Travis, but you can't order me around like this." I'm struggling to keep my voice calm and even, but I can feel my insides heating up. "This is my body, and I am responsible for taking care of it. If I want to do yoga, then I will. You know very well that I would not put my baby at risk."

I see the anger, hurt and pain written across his face immediately, and I realize I slipped up: I called the baby mine. I'm not sure what to say now. I've never seen him look like that before, and I'm kicking myself internally. But Marcia walks out of the house just in time and invites us in for dessert. It's just the two of us, and I'm relieved to be able to avoid Travis and Agnes, and the anger in their eyes.

# CHAPTER 20

Marcia appears to be in a bad mood herself, I imagine because of her mother's behavior. So we eat our dessert in silence, and when I drop my fork on the floor, she huffs loudly.

"I'll do it," she says when I try to pick it up. "You're not supposed to bend down like that." Her voice is tight with irritation.

I thank her when she gives me a clean fork, but the moment I take a bite of my coconut cake, my stomach lurches and I put it down again and push my plate away.

"I'm not feeling well," I say to her. "I'd better go back to the guesthouse. Thank you so much for the dinner." But as I attempt to stand, dizziness overcomes me, causing me to sit down again.

Still not smiling, Marcia helps me to the living room couch. "Lie down until you're feeling better, at least."

Nodding weakly, I sink back into the soft cushions, and rather than staying with me like she normally would to make sure I'm all right, she walks toward the door. "I'll check on you in a few minutes," she says and walks out of the room.

The only person who checks in on me is Beatrice, who has been sent by Marcia. Before long, I feel a whole lot better and I'm eager to get back to my own space. I tell Beatrice to let them know I've left, and make my way back, and once I'm on the other side of the guesthouse door, my shoulders sink in relief. Keeping my eyes closed for a while, I listen to my heart beating before turning on the lights. I go to the bedroom and remove my unflattering dark-blue maxi dress before putting on my bathrobe.

On my way to the bathroom to take a bath, I stop in the doorway, then take a step back, blood rushing in my ears. The tub is already filled with water, and it's tinted bright red.

"What the hell?" I take a step forward again, closer to the tub.

My nose fills with the scent of something sweet. It reminds me of the strawberry sherbet I enjoyed as a child. I feel sick, and I sit down on the toilet seat, my head reeling. Someone wanted the water to look like blood. I hear a scream and it takes me a few seconds to realize it's coming from me.

Finally, with trembling hands, I tighten the cords around my bathrobe and charge out of the guesthouse toward the main house. Both Marcia and Travis come to open the front door.

"Goodness, Grace, is everything all right?" Marcia asks, her face full of concern.

"Someone was in the guesthouse." My voice is trembling, and my temples are throbbing. "They... They—"

"Who?" Travis asks. "And they what?"

I swallow hard. "Someone was in the guesthouse and they colored my bathwater red to look like blood."

"I don't understand." Travis approaches me, placing a hand on my shoulder. "What are you saying?"

As I move away, I let his hand fall to his side. "My bathwater looks like blood," I say between clenched teeth as I look at Marcia.

"That can't be," she says, rubbing her forehead. "Come on, Grace, you're shaking. You need to sit down." She leads me to the living room again and turns to Travis. "Can you tell Beatrice to bring her a cup of sweet tea? I'll go and tell my mother that I'll drive her to the hotel a bit later. We'll be right back, Grace." She smiles at me and they both disappear from the room, closing the door behind them.

When Beatrice brings me the tea and touches my shoulder in a gesture of comfort, for a split second I wonder if I imagined it. Could it be that it was merely a trick of the light and that my mind had made it seem more sinister than it was? There's only one way to find out. When Travis and Marcia return, I tell them to come and see for themselves.

But when we enter the bathroom, I'm surprised to find the tub empty. It doesn't appear that a drop of water was ever inside of it.

I turn to face them. "I promise you it was... There was water inside. It was red."

Marcia puts both hands on my shoulders. "Grace, are you sure you're okay? There's nothing in there."

"You think I'm lying, don't you?" I move away from her, deeper into the bathroom, searching for signs that I didn't imagine it all, something to prove I'm telling the truth.

"We're not saying that," Travis says.

"You don't need to," I retort. "But you're thinking it." I fold my arms across my chest and meet Marcia's gaze. "I'm telling you someone was in here, someone who wanted to scare me. I think... maybe it was your mother."

Agnes was so disappointed when I rejected her offer. What if she decided to scare me?

I go to the living room and sit down heavily, my head in my hands.

"Grace," Marcia calls, coming to join me, "my mother could not have done this. She's in the library waiting for me to drive her back to the hotel."

I get up and push past her. "I need to talk to her."

We get back to the main house to find Agnes walking out of the library.

"What's with all the commotion?" she asks.

"I know it was you." I step close to her, pointing a trembling finger to her chest. "You messed with my bathwater. You wanted it to look like blood, didn't you?"

"What in the world are you talking about?" She places her hand on her chest, which is rising and falling rapidly. "How can you accuse me of something so hideous? How dare you even—?"

"She's lying," I plead with Marcia and Travis. "I can see right through her. She's a sick woman."

I hate that I sound like a schoolchild trying to convince the teachers that I'm being bullied.

"This is all too much for me," Agnes says, her voice weaker than before. Then, to my surprise, a tear rolls down her cheek, followed by another. "I need to get out of this house."

Her tears don't fool me for one second.

After Marcia takes her mother to the car, Travis turns his attention to me. "I understand that this is hard for you," he says. "Agnes is a difficult person, but I don't think she would do what you said—"

"Travis, I know what I saw. She got rid of it to make it look like I'm lying, like I'm going crazy."

"You know what I think? I think you need to get some rest. Let me take you back to the guesthouse."

"That's fine. I know my way there."

I leave him standing there, staring after me.

When I fall asleep two hours later, I collapse into another nightmare in which Peter returns to remind me of what I did. When I open my eyes, I still feel his presence in the room, and the words he said to me in the nightmare I had a few days ago, that the baby isn't meant to be born. I have been trying to suppress those words for days, but now they are surfacing again.

"Is it possible?" I whisper as my mind goes to the scarlet bathwater. "But how could it be?" I shut my eyes and press my hands against my ears to block out the sound of Peter's voice, and yet I can't stop the words from repeating over and over again in my mind. No matter how hard I try, I can't stop seeing his face.

I barely sleep all night, and first thing in the morning, I ask Marcia and Travis for additional locks on the guesthouse front door.

"But why?" Marcia asks, frowning. "Is it because of what happened last night? Isn't that a little extreme?"

I clasp my hands tightly in front of me. "Since I don't really know who did it, and your mother denied it, I'd just feel better with more locks. I hope you don't mind."

I'm certain getting locks on my front door is a better solution than making a rushed decision to move out, away from the Thorpes and their support.

Marcia glances at Travis then back at me. "That shouldn't be a problem. Anything that would make you feel safer in our home."

"Thank you," I reply. "I need it done as soon as possible, if that's okay."

Marcia squeezes my hand. "You know what, maybe Travis can do it later today."

When I look at Travis, he nods. "Yeah, of course."


Travis shows up with two more locks shortly before lunchtime.

"Thank you so much for doing this for me," I say when he's almost done. "I know it's an inconvenience."

He doesn't answer until he's done, then he turns to me, his toolbox in his hand. "No problem. We can't have you living in fear. It's not good for the baby." He pats my shoulder. "Take a nap after I leave. Both you and the baby need to rest." He hands me two new keys.

I curl my hand a little too tightly around them. It's great that he wants the best for their child, but his controlling nature is becoming increasingly difficult to bear.

"Maybe I will," I respond, even though I want to remind him that I'm not a child who needs to be told what to do.

After he's gone, I shut the door and scream into one of the couch cushions, letting all the frustration and anger I'm feeling out. I scream until I am gasping for breath, but I do not find relief from the tight ball of fear in the pit of my stomach.

What am I afraid of exactly? And who?

## CHAPTER 21
### FRIDAY, 20 MARCH 2015

I'm sitting on my bed one week after Rachel died, unable to sleep because my nightmares constantly take me back to that hospital room. My mind is still filled with the sounds of Rachel screaming in pain, along with that horrible silence when we went in to see her after the doctors pronounced her dead.

Leaning against the headboard of my bed, I close my eyes, hoping that sleep will soon come, but the air feels thick and oppressive. There is no point in trying to sleep if I can't breathe. I flick on my bedside lamp, slide into my slippers, and shuffle over to the window to peek through the blinds. On the other side of the glass is a heavy downpour, and the wind is howling, reminding me of my shame and guilt.

Through the water curtain, I see a silver Nissan parked across my driveway with its headlights on. With my nose pressed against the glass, I can make out that it's Peter's car and he's sitting behind the wheel. I haven't spoken to him since that day at the hospital when he looked me in the eye and told me it was my fault that Rachel died. As if I didn't have enough guilt already. My heart and mind are torn apart every day and night when I think about the one thing I could've done to save her life.

I throw on a warm bathrobe and, without thinking, I run downstairs, grabbing an umbrella on my way out the door. As soon as I step outside, the freezing rain hits me before I can open the umbrella, but I don't care.

"Peter!" I call out and when I reach the car, I press my palms to his window, which is slippery from the water. He glares at me, and I can almost taste the bile in my mouth as I see his bloodshot eyes, a stark contrast to his pale face.

"Are you okay?" I ask, my voice laced with worry.

The wind grabs my umbrella and rips it from my hands, causing it to fly away into the darkness as I get soaked. My hair is plastered to my head and hanging in ropes down my back. I shiver when the water seeps into my clothes, chilling me to the bone.

"Peter," I say when he rolls down the window, arms around myself, trying to keep myself warm, "are you okay?"

"Why do you care?" he shouts with such venom that I flinch. It's tempting to lash out at him, but I see the pain behind his anger, and I can't ignore it. "I'm here to remind you that what happened to my wife is your fault and I will never, ever forgive you." His voice chokes. "I don't want you to have anything to do with her funeral, you hear me?" He slams his hand against the steering wheel, and I take a step back, tears spilling from my eyes, his words piercing my heart.

"Peter, I'm so sorry for what happened. I really—"

"I'll never let you forget it." His teeth are clenched and his jaw is tight as tears stream from his eyes. "For the rest of my life, I will keep coming back to remind you of what you did until... until you're eaten alive by your guilt and regret." He wipes his eyes roughly with the back of his hand. "One way or the other, Grace, you will pay for what you did. I promise you that."

He starts the engine and reverses, taking off before I can move or say anything else. An hour after I get back into the house, my phone dings with a text message from him.

*I don't want you at the funeral. You will pay for this.*

Pretty princesses ride on the backs of unicorns, floating among the fluffy white clouds of the wallpaper. The nursery is everything I imagined it would be. I wanted to have a dedicated space in my home for my niece when I babysat her. It's the first time I have entered the room since she and Rachel died three weeks ago. My gaze moves to the personalized vintage crib on a round cream rug in the center of the room. Little Emma will never get to crawl around on it.

I spent a fortune decorating the room, telling the interior decorator that money was no object. I would visualize the baby sleeping in her crib, crawling on the floor, sitting with me in the rocking chair. Now my vision will only ever be a dream. I'll never get to meet her, never hear her cry. She will never play with the stuffed animals I bought for her, one for each month of Rachel's failed pregnancy. She will never spend quality time with me while her parents go out for date night.

I don't know what will become of the room. Sooner or

later, I will have to move everything out, donating some and selling the rest. But not yet. Now the room serves a purpose: when I enter it, I remember what I have done to my sister.

"It's not your fault," Sydney says, coming to join me in the doorway.

She has repeated those words to me more times than I can count, but it doesn't matter what she or anybody says. I know the truth, and I will never stop reminding myself of it, watering my guilt until it's big enough to strangle me.

"Should we go?" I ask.

"Yes. Are you okay?" Sydney places her arm around my shoulders.

"Does it matter if I'm okay?" My words come out a bit harsh, but that wasn't my intention. Sydney does not deserve it; she's been so kind to me. I press the heel of my hand against my forehead. "I'm sorry."

"You don't have to apologize for anything. You're going through a really rough time."

I lean into my friend and we walk out the front door.

Sydney has offered to drive me to the Crossroads Presbyterian Church, where Rachel and Emma's funeral services are taking place. Two days after Rachel died, I almost hit a pedestrian at a crosswalk. It freaked me out, and I don't want to be put in that position again, so I'm taking a break from driving.

Sydney follows me to the living room, where I pick up my phone and check if I have any missed calls.

"Has he called?" she asks.

"No." It's Rachel's funeral and Peter still won't speak to me, not since the day he showed up at my house in the middle of the night. Even though we used to have a close relationship, he has completely shut me out, and the rest of the world too. I have tried to call him many times over the last couple of days, but my calls and emails have gone unanswered. The fact that he's ignoring me hurts even more because we're sharing a similar pain. I thought we would heal together, comfort each other.

My shoulders sink as I continue to stare at the screen. "I really hoped he would reach out today."

"I'm sorry, honey. I think you should give him more time."

"Do you think I should approach him today?"

"No. I don't think that's a good idea. Let him come to you."

"Okay," I say. "Let's go."

Honestly, I'm dreading seeing Peter, but I must attend my sister's funeral. Even though it was hard, I respected his wish as far as possible by staying out of the funeral arrangements. After the pain my actions have caused, this was the least I could do. In a way, he did me a favor. It would have killed me inside to choose a funeral home and caskets, decide on flower arrangements, choose photos and memorabilia for display at the service, and everything else that comes with funeral planning. I hate to admit that a part of me is relieved Peter was handling it all.

In the car, I pull out my phone again and open the text I received from him the night he came to see me, the last communication we had.

*I don't want you at the funeral. You will pay for this.*

But he can't stop me from saying goodbye to my sister; I would never forgive myself if I didn't go.

"What if he asks me to leave?" I ask Sydney as we near the church.

"He doesn't have the right to do that," she says, pulling into the parking lot.

"He kind of does have the right." My hands tighten around the phone and I shut my eyes tight until pain sears my eyeballs. When I open them again, Sydney is watching me.

"Grace, you have to stop punishing yourself."

"Easier said than done," I say.

Sydney wipes away her tears. "You know what? Focus on your sister today. Think of the good times you had together."

I nod and unbuckle my seatbelt. "I'll try."

On our way to the front door, someone taps me on the shoulder.

"You're Rachel's twin, aren't you?" The blonde woman stares at me from beneath lashes covered in thick mascara. I want to say something, but like my tears, my words fail me. "I'm sorry for your loss." The woman pulls out a tissue and blows her nose. "Rachel designed my wedding stationery. She was such a nice person, we stayed friends."

"I'm sorry you lost your friend," I say to her, and she squeezes my arm and goes inside. More people approach me, extending their condolences. I recognize two of Peter's family members, including his stepmother, but they look at me like I am a stranger. Peter must have told them about me backing out of the surrogacy. I don't have the courage to approach them, even as I continue to scan the crowd for Peter. Unable to locate him, I place myself at the entrance of the church to greet the mourners. Someone has to do it.

Once everyone has disappeared inside, Sydney and I go in and find a place to sit. Out of respect to Peter, we choose the middle pew instead of the front, where his family is seated. The sweet scent of orchids and roses makes me queasy, and I scan the seats behind me. Still no Peter.

When I turn to face the pulpit again, I catch Pastor Paul White's eyes. He's getting ready to start the service, but I need to speak to him. He already knows who I am, since I have accompanied Rachel and Peter to services in his church in the past.

"I'll be right back," I tell Sydney and slide out of the pew. I make my way to the front of the church and ask to speak to him. I try my best not to look at the two white and gold caskets, one adult-sized with a miniature version next to it.

"I'm sorry for the loss of your sister," he says before I can speak. "She was a wonderful person."

"Thank you, Pastor. Have you heard anything from Peter?" I glance at the front pew and watch Peter's step-mother whispering to a woman next to her while throwing a look back at me.

"I *did* talk to Peter early this morning." The pastor scratches his full beard. "I'm afraid he won't be attending the service. He asked me to go ahead as planned."

"I understand. Thank you." As I make my way back to my seat, the lump in my throat threatens to choke me. I can't imagine the state Peter must be in to avoid his wife and daughter's funeral. When I'm seated, I text him, begging him to at least come to the burial, but he doesn't respond. The service is brief, and at the end of it, Rachel and Emma's caskets are carried out by people I don't recognize, total strangers. How well do these people know her? Do they love her? Will they even remember her name three years from now?

In the cemetery, my body and mind are numb as I stare

at the two holes that will be the final resting place for my sister and niece.

Sydney takes my hand and holds it tight. "I'm so sorry," she keeps whispering.

Some raindrops slip through the leaves of the tree above us and plop onto the fabric of the black umbrella we're sharing. It has been raining on and off all week, as if the sky is also grieving. I will my eyes to shed the tears building up behind them, but nothing happens. My twin sister is dead and I remain dry-eyed. What kind of person am I? No wonder Peter wants nothing to do with me. If only I could cry, it would help release the intense pressure in my chest. But maybe I deserve to suffer. I killed Rachel and her baby, and my punishment is to be trapped in my own grief.

Several other mourners glance at me from time to time, confused expressions on their faces. I wish I could explain to them that I *do* want to weep, but I don't know how to. Sooner or later, the tears will come. Maybe it will happen later today, or in a few weeks. I can't say. Perhaps my body needs time to catch up with everything.

As I tighten my fingers around Sydney's hand, something in the distance catches my attention. A familiar silver Nissan. Thank God he came. Peter did not respond to my text, but he's here and that's all that matters.

He sits in the car, staring at us.

The caskets are lowered into the two graves, and soil and rose petals follow them. Peter keeps his distance until the funeral ends and people start to disperse. I'm the first to leave: I need to catch him before he goes. By the time I reach the gate, he drives off, but I came close enough to see the pain in his eyes and the dark circles framing them.

I stand at the gate clutching the cool metal of my umbrella handle as his car disappears. Now that Rachel no longer connects us, I have no idea whether we will see each other again. I'm not sure if he still considers me family.

Back at the grave site, I approach Ron, one of the pall-bearers, who introduced himself to me as Peter's colleague and friend.

"He's sleeping very little and drinking too much." He scratches the back of his bald head. "I tried to get him to come to the service, but he refused. But he was here; I saw his car."

I nod. "Do you know if he has anything planned for after this?"

"Not that I'm aware of. I think he didn't want to give people an opportunity to speak to him. He's barely said a word to me since it happened."

"Okay," I say. It devastates me to think that my sister's send-off was so abrupt, as if it's simply another task to be checked off as soon as possible.

Back at home, I find a rose bouquet at my door. Chad never shows up in person, but he won't stop sending me flowers, begging me to take him back. I toss the flowers into the trash without bothering to read the note.

Then I run straight to the nursery and sit on the floor next to the crib with my legs crossed and eyes shut. Behind my eyelids, I see my sister, all smiles as she holds her baby in her arms, and pain flares to life inside my chest and spreads to the rest of my body, so strong it chases away the numbness. Finally, my eyes fill with warm, welcome tears. When the crying starts, I can't stop it.

As more and more images of Rachel appear in my mind, I weep for her. First, I see her the day we met up in person again after a year of estrangement, then in labor with an expectant smile on her face. Finally, I see her in her final moments. The last image on my mind is of Peter's crumpled face when we were told his wife and child had died.

I drop to my side and cry for all three of them, my tears landing on the carpet, and when I have no more tears left, I pull myself up, snatch a lamp from the table by the window, and hurl it at the wall.

# CHAPTER 23
## PRESENT

"Look who just walked in." Clayton gestures in the direction of the door.

Dressed smartly in a green blouse and black trousers, Cora looks a little different today. There's still no smile on her face and her red, graying hair is still tangled around her shoulders, but she seems more alert and is standing taller than the last time I saw her.

"Looks like someone feels a little better today." Clayton rubs his hands together. "Give me a moment. I'll get the lady her coffees."

"Okay," I say and return to my novel—something light and funny to help me forget my complicated life for a little while.

I show up almost daily at Clayton's café now that he has crowned me a regular and reserves a bistro table for me at the front of the shop. It's right next to the long, glossy counter, which displays pastel-colored coffee and espresso machines on one end and bottles of toppings and flavorings on the other. It's the perfect spot, but it's a struggle not to be tempted by the mouthwatering treats displayed in the glass case, and their aromas of chocolate, cinnamon, and caramel. Thanks to Marcia constantly hammering into me that I should eat healthily, I resist the temptation. Smoothies, salads, and healthy sandwiches for me. The muffins and pastries will have to wait.

I arrived early, as soon as the café was open. Since the bathwater incident, I've been finding it harder to stay at the Thorpes', even with the new locks on my door. Marcia is really trying not to be intrusive, which I appreciate, but Travis has started checking up on me obsessively again. I know he's just worried after what happened, and I appreciate his concern, but it's not helping my anxiety at all. So now, every day I leave the house early and get back late, and, as a result, I've been spending a lot of time with Clayton. Three days ago, I even accompanied him and Heidi to the petting zoo. Having a friend in Wellice does make things a lot more bearable.

I watch as Clayton places two cups of coffee in front of Cora and she nods with a small smile. I can't help wondering when she last laughed out loud, how she sounds when she's happy. When Clayton steps away from the table, Cora reaches into her purse and pulls out a piece of paper, placing it on the table. The photo of her daughter. I watch as grief descends upon her, and an ache throbs at the back of my throat. She reminds me of how I was in the months after Rachel's death, the numbness. If my feelings are anything to go by, Cora is probably still in shock, unable to release the pressure squeezing her lungs and suffocating her.

"I think I should speak to her," I say to Clayton when he returns to the front.

"Just keep in mind that, like last time, she might not be in a mood to talk," he says, just as Lillian O'Connor, one of the baristas—who must be in her mid-twenties—asks him if he can man the cash register while she goes to the bathroom. It's a busy time for them. The line is growing, and there are still many tables waiting to be served.

"I know," I say. "But I want to try, anyway."

"Go for it," Clayton replies before walking away. "It can't hurt to try."

I get to my feet and approach Cora's table tentatively.

"Hi," I say over the sounds of coffee beans in a grinder and the murmur of voices. "Do you mind if I join you?"

Instead of speaking, she picks up her daughter's photo and slips it back into her purse. Then she bends her head over her steaming coffee cup, like she does every day. A thin strand of her hair dips into the hot liquid, but she doesn't seem to care.

"I'm sure you know by now that I'm not very good company." She sighs and her gaze flicks up to meet mine for the first time. "I heard around that you're a nice young lady, but I really prefer to sit alone."

I nod and my t-shirt starts to creep up my bump, exposing the lower part to a light breeze. When I've tugged it securely in place, I smile down at Cora. "I'm sorry, I don't mean to disturb. I just... It's clear you're not a fan of the Thorpes, and I was just wondering why. You said last time that they don't deserve what I'm doing for them. What did you mean by that?" I wonder if talking about the Thorpes will help her to open up to me a little.

Her jaw tightens and she stares back into her coffee. "I meant just that. Good things shouldn't happen to people like them."

Surprised at the fire in her tone, I say, "I'm sorry. But can you tell me why that is?"

"I'm sure you'll find out soon enough," she says and puts her daughter's photo back on the table, face down.

I take that as a sign that our conversation is over and she needs a moment to herself.

"I'm sorry to disturb you." I back away from the table. "Enjoy your coffee."

"No success?" Clayton asks when I return to my table and he brings me my hummus veggie wrap.

"No, I couldn't get through to her." I glance back at Cora. She's still gazing into her drink. "I wish I could help her."

"You can only help someone who wants to be helped." Clayton pauses. "I'll be taking a thirty-minute break in a bit. Want to join me for a slow walk?" He emphasizes the word *slow*, and I laugh.

I close my novel. "Sure. Do you mind boxing up my wrap? I'll eat it at the guesthouse."

Sometimes I let it slip, but I try to avoid saying the word *home*. The Thorpes' guesthouse is not my home.

"Your wish is my command." Clayton takes the plate from me and reappears a minute later with a box. "Ready to hit the square?"

It's Saturday, 24 August, and the heat outside is still scorching and thick with humidity, but at least it's less stifling than the heavy air in the café, where the air conditioning has been broken for a few days now.

We are walking past Twisted Curls Hair Salon when I catch a flash of color in the corner of my eye. A red Jeep drives by, and seconds before it disappears, I recognize the driver.

"Travis," I say, coming to a halt.

"Are you okay?" Clayton asks, putting his hand on my shoulder.

"Yes, I'm fine." I gaze at the blur of red in the distance. "I saw Travis just now."

"Travis Thorpe?" Clayton follows my gaze.

"Yes." I start to walk again. "He drove by."

"Weird. Do you think he's following you?"

I shrug. "I don't know. Maybe not; it is a small town. But I do feel like he's constantly watching me."

"I don't know how you deal with them controlling your life like that." Clayton stops walking and stands in front of me, his expression serious. "If it ever gets to be too much, and you need to get away from it all, you're always welcome to stay with us. I'm sure Heidi would love that; my mother too. They both can't stop talking about how wonderful you are."

I put a hand on his arm. "I appreciate the offer, Clayton." Knowing he cares that much sends warmth through my chest. "I'm just so ready for this to be over." I continue to count down the days every night before I go to bed, crossing them out on my calendar one by one.

"Well," he says, "just know that the offer stands. If you ever need to get out, let me know and I will come and get you. No strings attached." He puts an arm around my waist, moving me out of the way as a skateboarder whizzes by. When he lets go of me, the place he touched feels like it's vibrating, and my cheeks tingle.

"You know what?" I say as we continue to walk, trying to distract myself from the sensations in my body. "I kind of feel worried about the baby sometimes."

"In what way?"

"I'm getting anxious that Marcia and Travis might end up being a bit controlling as parents. Imagine living with that as a teenager."

When I think of the baby's future, a weight presses on

my chest. *It's not your child*, I remind myself. I have no right to determine how the little boy or girl should be raised. And I know how desperate they are for a child; nobody will love this baby more than them.

"Do you ever think about how it will feel to give up the child?" Clayton asks when we find a bench in front of the fountain that sits smack in the middle of the square.

"It won't be hard," I lie and look away. "I can't let it be."

Even if I'm starting to realise just how painful it will be to detach myself in the end, I'm determined to follow through even if it's the hardest thing I've ever done. Marcia and Travis will be wonderful parents; I have to keep reminding myself of that.

"Grace, I'm only saying that because there are surrogates out there who decide in the end that they don't want to give up the babies."

"I won't be one of them," I say, my voice sharper than I intended. I shut my eyes and let out a breath. "I'm sorry, but I made a decision and I'm sticking to it. I signed a contract."

Of course, one day I want a family. I want to meet someone who loves me unconditionally, I want children, and the clock is ticking. If I wait too long, it might get harder for me to have my own baby. But I won't dwell on the future. Before I can think about a family of my own, there's a lot of healing that needs to be done.

"You're the strongest woman I've ever met," Clayton says, as we enjoy the fine spray of water cooling our faces. He smiles at me. "Grace, tell me about yourself. We spend quite a bit of time together, but you don't open up, not really."

He's right. Whenever he asks me personal questions, I brush them off and turn the conversation to him and his life.

"There's not much to tell, nothing interesting."

"Nonsense." He chuckles. "Everybody's story is interesting. Are you going to tell me why you left your job? It's quite a change you made from magazine editor to surrogate. I'm not judging, just curious."

My plan had always been just to tell him the basics and not go too deep into my life story. But I have now aroused his suspicions, and his eyes glitter with questions I don't want to answer.

"Sometimes our life goals change."

He goes quiet, staring at kids playing ball around the fountain.

"You're right about that," he says. "But I'm getting the feeling that you haven't quite let go." He looks back at me.

"Let go of what?"

"That editor job. Something tells me you didn't want to leave."

"You're wrong." I clutch my hands. "Leaving was the best decision I've ever made."

Possibly afraid of being sued for wrongful termination, Roman hadn't kept his promise of firing me for not attending the meeting with Jaden, Inc., in Seattle, but he had let me go two months after Rachel died because I was too depressed to pull my weight. I missed meetings and deadlines, cried and fell asleep at the office, went on leave too often, and made too many mistakes on the job. I was no longer a star employee, far from it. I was almost relieved when I was fired.

"Do you think you'll go back? You know, after this is over?"

Before today, Clayton never asked many questions. But now it feels like a dam has burst and he can't stop himself.

"I don't know, Clayton. Maybe I'll go on to do something else. In college, I dreamed of starting my own magazine."

"Then you should go for it. Do something for yourself for once."

If he only knew the truth. What I'm doing for the Thorpes is not completely selfless. Sitting next to him, I feel like a liar and a crook. Maybe I am, but it doesn't matter anymore: I've almost reached the end of this chapter in my life. Everything needs to happen this way; it's the only way to wipe the slate clean. And before that happens, I can't allow myself to think about the future.

We sit in silence, and eventually Clayton stands up to kick a ball around with the kids for a while, and I can't help smiling as I watch him.

He comes back after a little while and takes a swig from a bottle of water. "So, did the Thorpe matriarch come back to demand you accept her offer?"

"No. She hasn't come over, at least not when I was there."

"If she does, be careful. The woman sounds dangerous, like she's not in her right mind. Anyone who leaves a threatening note like that on the doorstep of a pregnant woman must be unhinged."

It's a good thing I didn't tell Clayton about the bathwater; he'd be so worried.

"I know," I say. "But, unfortunately, Marcia doesn't see it that way."

"Of course she doesn't. It's her mother."

"Yeah. I just don't understand why Agnes hates her son-in-law so much. Travis is obsessive when it comes to my pregnancy, but he's really a nice guy at heart."

"I bet it has something to do with money. But you know what? I guess it's none of our business."

"True," I say. "So, have you decided yet whether you plan on being in the coffee business for good?" Lately, he's been thinking out loud about his and Heidi's future, weighing his options.

He laughs. "Looks like someone prefers asking questions to answering them."

I nudge him in the ribs. "I did answer your questions."

"Not really." He places his hands on his thighs and rubs them up and down. "Actually, I recently spoke to one of the partners at the firm where I worked back in DC. They said they will take me back when I'm ready to return to law. If I'm ever ready to go back, hopefully my mother wouldn't mind running the café again. It used to be her baby for years, after all."

"She's so sweet, I'm sure the customers loved her," I say, smiling. "But do you think you'll ever be ready?"

"I'm starting to think so." He runs a hand through his hair. "I came here because I wanted to heal from everything that happened. For months I didn't feel as though anything was changing, and then, just like that, everything did. It's like I was in a deep sleep and now I'm starting to wake up."

"That's really great, Clayton." That's exactly the kind of shift I'm waiting to experience, and I wonder how long it will take. I put a hand on his. "I'm happy for you."

Our gazes lock, and he places his other hand on top of mine. When he speaks again, his voice is low. "I think it has everything to do with a certain somebody who came to town."

A jolt of electricity shoots through me. Even in the cool mist of the fountain water, my body is heating up. I return my hand to my lap. "I don't understand."

"I think you do," he says. "You're the first person I've

opened up to since it happened. You've helped me so much, Grace."

I force myself to look back at him. "You've helped me too. I hope we can remain friends after all this is over."

"I wouldn't have it any other way," he says. "Let's promise to keep in touch."

I smile at him, but I'm not sure I'll be able to keep my promise. I don't tell him that when all this is over, we will have to go our separate ways. I won't see the Thorpes again, and I won't see Clayton again either. I don't want anything left that ties me to this place, to the child I'm going to leave behind.

# CHAPTER 24

The walls are painted pale pink, and the floor is covered by a snow-white shaggy carpet, but the crib hasn't been put together, and most of the nursery items have been stored in the guesthouse. Marcia's ready to prepare the nursery, and she's asked me to help. My job at this moment is to hang three identical photos of a cow flying over the moon on the wall. We're twenty days away from my due date and I can't believe I've made it through these last stressful months. I can guess why Marcia waited until now to finish the nursery. She wanted to be sure nothing would go wrong with the pregnancy, that she wouldn't be disappointed yet again.

An uneasy feeling comes over me as I watch her sitting on the floor, stuffing a pillow into an ivory cover. She has zoned out, focused on the task at hand. I say something to her, but she doesn't react. Maybe she doesn't even hear me. Something is not right with her lately and she's been crying a lot. Maybe she thinks I don't notice, but no matter how much makeup she wears, the signs of crying can never be completely covered up. She and Travis have been fighting quite a lot too. When it gets to be too much, Marcia locks herself in her studio, sometimes for hours. Once I walked by while she was inside and heard her crying, followed by the sound of things being thrown at the wall.

What worries me is that one minute she seems to be there and the next she's gone, sinking into a different world. She told me that it's just the stress of the pregnancy, worrying that something might go wrong. So I hold on to the hope that things will change once the baby comes.

"Wow," Travis says, joining us in the room. "You guys did a great job."

He's been out most of the day. He's hardly at home lately, and when he is, he's constantly touching my stomach and talking to the baby. Normally he leaves right after breakfast, but today we're doing a photo shoot. They want photos of my belly to keep as a memory, and I agreed on one condition: my face will not be shown in the photos. Travis objected at first, but I refused to have it any other way.

"Are you both ready to get started?" he asks.

"Sure," I say through my tightening throat. It's a strange feeling knowing that when I leave, photos of me will remain, a trace I will leave behind.

Travis calls Marcia's name, and she snaps out of her trance, smiling up at him. He goes to get his camera equipment, and we all walk to the guesthouse together. I'm not sure why, but Marcia suggested we take the photos in the guesthouse living room. I don't really mind where it happens, I just want it to be over.

I'm already dressed for the photo shoot, in a flowing white and silver print dress Marcia bought me yesterday. It feels more like a wedding dress to me, but I don't want to mess with her vision.

After Travis sets up everything, creating a mini studio, he asks me to lie on the couch, and while the camera clicks away,

Marcia stands by the TV, watching us with a tight smile on her face. Even though she wants the photos, I can only imagine how hard it must be for her. I'm sure she wishes she could be in my place, pregnant and having photos taken of her by her husband. To be the one to bring their child into the world. She's doing her best to hide her pain, but I sense it, and halfway through the session, she excuses herself to go to the bathroom.

The photo shoot was Travis's idea. Once this is all over, I doubt Marcia will be looking at the photos much. They will be a constant reminder of what she was not able to do herself.

"How are you feeling?" Travis asks as he stops to adjust some settings on the camera.

"I'm fine." I don't know what else to say. Being alone with him in the room while his wife is obviously crying in the bathroom is making me uncomfortable. I really wish he would go and comfort her.

"You're doing great," he says. "Grace, I've told you this many times, but we really appreciate what you're doing for us."

"It's my pleasure. I'm happy for you both."

"You must be looking forward to the end." He takes several photos, then peers at me over the camera, waiting for a response.

"I am," I admit. "It's been quite a journey."

"That's true. But it will all be worth it. Now show me that smile."

"Why? My face won't be in any of these."

"You're a bit tense, and smiling will help you loosen up. It affects the entire body, not just the face."

When Marcia returns to the living room, she's all smiles, but her eyes are red.

"How's it going, you two?" she asks and turns to Travis. "Did you get some nice shots?"

"Absolutely. Grace is a great model."

Does he not notice that she's hurting? Does he see her red eyes? Does he care? I'm waiting for him to stop doing what he's doing and pull his wife into his arms, but he doesn't. He continues to take pictures of me, the woman who will give birth to his baby.

"Great," Marcia says and walks to the door. "Looks like you have everything under control. Since I'm not needed here, I'll go take a walk. Carry on."

"Sure," he says briefly. "See you in a bit."

The photo shoot lasts another thirty minutes, and Travis continues trying to make small talk, but I give one-word responses. Finally, he's done and he asks if I want to see the photos. I decline.

When he finally leaves the guesthouse, I strip off the dress, and back in my stretchy jeans and t-shirt, I feel a little better. I'm on my way to the kitchen for something to drink when my phone rings from the bedroom.

I'm expecting it to be Clayton, but it's Sydney. We haven't spoken for days.

"Hello, stranger," she says over the sound of laughter from one of her daughters.

"Hey, you." I take the phone with me to the couch.

"How are things going? It's almost the end of the road, isn't it?"

"Three weeks, and I can't wait."

"You're amazing," Sydney says. "I still can't believe you went through with this. I know I wasn't supportive at the beginning, but I really am proud of you."

"I'm glad I did this, Sydney." It's not over yet and

anything can happen in the next few days, but I'm choosing to remain positive.

"I can't wait for you to come back to Miami, to start living your own life."

"Yeah, me too." Worry snakes through me. What if I give birth to the baby and don't get the peace I'm searching for? What if the feeling of emptiness remains, and I find myself exactly where I started?

"I know what you're thinking," Sydney says. "You're thinking that you have no place to stay. But you do. You can come and stay with us until you find a place of your own. Jeff doesn't have a problem with it."

"That's really kind of you," I say. I know that in the first few months after giving up the baby I'll probably be struggling emotionally and having Sydney close by might help. But I'm finding it hard to think beyond the birth right now.

"I spoke to Camille," Sydney adds before I can respond to her offer to move in with her and her family again. "She's willing to give you your job back at Dear Blooms, if you need a place to start."

"Thanks for doing that. It means a lot, but we both know it won't work out. My passion is in magazines."

There's no way I'm going to let her and her sister down again.

"Will you try to get your job back at *Living It*?"

I shrug. "Maybe. I don't know yet."

"Grace, I hate to push you, but you'll be giving birth in less than a month. You need to think about the next steps."

"I am," I lie, "and I'm thinking I might want to start my own magazine." It's always been a distant dream, but if I go down that route, I will need some money to make it happen.

I move to the window and stare out at the river. The water is glistening in the sun, as if silver-winged fireflies are dancing on its surface. The beautiful view lures me out of the guesthouse. Still trying to sell Sydney on starting my own business, I find myself walking toward the river, following the glitter of sunlight on the water.

"That's not a bad idea," Sydney says. "You should do that, create something of your own. I hated that you had to work so hard at *Living It* and the credit went to someone else." I expected her to be against the idea, reminding me of my bleak financial situation, but she really does sound excited about the whole thing.

After we talk about me for a while, she tells me that she and Jeff are planning a one-month-long vacation across Africa for the whole family. Sydney loves to travel, and when she's not working, she's always planning their next vacation. She's been talking about seeing Africa for a long time.

"Maybe one day we'll go there together." I've never been outside the US, but in the last year, I've done a lot of things I never thought I would do.

"I'll hold you to it," she says, and lets out a loud breath. "Grace, I don't mean to ruin your day, but Chad showed up here last night. He brought flowers and demanded to know where you are."

Panic sweeps through me. "You didn't tell him, did you?"

"Of course not. But I did give him a piece of my mind and told him to stay the hell away from you or we'll call the cops. I have a feeling he won't bother you again."

"Thank you. I hope he stays away." Even as I say the words, my stomach churns with anxiety. Over the years, Chad somehow always figured out my address. Hopefully, not this time.

Sydney and I end the call before I reach the river's edge.

I push the phone into my pocket and tilt my face to the sky to enjoy the warmth of the sun on my skin.

I turn at the sound of footsteps. Beatrice is approaching one of the cushioned benches. Today, instead of hanging down her back, her braid is wrapped around her head like a halo.

"Hi there, Grace," she says, sitting down and unwrapping a sandwich. "Come and join me. It's been a while since we sat down for a chat. Are you feeling okay? You're almost at the finish line."

"That's right." Panting a little from the effort, I lower myself next to her on the bench. "Time went by so fast and so slow at the same time."

"That's how time works sometimes," she chuckles. "It's been years since I first stepped into this house, but it feels like yesterday." She takes a bite of her sandwich. "Did I ever mention that I started as Marcia's nanny?"

"No, you didn't. That's amazing. You must feel like part of the family."

"Not really, not when things are like this... different."

"In what way?" I ask.

She takes another bite and chews before answering my question. "It's hard to be a witness to an unhappy marriage. I'm afraid he's not the right man for her."

I never expected her to be so open with me. I sit up straight, ready for more.

"Maybe a baby will bring new life into the family," I say when she doesn't elaborate.

"Maybe," she says and stands up, her unfinished sandwich still in her hand. "I should go back in, I think I forgot to switch off the iron. I'll see you when I come to the guesthouse in the morning. I'll bring you some of my Daphne's lemon cupcakes."

"I'd love to taste them," I say, standing up as well. She's often told me what an amazing cook her daughter is.

As I watch her walk back to the house, I can't stop thinking about what she said. I'm not surprised that she noticed the fighting, that she feels the tension too. Even I have experienced some of the unpleasantness between Travis and Marcia, and she's around them much more than me. Will the fighting continue once the baby comes? Will it get better, or will the demands of a newborn make it worse? Am I leaving my baby in the right hands?

Sudden nausea hits me, and I hurry back to the guest-house. When I reach the door, I no longer feel like throwing up. I just want to climb under the covers and take a long nap. Lying in bed, I stare up at the ceiling and, for the first time, I seriously think about the future. If I had accepted payment from Marcia and Travis, it would have been easier to start my own business. But there's no point thinking about that now.

Exhaustion finally takes over and I fall asleep, but an hour later, I awaken from another nightmare about Peter. In my dream, I walked out of the front door to find him right there, staring at me with his eyes full of pain and anger.

This time, instead of screaming, I pull myself out of bed and sit in the closet, breathing slowly until I calm down.

# CHAPTER 25

My hands are shaking as I dial Marcia's number, but a man answers the call, a familiar voice.

"Clayton?" I pull the phone from my ear and glance at the screen. I *had* called him by mistake, in my flustered state. "I'm so sorry. I was calling Marcia."

"Grace, are you okay?" he asks. "You sound like you're crying."

"I'm..." I stammer. "I'm fine."

"You're not fine. I can hear it in your voice. Come on, tell me what happened." The gentleness in his voice soothes me, and I contemplate whether to talk to him about something so personal.

"Are you in pain?" he asks. A shuffling sound on his end signals he's probably trying to sit up in bed. "You can tell me anything."

"I had some spotting," I blurt out, holding back tears and praying nothing is going wrong only two weeks before the due date.

He lets out a harsh breath. "Spotting."

"Yeah. That's when—"

"You don't have to explain it to me. I had a pregnant wife once." I'm grateful for that because the last thing I want to do is go into detail.

"Do you feel any pain?" he asks again.

"Not really. Not anymore. I felt cramping earlier. When I went to the bathroom, that's when I saw it."

"Was it a lot?"

"It was enough to scare the hell out of me." I slide out of bed and use my free hand to remove my night dress. "I'm going to the hospital."

"That's a good idea. Will Marcia or Travis take you?"

I walk into the closet and pull out a pair of jeans from the shelf. "They're out... attending their baby shower at the Sawyer Hotel. Well, the baby shower was earlier, but they wanted to have a dinner party afterwards. That's why they're still not home."

Most people throw baby showers four to six weeks before the due date, but I do understand why Marcia and Travis waited this long to celebrate. They wanted to make sure nothing can go wrong with the pregnancy.

They asked me if I wanted to go with them, but I refused. It would be way too awkward for me, and I like being home by myself. I also didn't want to see Agnes and there's no way she wouldn't be invited. Travis had not wanted to go to the party either, saying that baby showers were for women only, but Marcia insisted.

"Are you thinking of driving yourself to the hospital?" Clayton asks.

"Sure. It's not far from here."

"No, you're not going alone. I'll come and get you."

"It's really not a big deal." I struggle to get into my jeans with one hand. "I'm not in pain, but I don't want to take chances."

"That's smart, but I don't think you should drive yourself."

"Then I'll take a cab."

"It's Wednesday, and taxis in Wellice don't operate after midnight during the week." He must be in the bathroom or kitchen as I can hear running water. "Stay where you are, Grace. I'll be there in twenty minutes max. My mother is here to take care of Heidi."

"Thank you, Clayton."

I'm grateful for his offer, even though I feel guilty, because I'm terrified of being alone. What if I receive bad news at the hospital? Perhaps I should call Marcia and Travis, but I don't want to worry them without knowing anything, especially on the day they're celebrating the upcoming birth of their child.

Clayton arrives soon and pulls me into his arms as I start crying. He helps me into the car, my legs trembling.

"You really didn't have to do this." I buckle my seatbelt.

The interior of his car smells like mint chewing gum and fresh coffee.

"I know." He glances over his shoulder as he backs out of the driveway. "But I want to."

I look out of the window, turning away from him as the tears keep coming. The fact that he would get up in the middle of the night to come and help me means more to me than he could ever imagine.

"Tell me about the baby shower."

"Are you trying to distract me?"

"Maybe." His laughter ripples through the air. "I'm also curious. Why aren't you there?"

"Marcia wanted me to go, but I refused. I don't want to divert the attention from her. She's the mother."

"I get that." He touches my arm. "I'm glad you called me."

I stiffen, feeling pressure build in my stomach, and take a sharp breath in.

"Are you okay?" Clayton asks, throwing a glance at me.

"I think so. My stomach just went hard."

"Braxton Hicks contractions, huh?"

I look at him in disbelief. "What don't you know about pregnancy?"

"Not much. When my wife was pregnant, I wanted to be fully involved in the whole process. It wouldn't have been fair for her to do it all on her own. So, I read all the books and watched all the videos. I'm glad I did." He throws a glance my way. "If I remember correctly, Braxton Hicks are often harmless. I'm sure the baby's fine."

"I hope so." This cannot go wrong, not so close to the due date. Surely, fate wouldn't be that cruel.

When we pull into the hospital parking lot, Clayton comes to open my door and helps me out. But my stomach has hardened again, and I ask him to wait a few seconds until the discomfort passes. When it finally does, he escorts me through the automatic doors into the hospital. From the outside, we might look like we're together, a happy couple expecting a child. They would never guess that we're just two people trying to heal together. Nothing more.

A doctor agrees to see me immediately, and a short time later, the checkup is done and I'm waiting for her to tell me the results. But she's typing something on her computer, her expression serious. Without warning, my mind goes back to the day I swallowed those pills. If something goes wrong, will I be tempted to escape the pain again?

The doctor looks back at me finally and her face breaks into a warm smile as she confirms I was indeed having

Braxton Hicks contractions. "The baby is fine and you have nothing to worry about."

"What about the spotting?" I ask, still a little worried.

"Some women do experience spotting, and it's good you came to get it checked out. But everything is okay."

"Thank God everything is fine." Clayton pulls me into a quick hug when I return to the waiting room and tell him the news. He didn't feel it was right for him to come into the examination room with me. Overwhelmed with relief, I sit down next to him, cover my face with my hands, and allow the tears to fall. I had no idea how worried I was. He doesn't speak as he puts his hand on my upper back, rubbing in circles until I stop crying.

Finally, I look at him with sore eyes. He's my only friend in this town, and he dropped everything to be by my side. I really want to tell him the truth, to open myself up to him.

"My twin sister died during childbirth. She had a stroke, and she and her baby didn't make it."

"Jesus." Clayton's hand claps his mouth. "That's terrible. I'm so sorry to hear that."

"A few months before that, she and her husband, Peter, asked me to be their surrogate. I said yes, but then I changed my mind." I stare at my hands, clasping them together to stop them from shaking. "If I had gone through with it, Rachel would not have gotten pregnant again. She wouldn't have died."

"That's why you're doing this?" Clayton's voice is low against my ear as he puts an arm around me, pulling me close. "Because you feel responsible?"

"Don't. Please, don't tell me it's not my fault."

"Okay, I won't. But that doesn't mean I'm not thinking it."

He holds me a while longer, the silence between us filled in by the sounds of hospital staff being paged over the intercom. When the woman sitting opposite us starts to cough and sneeze uncontrollably, we stand up to leave.

In the car, I lean back my head and stare through the window at the other parked cars. A man is pulling a folded wheelchair out of the trunk, and he helps an old woman into it. Clayton puts a hand on my cheek and turns me to face him, with glistening eyes.

"You need to stop punishing yourself." He leans into my direction and brushes his lips with mine, barely. "You deserve to be happy," he whispers against my lips, then pulls away to start the car. "Give yourself permission to be."

What we just shared is not a kiss, not really, but it still sends my senses spinning out of control. The engine of the car springs to life and the sound brings me back to reality. What am I doing? Why am I letting down my guard? Clayton and I can't work. I'm leaving soon and, even if I wasn't, he deserves someone who has her emotions under control. Someone who knows where her life is headed. I'm not good enough for him.

We drive back to the Thorpes' in silence.

"Thanks, Clayton," I say when we arrive. "I'm sorry you had to come all the way out here because of a false alarm."

"Call me if it happens again, anytime." He cups my chin with his hand. "I mean it. I'm always here if you need me, and you need someone to take care of you right now." He pauses. "I'm not at the café tomorrow, but feel free to drop by the house anytime."

"After what happened tonight, it might be a good idea for me to stay in." In fact, he won't see much of me from now on. I plan on taking it easy the last two weeks before the baby comes.

"You're right. I'll see you around. Let me know if the baby decides to come ahead of schedule."

"I will." I step out of the car and Clayton drives off.

Travis and Marcia have returned home, but most of the lights in the main house are out except in the living room. I have barely inserted the key into the lock of the guesthouse when the door opens, and I jump back, startled. Travis is standing in front of me.

"Travis, you scared me." I hold my chest to calm my heart. "What are you doing here?"

"After we got back from the baby shower, Marcia came to bring you some cupcakes but the door was open and you weren't home. Where were you?"

I glance down at my keys as I enter. "Oh no, I didn't know... I thought I locked up. I'm sorry."

We had left in such a rush that I must have forgotten to lock the door.

Travis rubs the back of his neck. "So, where were you?"

I shut my eyes and let out a breath. I don't want to tell him about what happened; it would only make him more protective.

"I just had to... go out for a little while," I say, hoping he will drop the subject.

"No, Grace," he says softly, but his tone is firm. "We've been over this. You can't just disappear without letting us know where you're going, and definitely not in the middle of the night, leaving the door wide open. Can you imagine how worried we were? You could not even be reached on the phone. I was about to call the police."

"Come on, Travis. That's a bit extreme, don't you think?" I place my hands on my hips. "I'm a grown woman, I do not need anyone watching over me. And the baby is fine."

"Grace, as long as you're carrying our child, we need to know where you are, especially late at night." He gives me a stern look and rubs his forehead with his fingertips. "If something happens to you, or to the baby or—"

Anger rises in me like steam from a boiling pot, and I cannot contain it. "I'm sorry, Travis, but I can't always tell you where I'm going and what I'm doing. I have my own life too, you know?"

"Well, right now, that life of yours revolves around our baby." He turns and walks away, leaving me feeling as if he's slapped me across the face.

Suddenly, I feel the baby move inside me. I place a shaking hand on my belly and speak to it in a soft voice. "It's okay, honey. Everything is going to be okay."

But is that really the case? If so, why are my hands trembling?

## CHAPTER 26

During my early morning walk the next day, I call Sydney as I'm bursting to speak to her about Clayton.

"There's something I need to tell you," I say when she picks up.

"Something good, I hope."

"Something complicated."

"Does it have to do with the baby?"

"No, the baby is fine."

"Then spit it out, woman," she pushes. "Hang on a second. Is this about a boy?"

I laugh. "It's about a friend."

"A *boy*-friend? Grace, have you met someone out there?"

"We're just friends. We've been hanging out, that's all. He's been showing me around town."

"Oh, my goodness. That's great. It's high time you start dating again."

Although I dated from time to time, I haven't had any serious relationships since Chad and I broke up. And when Rachel died, I had other things to think about than men.

"I'm not dating him." I shrug. "It's complicated."

"It always is, isn't it? Tell me about him. Pretend it's an ad for a dating site."

"Tall, dark, and handsome, lawyer and widower in his late thirties with an adorable five-year-old daughter."

"Aha! I get now why that might be complicated. He's got a broken heart too, then."

"Something like that. And then there's me and my baggage."

I'm not even sure why I'm telling Sydney about Clayton. I know it can't go anywhere.

"What does he think about what you're doing for the Thorpes?"

"He thinks it's wonderful, actually."

"Well, that's a few points for him. He's not another Chad."

"Definitely not." There's nothing similar about the two men at all.

"I think you should let down your guard and see where this takes you."

"You know what?" I say, changing my mind. "Let's talk about something else."

Sydney laughs but doesn't object as she fills me in on her travel plans. But my mind is still on Clayton and the kiss we almost shared. *Stop it, Grace. Just stop.*

Before long, she pivots the conversation back to Clayton, and to change the subject I find myself telling her about the red bathwater, and the fact that I think it was Agnes again, trying to scare me away. Big mistake. Sydney freaks out and insists on me packing my bags immediately, getting out of the Thorpes' home right away.

"You know what I think, honey?" she says with a sigh. "I think you've bonded with the baby and being there makes you feel like you're somehow connected to its future."

"I think you're wrong," I say, but deep down I wonder if she could be right. Lately, while moving around the property, I've been imagining my little child running around and playing in the garden and paddling its feet in the river, and even sleeping in the guesthouse. It's hard for me to tear myself from that. But I can't admit it to Sydney or anyone else.

It takes a while, but I manage to talk her down from the ledge and hang up finally, feeling exhausted.

A short time after I return from my walk, Beatrice comes to the guesthouse and tells me that Marcia wants to see me in the house. As I arrive at the front door, I bump into Agnes, who's just leaving, and she has the audacity to remind me of the offer she had made.

"I've already told you I'm not interested," I reply firmly and almost too loudly. "If you don't stop this, I'll go and tell Marcia. I can do it right now, your choice."

"You wouldn't dare," she hisses, grabbing my arm.

"I'm not afraid of you," I say in a hiss to match hers as I wriggle my arm from her grip.

"Are you sure about that?" she asks before I'm out of earshot.

Marcia is waiting for me in the library, wearing a crisp gray and white pantsuit. Her hair is pinned back and styled into a neat bun to show off the pearl and diamond earrings in her ears, which I suspect are one of MereLux's pieces.

There are huge bookshelves lining the walls of the library, and large windows let in sunlight, creating a warm glow. A fireplace in the corner of the room makes it feel warm and inviting, even if it isn't lit, and Marcia sits behind an oak desk on top of a Persian rug in the center of the room.

"Thanks for coming, Grace. I hope you have a few minutes for me," she says with a smile. "Please, have a seat. I wanted to talk to you about something."

"Is everything all right?" I have an uneasy feeling that this has to do with what happened last night, and if she, like Travis, decides to forbid me from going out, I'll lose it.

She folds her hands on the table. "I just wanted to apologize for Travis last night. He was... he's worried about the baby, as you already know."

"I know, Marcia, and I understand." I take a deep breath. "But I just can't let him control my life. I have to do what I feel is right. I need my freedom."

She nods. "I fully understand that you need your freedom, but please just be careful. Travis just wants to make sure nothing goes wrong... again."

I nod and run a hand through my hair. "And I'm sure you know that I want you to have this baby as much as you do." I tap my fingers on the edge of my seat. "As far as where I was, I was out with a friend, and I think I have a right to meet people."

"Yes, of course, and I understand. I'm sorry if we overreacted. It's just that you haven't been out that late before." She takes a deep breath and smiles at me. "Listen, Grace. I've been wanting to tell you something, but I couldn't find the right time."

I look at her with curiosity, but she says nothing more.

"What... is everything all right?"

"I have something to confess, something that has been burdening my conscience."

She looks down to hide her flushed cheeks and my heart

skips a beat. I feel like I'm suffocating. What is she trying to tell me? And why am I fearing the worst?

"The red bathwater," she starts and I straighten up.

I narrow my eyes as my pulse starts racing. "What about it?"

"When you went out for a walk, I was in my studio, and through the window I overheard you tell someone on the phone about it, so I think it's time to come clean." She takes a deep breath. "It was me, Grace. I made the water red, but not because—"

"You did what?"

She stands up and comes to me, taking my hands into hers. "I'm so sorry I scared you that night. It wasn't my intention. I just... I wanted to treat you to a nice warm bath, to help you relax. I put a strawberry bath bomb in the water and that's why it was red. I didn't think it would—"

"Why?" I ask, still reeling from the shock of her confession. "Why didn't you say anything?"

She lets go of my hands and moves back to her desk. "The scare the red water gave you could have been dangerous for the baby, and I felt so guilty. Travis would have been furious with me. I guess I was also ashamed that I hadn't thought things through, and I hadn't spoken to you before doing it after you'd asked for privacy. I should have known that not everyone likes surprises."

"Yes, you are right. It did give me a scare." I stare at her, unsure of what else to say. I feel relieved, but also angry that she would keep this from me and allow me to be afraid and suspicious all this time.

She takes a deep breath and lets it out slowly. "I am so sorry. I hope you can forgive me," she says. "I was just trying to do something kind for you."

"Marcia, I'm not mad at you," I say finally, and stand

up. I'm too tired to handle this. "It's fine. I just wish you had told me before I accused your mother, that's all."

"Thank you." She gives me a warm smile. "Thank you for not being upset with me." She stands up as well and comes to stand in front of me. "Can you do me a favor?"

"Sure," I say.

"Please don't mention it to Travis. You know how protective he is. He'll be apoplectic."

"Okay, I won't say anything," I promise. "And Marcia? I appreciate you telling me what really happened."

"It was the right thing to do," she says. "I'm so glad we talked about this. I feel so much better."

"So do I," I say weakly.

"By the way," she says as I'm about to walk out the door, "my mother came over today to ask if she could move back into the house. How do you feel about that?"

"Marcia, she's your mother, and this is her home," I say with a forced smile. "I'll speak to you later."

I'm desperate for some calming herbal tea and plan to make some and take it with me to the river, but when I arrive at the guesthouse, I find a massive gift basket covered in cellophane on the doorstep. It looks like one of those self-care baskets with soaps and bath salts. Marcia has already apologized for Travis's overprotectiveness, so I imagine the basket is a gift from Travis, himself, an attempt at making amends.

I take it with me into the guesthouse and sit on the couch with it on my lap, then I pull the ribbon at the top to release the opening. It's filled to the brim with several bottles of shampoo, scented shower gels, bath bombs, candles, and perfumes. I lay everything next to me on the couch until there's only one thing left in the basket.

A miniature doll without a head, arms, or legs.

As I jolt back, the basket falls from my lap onto the floor, and the headless doll rolls out and lands in front of me.

I can feel the blood draining from my face. Agnes may not have turned my bathwater red, but I know she did this. The veiled threat she made me on her way out the door was real, but I underestimated her. As if I am in a trance, I get up, put the doll back in the basket, then take the basket and everything in it to the main house, where I find Travis with Marcia in the library.

"I found this on the doorstep," I say, holding up the basket in front of me. "Agnes must have left it there. She's trying to scare me, so I'd leave and take the baby with me."

I drop the full basket on the table and they both come to take a look. As soon as they see the doll, they both suck in a breath.

"How dare she do such a thing?" Travis's face flushes red with indignation as he turns to his wife. "I know she's your mother, but her behavior is out of control. She's gone too far."

"I agree." Marcia's face is pale from shock, and she's on the verge of crying. "I'm so sorry, Grace. I really am. I'll talk to her. I know she can be over the top at times, but trust me. She would never want to cause you or the baby harm."

"How can you even say that?" Travis asks. "She just traumatized the woman carrying our baby. I'm sorry, but she can't move back in here. She needs professional help."

I agree. "Please, Marcia. I don't want her around me or the baby."

"I understand," Marcia says after a long silence. "It's important for you to feel safe and protected." She looks at Travis and then at me. "I will take care of it, I promise. My mom will not move back in until the baby is born, and again, I'm deeply sorry, Grace."

Travis nods as he paces around the room. "You better talk to her or I will."

I'm still shaking, but my voice is clear and firm. "If Agnes pulls anything like this again, I'm moving out. I mean it."

# CHAPTER 27

Two days after Clayton drove me to the hospital, I'm lying in my bed fully awake, staring into the darkness. I've only slept three hours in total, but my body and mind are well rested, like I've had a full night's sleep. Aside from the usual aches and pains of pregnancy, I'm buzzing with energy. But my watch says it's five minutes after midnight, far too early to get up and start the day. I push aside the starched sheets. The moonlight flooding in through the corners of the curtain is luring me outside, and the idea of taking a walk in the garden when everyone is sleeping is tempting.

Without switching on the night light, I make my way around the bed, guided by the gentle natural light, and at the foot of the bed, next to the ottoman, my bare foot comes into contact with something soft. I jump back before realizing it's Marigold. She lets out a hiss of disapproval and flees to hide under the vintage desk by the window. I switch on the lights to find her eyeing me suspiciously.

"I'm sorry, Marigold," I say. "I didn't mean to scare you; I didn't see you there."

Marigold has been visiting me more and more, and she

now spends most of the nights with me in the guesthouse. Marcia doesn't mind and keeps saying that having a pet around instead of being all alone is good for my mental health. She's right; having Marigold around does me good. Since she moved in, I've had fewer panic attacks. When I find myself going to that dark place, I focus on giving her attention.

"I'm going out for some air," I tell her.

As I grab a light-knit cardigan from a chair, something falls to the floor. It's a newspaper Marcia brought me yesterday, thinking I might want to know what's going on outside our little bubble. The front-page story springs out at me, and a woman with mesmerizing violet eyes draws me in. Her name was Lorie Dawn, a thirty-two-year-old bank clerk who was found stabbed with her own kitchen knife in her Tallahassee apartment. The story has received renewed interest as new evidence has recently emerged.

Marcia already talked to me about this case, along with another woman who was found floating face down in a lake. Both cases have yet to be solved. She is obsessed with true crime stories and crime thriller novels, and she continues to lecture me about how dangerous it is out there, especially for women.

Picking up the newspaper and tossing it into the trash, I throw the cardigan over my nightdress and step outside into the cool night air. Very soon I wish Marigold had come with me. The darkness is making me shiver, especially after looking at that article. But I can't stand the stifling heat indoors. It's stupid for me to worry; Wellice is a safe place, I tell myself. I go a short way down the path, until my ears catch a sound. It seems to be coming from Marcia's studio. But the lights are off in there.

Voices. Not inside the studio, but behind it. They grow

louder as I draw nearer, but I can't hear the words, just murmurs. Switching off the flashlight on my phone, I stop by one of the rose bushes to listen. It must be Marcia and Travis talking, I realize, immediately feeling guilty for snooping. I wouldn't want to be caught listening to their private conversation. Unlike them, I do my best to respect other people's privacy. But just as I turn my back, the voices grow louder. I stop in my tracks, then step closer to the studio. I recognize Travis's voice, but not Marcia's.

Common sense tells me to return to the guesthouse, but curiosity gets the better of me. I hurry to the studio, my back pressed to the wall as I move along it. My heart is beating fast now and sweat is cooling my back. One short peek, just to see if the woman Travis is talking to is really Marcia. The conversation grows more intense. In fact, it sounds more like an argument.

When I get close enough to the end of one wall, I stop, and I'm about to take a look when the woman's voice drifts toward me, and I recognize it. I've never heard Beatrice angry before, but there's no doubt in my mind the voice belongs to her.

"I know what you're planning," she threatens. "It's time she knows who you really are."

"I'm warning you, Beatrice," Travis snaps. "You have no idea who you're dealing with."

I flinch at the sharpness in Travis's tone.

"Are you threatening me, young man? You don't want to do that, trust me." She pauses. "One word and you're out of this house and her life. You won't even be allowed to use her good name. I'm tired of standing back and watching you break that girl's heart. Marcia deserves to know the truth."

I start to tiptoe away, but something cracks under my

feet. I cringe, thinking I stepped on a twig. But no, the sharp sound came from them.

A slap.

I stumble, my heart pounding, and hurry back to the guesthouse.

In the bedroom, I sit in the dark as Marigold rubs her body around my legs and the conversation replays in my mind. Something is badly wrong. What exactly does Beatrice have against Travis that would drive her to threaten him?

The posts Marcia continues to share on social media make the world believe she and Travis have the perfect, happy marriage. That's what drew me to them. I wanted to bring a baby into a marriage that was loving and intact, like Rachel and Peter's was. Not even the lack of a child in their marriage stopped them from loving each other.

I close my eyes and moan with frustration. This is not how I wanted things to go. It's all wrong, and I feel so stupid. I've been ignoring the signs, the arguments, the silences between them, the cracks in the marriage. I thought it was a phase, that it would pass and they would go back to being the perfect couple I'd envisioned them to be.

I clench my fists in my lap. I can't help feeling betrayed. I should have known better; social media is just a place where people spread lies about themselves. Most of the photos featured on the perfect, color-coordinated grids and profiles are altered and meant to fool the world. I should have studied Marcia better, dug deeper into her picture-perfect life, asked more questions. Instead, I'd wanted so badly for this to work that I fell for a fairy tale.

What now? Where do I go from here? I need to know the truth. What secret is Beatrice hiding? Maybe if I talk to her, she'll let down her guard and confide in me. But then what? What can I do with only days left before the baby comes, and a contract already signed?

I lie on the bed, still clad in the cardigan despite the heat. Sleep is no longer on the agenda tonight. After a while, I get out of bed again, careful not to trip over Marigold, and walk to the window. From this side of the guesthouse, I can see the studio.

A short time later, they emerge from behind the studio. Beatrice stomps off toward her car, and Travis walks in the direction of the main house. I watch until they both disappear from view. My thoughts whirling, I climb under the covers and pull them up to my chin. Why did I have to go out there? If I had stayed inside, I wouldn't have heard the conversation and wouldn't be desperate for answers. But as much as I want the answers, I'm also afraid of what I'll learn and that it might change everything. Maybe it's better not to know.

I lie awake, stewing in my own thoughts until I fall into a restless sleep. I'm shaken awake by the sound of a shot ringing through the night, but I don't open my eyes because I know it's not real. It has to be in my head, another memory returning to haunt me.

# CHAPTER 28

Saturday morning, Marigold is curled up next to me instead of at the end of the bed, where she fell asleep last night. She's in such a tight ball that I can't even see her face. When I shift in bed, she stirs and hops off to stand in the bedroom doorway. I left the door open last night, so she didn't feel trapped and could roam around the house if she liked.

"Meow!"

I yawn and stretch. "Good morning to you, too," I say. "Give me a moment to brush my teeth, and I'll get you your breakfast, okay?"

Another meow, and she disappears into the hallway. In the bathroom, I'm groggily reaching for my toothbrush when I remember the conversation last night between Travis and Beatrice. Before I finally fell asleep, it had played in my mind for hours. Why were they arguing?

I'm nervous about seeing Travis again today. He sounded dangerous last night, and I'm worried that he hit Beatrice. If he did, any respect I had for him will be wiped away, and I don't know what I'm going to do.

I brush my teeth and force myself not to think about the conversation, at least for now. Once I've fed Marigold, I get ready to head out. I need to speak to Clayton. He might be able to help me decide what to do with this new information. I'll talk to Beatrice later, when she comes over to clean.

I take a shower and sneak out of the guesthouse. For the first time since I moved in with the Thorpes, the curtains and shutters of the main house are closed. It's my lucky day: no one is watching. After the night Travis had, I won't be surprised if he's still asleep. But when I reach the driveway, I only find my car standing there. Marcia and Travis are not home.

Strange for them to leave without a word to me, and without their daily checkup on the baby.

My spine tingles. Something doesn't feel right.

Maybe they had a fight last night and Marcia was so upset that she left the house early? Did Beatrice keep her promise and tell Marcia whatever secret she has been holding over Travis's head? And if Marcia left, where is Travis?

I drop my car keys back into my purse. Change of plans. Since no one is home to hover over me, I'll stay. I'm too drained to go out, anyway. What I have to tell Clayton can easily be said over the phone.

Clayton doesn't answer, but he soon calls back. "Hey, Grace. Sorry, my phone was in the back."

"That's all right," I say. "Are you at the café already?" I glance at the clock on the living room wall. Six-thirty.

"Yes, early start today. Will you drop by later?"

"I'm not sure. I should take it slow, remember?"

"Right." He sounds different, distant somehow, and my heart sinks. He's been pulling away from me since the day we almost kissed, and my gut tells me he regrets getting too close. He did mention once that he has not dated anyone since his wife died, partly because he didn't want to confuse Heidi. Maybe I should stop involving him in my issues. I've been leaning on him too hard lately, and it's not fair to him. He has his own life to live, and I don't want to disrupt it.

"I better let you work. Sounds like you're busy."

"No, no, I have a moment. Is everything okay?"

"Yes." I rake a hand through my hair. "Sure."

"Grace?" He draws out my name. "Something's going on. What is it?"

Marigold appears from the kitchen and hops onto my lap. I lay a hand on her warm body and calm sweeps through me. Having her near gives me the courage I need to change my mind and get the words out. Clayton is a friend, and talking to him doesn't have to mean anything. The loud whirr of a coffee grinder on his end gives me a chance to weigh my words, and when silence returns, I fill it.

"At around midnight, I couldn't sleep, so I went out for a late walk in the garden. And I heard Travis talking with Beatrice, their housekeeper."

"That's strange. What would they be doing outside so late?"

"I asked myself the same question. And they looked as though they were hiding behind Marcia's studio. It was weird."

"Did you hear what they were talking about?"

"They were having some kind of confrontation— throwing around accusations and threats."

"Threats?" Clayton asks.

"Yeah. I only showed up when it was escalating, so I have no idea what they were talking about exactly. But it seemed like Beatrice knew something... a secret she was holding over Travis's head."

"What do you think it is?"

I shrug. "I don't know. I had to get away, I didn't want them to catch me and it was so creepy, late at night in the dark. But it sounded like something that could destroy Travis and Marcia's marriage."

"What does she know?" Clayton asks slowly, deep in thought.

"That's the question."

"Well, it all sounds very intense. What time of night was this again?"

"Around midnight." I pause. "Beatrice mentioned something about Travis having hurt Marcia enough, and that it was time for her to know the truth."

"Right." Clayton draws in a breath. "I know Beatrice was working for the Thorpes long before Travis and Marcia got married. It wouldn't be a surprise if she's protective of her."

"True. She was her nanny." I pause. "I actually had a conversation with Beatrice recently and she made it clear to me that she doesn't think Travis is the right man for Marcia." I can still remember the bitterness in her tone, and I suck in a sharp breath. "Clayton, there's something else. Whatever secret they're keeping between them must be serious because it got physical. I think I heard a slap."

"Are you saying Travis struck Beatrice?" Clayton sounds horrified. "Why would he do something like that?"

"Maybe it was Beatrice who hit him; I can't be sure because I didn't see it. All I know is that what I heard did sound like a slap. Somebody got hit."

Giving my baby to a man who might be capable of hitting a woman terrifies me. My goal from the start has been to care for and protect the baby I'm carrying, and I trusted that when I handed it over to its parents, they would take over that task. Now I'm not sure what to do.

"Clayton," Lillian calls in the background. "Come help me with these boxes."

"I'm sorry, Grace," Clayton says. "I have to get to work, but let's talk about this later. Why don't you join us for dinner tonight? Mom promised to make her famous roast beef. Then we can try to figure out this big mystery."

"Sounds delicious. I'll let you know later if I'll be able to make it."

After hanging up, I stare at the blank screen of the TV and continue to stroke Marigold. I only stop when I hear cars pulling into the driveway.

They're back.

I put Marigold on the couch and go to the window, my heart thudding hard in my chest. The tables have turned. The Thorpes are no longer watching me. I'm the one watching them.

I watch as Marcia and Travis exit their individual cars. Why would they use separate cars if they went to the same place? If they went to different locations, then how did they happen to return at the same time?

They don't seem to be talking to each other as they make their way to the house. Marcia's shoulders are hunched forward, and she's wiping her eyes. Travis attempts to put an arm around her, but she shakes him off. I groan when they disappear into the house, where I can no longer see them. I've seen enough to know that Marcia probably knows the secret. Maybe she also heard Travis and Beatrice talking last night. They could have started the conversation at the house before moving to the back of the studio.

I don't see Marcia or Travis again until after lunch, when they both show up at the guesthouse, and barely say a word to me before they make their way to opposite ends of the couch.

Fear drips down my spine.

Maybe their marriage is over? Then what?

I try not to get ahead of myself as I sit in the armchair across from them.

They exchange looks with each other before looking back at me. Marcia's eyes are swollen and red, and a dried river of tears and mascara runs down her cheeks. When our eyes meet, hers well up again.

"Is everything all right?" I ask, my throat dry.

Travis shakes his head and Marcia drops her gaze to her lap. I watch as a tear drops onto her hands. Travis doesn't say anything.

"What's going on? Marcia?" I can't bear the pressure in my chest.

"Beatrice is..." she wipes her eyes. "Beatrice is dead."

A cold wave of shock sweeps through me from the top of my head to the tips of my toes and fingertips.

"She's dead? She—how?"

"We received a call this morning from her granddaughter. She found her lying at the bottom of the stairs. She must have fallen last night."

"But that's impossible," I say.

"It's a shock to all of us," Travis adds quickly. "Beatrice was a good woman; we loved her very much. But she was also tired and weak; she was getting older. It wouldn't be a surprise if she really just fell."

*Liar*, I want to scream. The way he talked to her last night made it clear he didn't think much of her. I'll go as far as saying he hated her. And Beatrice was no weak woman.

They continue to tell me more about the accident, Marcia mumbling and choking through her tears, but I'm not interested in what they have to say. My mind is now focused on one single question.

Was it really an accident?

# CHAPTER 29

"Have you eaten?" Clayton asks as he steps through the door. I shake my head and he holds up two goodie bags. "I brought you a roasted sweet potato salad and some avocado brownies. You sounded over the phone like you might need a treat."

He had called me again during his lunch break, wanting to know if I had decided whether to have dinner with them. When I'd told him something terrible had happened, he'd ditched the dinner plans and told me he'd come see me after work instead. Even though it would be the first time I'd invited someone to come see me at the Thorpes, I said yes. I'm an adult. I'm allowed visitors.

"Thanks, Clayton. That's really kind of you." I close the door.

I don't have much of an appetite, and he doesn't mind when I put it in the fridge to eat later.

"Are you okay?" he asks when we take a seat in the living room.

"I think so," I say, unsure where to start.

"You don't have to lie to me." He draws closer, placing

an arm around my shoulders, like he did in front of the
fountain a few weeks ago.

Despite the circumstances, my body reacts the same
way and I find myself leaning into him, resting my head on
his shoulder. "Okay," I say. "You're right, I'm not okay." The
tears come and I'm unable to stop them. Even though I
haven't known Beatrice for as long as Marcia has, I really
did like her, and I feel the loss deeply. I can't believe she's
gone, just like that.

After sitting in silence for a few minutes, Clayton pulls
away and looks into my eyes, his brow knitted.

"What happened?" he asks. "Please tell me it has
nothing to do with the baby."

"No. The baby's fine." I pull a tissue from my pocket
and blow my nose. "It's Beatrice."

"What about her?"

I sniff and blow out a breath. "She's dead."

The silence that follows is heavy and long, as if the
whole world has stopped and there's nothing left in it but
the two of us.

"What do you mean, she's dead?" Clayton asks. "Didn't
you say you saw her last night?"

"I did. I mean, I heard her voice. I'm pretty sure it was
her."

Clayton scratches the back of his head, confused. "So
she died afterwards? That quickly?"

It's not that out of the ordinary, I want to tell him.
People die overnight all the time. One second they're in
front of you and the next they're nothing but a memory.

"I don't know, Clayton. I don't know what to think."

"How did you find out about this?"

"Travis and Marcia came over this afternoon to
tell me."

He runs a hand through his hair. "Did they say what the cause of death was?"

"Apparently, she fell down the stairs at her place. Beatrice's granddaughter was the one who found her at the bottom." I bite down on my trembling lip.

Clayton rubs his chin. "What a horrible way to die."

"It is a painful way to die, yes, but what if that's not really what happened?" I turn my body to face him. "What if it was not an accident?"

"What do you mean?" Clayton's words are low and measured. When I look into his eyes, I can tell he knows exactly where my thoughts are taking me. "You don't think he has something to do with it, do you? After last night?" he whispers, then shakes his head. "No. He couldn't have. This is crazy."

"You're right. Forget what I said. I just think it's strange that he was the last person she argued with. He threatened her, for God's sake. And now she's gone."

"It certainly raises a lot of questions. But surely they didn't have a secret so terrible it would lead to murder?"

I glance at the windows, making sure they're closed and that no one can hear our conversation.

"I have no idea." I close my eyes and keep them that way, trying to clear my head. Everything in my mind is a jumbled mess right now, and I need to be able to think straight.

"What are you thinking?" Clayton asks.

I meet his gaze. "I'm thinking that if there's a chance it wasn't an accident, and he had something to do with it, I can't... I won't give this child to them. Of course I can't."

He raises an eyebrow. "You're thinking of keeping the baby?"

"Look, when I came into this, I never planned on

keeping the baby, of course not. But I don't know what else to do at this point, a few days before my due date. Can I really give my baby to someone I suspect is a murderer?"

"We don't know that for sure," Clayton says. "There's no proof, let's not get carried away."

I don't say anything and, as I sit there, I listen to the heavy beating of my heart. My chest feels so tight, and I wish I could give up and crumble. But I can't do that. I need to be strong. This is not just about me. I may be about to break one promise, but I will keep the other. I will protect this child.

But Clayton is right: there's no proof Travis had anything to do with Beatrice's death. Maybe it was exactly what they said it was: an accident.

"You know what I think?" Clayton asks. "I think you should wait a little and see what turns up. If there was really any foul play involved, the cops will uncover it."

Unless Travis is smarter than the cops. People get away with murder all the time.

"You really don't think I should go to the police?"

"Not without any concrete evidence." He pauses. "Look, I don't want you to get caught up in this mess, Grace. If Travis finds out you suspect him, you don't know how he might react."

"True." I pick at my fingernails, still deep in thought. "I just have such a bad feeling about this, Clayton." What if, by not going to the cops, I'm doing something wrong? Isn't it my obligation as a citizen to tell them what I heard?

Clayton squeezes my hand. "Give it a few days and see what happens."

"Fine," I say eventually. "I'll keep my mouth shut until I know more."

Never in my wildest dreams did I think being a surrogate would end this way, that I would come to a place where I would consider not handing over the baby. And here I was thinking that dealing with Agnes was my only obstacle.

Maybe I'm reading too much into it. The secret Travis and Beatrice were talking about could be something simple, a misunderstanding. That's it. That's what I'll hold on to.

When the sound of a car engine breaks the silence, we both go to the window. This time, Travis and Marcia are getting into Travis's Jeep, and they don't even seem to notice Clayton's SUV. Again, they haven't told me they're going out. They don't need to; it's their business. It's just a big change from their normal routine since I arrived here. But I can't help myself from feeling that the one good thing that has come out of this whole mess is that I finally have some peace. They have something else to worry about instead of me.

I step away from the window. "I feel so sorry for Marcia," I say. "She's known Beatrice since she was a child. I bet Beatrice was more of a mother to her than Agnes ever could be."

After they drive away, Clayton and I change the subject because talking about what happened to Beatrice is just too painful, and my head is pounding. I need to stop crying, and I take slow sips of water as we talk about Heidi's school and his struggle with deciding to return to law.

"Moving Heidi again after she's settled here would be tough, and my mother wants us to stay. She won't even discuss it."

"Clayton, whatever decision you make will be the right one for you and your daughter, and if you decide to return to the big city, maybe Nina will get over her discomfort and come visit. Now that she's used to having you and Heidi around, she will miss you quite a bit." I pause. "What I'm trying to say is, you're a great dad. You'll help your daughter flourish anywhere."

"Thank you for saying that." He draws me into a hug. "Whatever decision you make will be the right one for you, too. Whatever comes your way, you will be strong enough to handle it."

"Copycat," I say, laughing as we draw apart and our eyes meet. Then he suddenly stands up, pushing his hands deep into his pockets and looking away.

"I should go," he says.

"Sure. Thanks for dropping by, and for the food."

"No problem. That's what friends are for."

At the door, he leans slightly forward, like he's about to hug me again, but he steps back before our bodies touch.

"If you need anything, you have my number." He disappears through the door, leaving me feeling empty inside.

# CHAPTER 30

The first thing I do when I open my eyes on Monday morning is think of Beatrice, the lovely, kind woman whose face lit up when she talked about her daughter and grand-daughter. It's been forty-eight hours since I heard she died and it still hurts. I can see the loss has also hit Marcia hard, and she copes by locking herself away in her studio. Travis, on the other hand, has been pretending to be affected by the loss of their housekeeper, but it's obviously an act. I know he must be relieved that Beatrice died with their secret.

Their obsession with the baby has waned a little, and that is giving me the time I need to come to a concrete deci-sion about what to do when it is born. My decision would be clear if the cops showed up to question Travis about Beatrice's death, but that hasn't happened yet and I'm not sure whether to be disappointed or relieved. The thought of giving them the baby without knowing the truth terrifies me. I can't do it, not when I have so many doubts about Travis's innocence.

My stomach is rumbling as I get out of bed and brush my teeth. For the first time since Beatrice died, I'm craving food instead of just forcing myself to eat for the sake of the baby. But any time I spend in the kitchen reminds me of Beatrice, especially when I see the pot of herbs on the windowsill.

To distract myself from the memories, I grab my phone to call Sydney. I'm dialing the number when I enter the kitchen, but the moment my bare foot lands on the tiled floor, it slides forward and, the next thing I know, I'm falling.

A scream explodes from me as I land hard on my bottom, and pain shoots from the area of impact to my lower back. I place a protective hand around my belly. "No," I whimper, my voice filled with panic. The sound I make brings Marigold to my side, and she paws at me with concern in her big emerald eyes.

I need to get up and do something. I can't sit here and hope the baby is fine. Gritting my teeth, I crawl across the slippery floor to my phone, which has landed in the middle of the kitchen, and I call Marcia with shaking hands. Within minutes, she and Travis enter the guest-house without me opening for them. They must still have another key for the door, even though I thought they gave me the spare. But I'm in too much shock to care about that.

"Are you okay?" Travis asks, putting his hands under my armpits to help me to my feet. It's a struggle, as we both keep slipping and sliding, but eventually we make it out of the kitchen and into the living room.

"What happened?" Marcia asks.

"I don't know how that liquid ended up on the floor," I say, my voice high-pitched and frightened.

"We need to have you checked out," Travis says urgently.

Marcia's eyes are wide with fear and her face has gone pale.

Since I hit the floor hard, I walk with a slight limp as Travis escorts me to his car.

I am certain that it was no accident. Whoever spilled the liquid is out for blood. They want to harm me, and my innocent baby, just days before it's due to be born.

# CHAPTER 31

Half an hour later, I'm on Dr. Miller's examination table. The doctor is a stocky, dark-haired man in his late fifties with a soothing voice, warm, gray eyes, and a firm handshake that reminds me of my late father, who used to believe that firm handshakes were a sign of confidence, and could tell you a lot about a person. Dr. Miller's wife, Barbara, works as his receptionist.

"Everything looks great," he says, removing the ultrasound transducer from my belly before handing me a tissue to wipe off the ultrasound gel. "You'd be surprised, but babies are well protected inside a woman's womb." He smiles at me before continuing, "They can survive a lot of bumps during pregnancy."

I send up a prayer of thanks, my gaze focused on the exposed skin of my belly as I wipe it clean. The doctor snaps off his rubber gloves and tosses them into a silver wastebasket. "Grace, I suggest you take it easy for the next few days and get as much rest as possible. Come back in if you experience any intense pain or bleeding."

"I will," I say and ease myself off the exam table,

allowing my linen blouse to fall over my stomach. Then I follow him out of the exam room and into his office, where Travis and Marcia are waiting.

Sitting behind his desk, he tells them what he told me. "Her blood pressure levels are no longer as low as they were at the last checkup. The due date is fast approaching, but the baby is healthy, so I do not expect any complications. If anything unusual occurs, please contact me immediately. As always, you can reach me by phone and cell, anytime."

"Thank God the baby is fine," Travis says, running his hand through his hair before clasping both hands behind his head. "We look forward to seeing him or her."

The doctor nods with a smile, then he leans forward. "Keep in mind, however, that most babies don't arrive on their scheduled due date. They can come early or late, depending on how ready they are to make their appearance. You should be prepared for either scenario."

While Marcia stares into space, Travis asks the doctor more questions about how they can help me prepare for the birth. Marcia still looks rattled, and her cheeks are streaked with tears. We both came very close to losing something that means everything to us.

When my gaze returns to Travis, the doctor's words fade away as I notice a red mark peeking out from underneath the cuff of his long-sleeve shirt, stamped on his wrist. He glances at me and covers it up again. Could Travis have followed Beatrice home, and pushed her? What if she scratched him, to stop herself from falling?

Am I being crazy? I look over at Marcia, whose jaw is moving back and forth like she's chewing gum. Does she suspect something and is saying nothing to protect her husband?

The mark on his arm is not enough to prove murder. It

shouldn't be enough for me to suspect him either, but I can't stop the thoughts from churning in my mind, even after what just happened to me.

"I still don't get it. Exactly what happened?" Travis asks as we walk out and stand outside the building.

Thanks to Marcia grabbing a pair of jeans and a blouse for me on our way out of the house earlier, I'm no longer drenched in oil.

"I don't know." I rub my forehead. "Like I said, I went into the kitchen to get the cat some food and I slipped."

"You didn't see the liquid on the floor?"

"No." It was vegetable oil, I smelled it on my fingertips.

Travis shakes his head, confused. "Why would it be all over the floor? Did you accidentally spill it?"

"I'm sure I didn't. The only time I was in the kitchen was last night before I went to bed. And I didn't cook anything with oil as an ingredient." Anger is beating like a pulse at the base of my throat. I have to get out of here. "Someone must have poured it onto the floor."

Travis turns to Marcia, his face puce. "Did your mother go to the guesthouse anytime last night?"

Marcia presses a tissue to her eyes. "I don't know. I don't think—" She covers her cheeks with both hands. "Oh my God. The guesthouse spare keys were not where we normally keep them."

"She has to be behind this," Travis's voice is harsh, his eyes wild.

"I really don't think she'd—" Marcia starts and then stops talking. "I'll talk to her."

"Don't bother," Travis snaps. "I'll do it myself this time. She's gone too far, Marcia; she could have killed my child. She can never live with us again."

I've never seen Travis angrier. His face and neck are red, and veins are popping through his skin.

"You can't do that, Travis. We can't kick her out completely. It *is* her home."

"No, it's *our* home. Your father left it to you. She has enough money to buy another house, or ten if she wants. Why would she want to stay with us when she doesn't like being around me?"

"She's my mother, Travis." Marcia's voice is trembling now. "And we can't prove she did this. Maybe something spilled last night when Grace was cooking, and she forgot about it." Marcia looks back at me and gives me a tight smile. "But you're right. Grace and the baby should be our priority right now. I'll take care of them."

"So will I," Travis says, striding toward the car. "I'll never let your mother come near Grace again. She will not do anything to harm my baby."

*My baby.* How could he say that? He must know it will hurt Marcia's feelings.

Marcia says nothing as she opens the car door.

"I'll take a cab back," I say, instead of getting in with them.

"Why?" Travis asks. "I don't think you should be alone right now."

"I won't be alone; I'm meeting a friend." I've made my decision. I can no longer bear to be around them, not after what happened to me today. It's not safe. And I can't allow my child to be raised by a man I suspect of murder, or at the very least of hiding damaging secrets from his wife. I can't stay, and I certainly can't give them the baby.

"But Grace," Marcia says, getting out of the car again, "you need to rest after what happened. You heard what the doctor said."

"Marcia is right," Travis adds. "You're carrying our child and we'd appreciate it if you take it easy, especially after the fall you had. And you're only a few days away from your due date. What if the baby comes early?"

Too frustrated to answer right away, I count to ten. Then I try again in a calmer, but firm tone. "The doctor said many babies come late, too. You heard him. And the baby and I are fine." Even though I still feel sore, my heart is more bruised than my body.

"Is it Clayton Price you're meeting?" Travis asks. "I heard you've been seeing quite a lot of him lately."

"I have. And yes, he's the one I'm meeting." I frankly don't understand why it's their business. "Is that a problem?"

"Kind of. We would prefer it if you don't have a boyfriend while pregnant with our child," he says.

"Clayton and I are just friends," I say coolly, trying to keep myself calm. "I should go. I'll see you later." I walk away before I say something I might regret.

I feel his gaze following me, but I don't stop walking. I need to get to Clayton, to ask for his help because I feel like I can't do this alone.

The distance between Dr. Miller's practice and Clayton's café is no more than ten minutes, but, as a heavily pregnant woman, it feels like I've been walking for miles. When I reach the café, my armpits are damp and my blouse is sticking to my back. A teenage girl in a pink cowboy hat and matching sandals opens the door for me. My eyes search for Clayton. Normally, he spots me first and waves me over.

"He's not in until evening," Lillian says in passing. "Give me a moment. I'll be right with you."

"Thanks," I say, more than a little disappointed.

If I had told Clayton I was coming, he'd have reminded me that on Monday, he works the evening shift. But stopping by was a spur-of-the-moment decision. As it is, the grueling walk was all for nothing. All tables are occupied, including mine.

"I'm so sorry," Lillian says when she comes back to me. She toys with her silver eyebrow ring. "It's crazy busy today. Do you want to wait for a table? I'm sure one will be free soon. It's always nice to have you around."

I look around the packed café again and spot Cora at her table with her two cups of coffee. I could ask to join her, but she wouldn't want that. The empty seat is reserved for her daughter, and I won't intrude again.

"Don't worry about it," I say to Lillian. "I'll come another time."

"Are you sure?" She points to a table in the back. "Sandy Brown should be leaving in about five minutes. She has a dentist appointment."

"It's really fine, Lillian. I'll see you soon."

"All right then. You're welcome anytime."

On my way out, my phone pings with a text from Marcia.

*We're not going home straight away. I'm going to meet my mother at the hotel. I need to speak to her. Travis is running errands. Please get some rest, and I'll be home as soon as I can.*

Perfect. Having them out of the house will make it easier for me to get the hell out. I'll move into a hotel for the night while deciding what to do next.

But by the time the cab drops me off at the Thorpes, my plans are dashed. Travis is there, emerging from the main house. I move forward slowly, watching him walking like a man on a mission. Without knowing why, I crouch behind my car, an almost impossible task thanks to my protruding belly. But his back is turned anyway. He's walking in the direction of the shed now, a large, white envelope underneath his arm. Why is he home when he told Marcia he was running errands?

I should go to the guesthouse before he sees me, but my feet are glued to the ground. I force them to move and hurry to the back of the house, hiding behind one of the larger bushes. At first, I think he's about to walk past the shed, but he stops suddenly and looks around as if checking whether someone is watching him. I disappear out of view. Can he feel my gaze?

I head over to the guesthouse, but by the time I get there and look out the window, Travis is gone. I'm not sure whether he's inside the shed with the door closed, or if he went back to the house. I continue to stare at the shed, and three minutes later, he emerges. He's still looking shifty, his head moving from side to side as his gaze sweeps the grounds.

Finally, he returns to the main house. He only stays inside for about five minutes before coming out again, carrying his golf clubs, then he gets into his car and drives off.

He's hiding something, and I can't leave this house without knowing what it is.

# CHAPTER 32

The spare key to the main house is kept under the front door mat, and Marcia gave me permission to use it whenever I like. I'm positive that the key to the shed hangs on a hook behind the door, along with the one to Marcia's studio. I look under the mat, but there is no key. I guess I need to wait for them to come home. I'm determined to find out what Travis is hiding in that shed.

Marcia returns home a few minutes after 7 p.m., and her first stop is the guesthouse. I open the door before she knocks.

"Goodness," she says, putting a hand on her chest. "You frightened me."

"I'm sorry. I heard your car, and I wanted to come and talk to you."

"Oh," she says. "About what?" She looks at my stomach. "Are you feeling okay? Do you want us to go back to Dr. Miller? I'm sure he'll fit us in even after business hours, or we could go to the hospital and—"

"Marcia, I'm fine... physically. I was wondering if I can join you for dinner tonight. I need company."

"Oh, well, that's a pleasant surprise... I thought you preferred to eat alone."

"I do, most of the time." I pause. "But there are only a few days left until the baby comes and I have to go back to Miami. I thought we should spend some time together."

"Sure," she says. "I'd love that. I passed by the hotel to pick up some salads for dinner. Come to the house in thirty minutes; Travis should be home by then. Let's keep it casual."

As she walks away, I wonder why she came to the guest-house, since she didn't act like she expected me to be inside. But I'm relieved that I at least don't have to dress up for the dinner. The only thing I want to do is get inside, eat with them, and grab the key on my way out.

Dinner with them is uncomfortably quiet and I almost regret joining them, my mind swirling with anxiety. During the meal, my phone vibrates in my lap. It's Clayton, but Marcia has a "no phones at the table" rule. I'll call him back later. A text follows the phone call, but I don't read it.

After sitting in silence for half an hour, I stifle a yawn.

"I'm so sorry," I say. "I get exhausted so quickly these days. I think I should go to bed early."

"That's a good idea," Travis says. "Get as much rest as you can."

"I will." I get to my feet and wish them good night. "I'll show myself out." Thankfully, neither of them follows me to the front door.

The keys have all been labeled, making it easy to pick up the right one, and I reach for one of the two older-looking keys. One belongs to the shed, the other to Marcia's studio. Before long, I'm back inside the guesthouse with the key in my hand, waiting for darkness to fall and praying that they won't notice it's gone. If they do, I'll have to deny that I have it. I haven't even thought about how I'm going to get it back inside the house. Maybe Travis will think he dropped it somewhere outside.

Shortly after ten, the lights in the main house go out and, wasting no time, I throw on a bathrobe and sneak out of the guesthouse. Normally, I find the sound of chirping crickets soothing, but not tonight. It's not the only sound distracting me, either: my heart is beating way too loudly in my ears. I glance at the main house to make sure the lights are still off, then dart across the yard and past Marcia's studio. By the time I reach the door of the shed, I'm panting, both from exertion and the fear of getting caught.

I slide the key into the lock and twist to the right, only to be met with resistance. After I went to all that trouble, the door is unlocked. You'd think Travis would have locked it if he was hiding something in there.

I pull the door open and enter. Enveloped by the darkness, I switch on the flashlight on my phone. Spades, trowels, garden rakes, and every other tool required to tend a garden fill the surrounding space, but I don't see anything unusual.

I don't give up, though. I follow the light over every object in the room until it lands on a large metal storage box at the back of the shed, next to a rusty wheelbarrow full of seed and fertilizer bags. The perfect place to hide something, especially in a hurry. But when I open the box, I see it's filled with garden furniture cushions and throws. Disappointed, I put the cushions back inside and stare at it.

That's when I notice that the dust is disturbed on the ground, by the box. It's been moved, recently. Adrenaline is pumping through my veins as I push it aside, straining at the weight. There's nothing underneath it, but the surface is uneven. Some pieces of the wooden floor are slightly raised. I pick up a heavy-duty digging trowel and use it to pop open the piece of wood that stands out most. It gives way without much resistance.

Bingo. There's an envelope, folded and pressed as far to the bottom of the small space as it would go. My hands are shaking as I pick it up. What am I going to find?

The flap is not glued to the envelope, so I slide it out and reach inside, and my hands come into contact with something glossy. I grab the contents and pull them out.

I stare at the photos in my hands. These are the photos Travis took of me the day of the photo shoot. The photos that were not supposed to show my face.

But they do. And there are more photos of me. Most of them not taken on that day. Photos of me sleeping, eating, washing dishes, lying in the bath with my eyes closed, and even several of me at the Sawyer Hotel.

I feel sick to my stomach. He has been following me. He must have been spying on me through the window, coming in while I was asleep, watching me even when I was at the hotel. My throat goes dry and my knees weaken, but I can't stop looking at them. There have to be at least thirty photos of me.

When I reach the last one, something else falls to the floor and my head swims as I pick up what look like folded newspaper pages. I set the photos aside and stare at the three articles, one by one. Two of them are about the two murdered women I heard about—one found in a lake, and one in her kitchen. One brunette and one blonde, both women from two separate towns neighboring Wellice. They died about two years apart, and the woman in the lake is the most recent. Why would Travis have the articles about them? Why would he hide them? I move on to the third, torn from the *Wellice Gazette*, and something inside my gut shifts. My eyes move to the headline.

> H*IT-AND-RUN KILLS THIRTY-YEAR-OLD* W*ELLICE*
> *RESIDENT,* D*AISY* L*ANE*

Blood rushes to my head. It's Cora's daughter; I saw her photo on the table at Clayton's Coffee Lounge. I memorized her face the day I picked it up from the floor.

I hear a creaking sound outside and my heart jumps to my throat. I stuff everything back into the envelope, breathing heavily. But I don't have time to put it back in its place before I hear another sound. Someone is out there. Is it Travis? What will he do if he catches me with this?

I drop the envelope to the floor and creep out of the door, my heart in my mouth, and to my relief I don't see anyone outside. But something is moving out there, I'm sure of it. I can hear it even over the crickets chirping.

My arms around my body, I hurry back to the guest-house. Once inside, I collapse against the door and close my eyes, trying to get my breath back to normal before I call the police. But when I open them again, I freeze.

Someone's there, staring at me.

# CHAPTER 33

"You look flustered, Grace," Marcia says. "Are you okay?"

"I—sure." I press a hand to my chest. "You startled me. What are you doing here?"

"I'm sorry about that. I didn't mean to scare you." She puts a hand on my arm. "I saw you go to the shed. Is there something you needed?"

What do I say? Should I tell her? I'm afraid to do so: what if she goes to get Travis? I just have to get her out of here, so I can call the police. I blurt out the first thing that comes to me. "I couldn't sleep. I thought fresh air would help."

Marcia pushes her hands into the deep pockets of her long camel cardigan. "In the shed?"

I let out a stifled chuckle and swipe a film of sweat from my upper brow. "No. Of course not. The door was open, so I went to close it."

She takes a step back. "Silly me, I thought I saw you disappear inside."

*Act normal. You did nothing wrong.*

I try again. "Yes, I did. I checked to see if someone was inside first before closing it."

"I see." Her eyes are now narrowed to a squint. She doesn't believe a word I'm saying. I wouldn't either, if I were her.

"Did you also have trouble sleeping?" I jam my hands into my armpits, force a smile as I silently plead for her to leave.

"I heard a sound outside," Marcia says. "It woke me up."

But she couldn't have heard me. The door to the shed creaked when I opened it, but not loud enough for the sound to reach the main house.

"Okay," I say. "Marcia, if you don't mind, I'd really like to go to bed. Can we talk in the morning?"

"Sure. You and the baby should definitely get some rest." She touches my cheek with a forefinger. "You look a little pale."

"I'm just tired," I say quickly, stifling a pretend yawn.

"All right then. I'll see you in the morning, Grace. Good night." She opens the door and steps outside, closing it behind her.

"Good night," I murmur, but I'm not sure if she hears me.

I remain standing at the door, and I can't hear her footsteps. She must be standing on the other side. What is she waiting for? What's going through her mind?

When I finally hear her footsteps retreating, I hurry to the window and watch her dark figure walking toward the main house. In the middle of the path that separates the two buildings, she stops for a few seconds before changing her mind. I panic as I watch her change direction, moving toward the shed. What will she think when she sees what her husband is hiding?

*Stop panicking. Maybe she's going to the studio.*

No such luck. It's not long before the light in the shed is switched on, some of it spilling through the open door, illuminating the boxwood hedges and flowers outside. About a minute later, she's out. The light is switched off again, so I can't make out whether she's holding anything. She goes to the house, and I wait until the front door closes before stepping away from the window.

My hands are shaking, and my throat feels like it's closing up. Inside my room, I sit on the bed with Marigold at my feet, my phone in my hand. I feel so lonely, and afraid, and I know that if I don't calm down soon, I'll have a panic attack before I can tell everything to the police. I need to talk to someone, but if I call Sydney, I'll have to do too much explaining before I get to the point. Clayton, on the other hand, already knows most of what has been going on.

I close my bedroom door and unlock my phone to read the text he had sent me.

*Just wanted to see how you're doing. Lillian told me you stopped by at the Coffee Lounge. Call me when you can.*

I do just that.

"Just the person I was thinking about," he says when he picks up. "How are you?"

"I'm... I'm not good, Clayton. Something's happened."

"What? Grace, what's going on?" Worry is dripping from his voice now.

"When I got home, I saw Travis entering the garden shed and he was looking very suspicious. He kept glancing around, like he was checking to see if someone was watching. Then he came out, and he left."

"Let me guess," he says, "you went to investigate."

I pluck one of Marigold's pieces of fur from the bed sheet with trembling fingers. "Yes, I went to the shed, and I found an envelope hidden under the floorboards."

"What was inside?"

I close my eyes, hardly believing what I'm about to say. "Some newspaper articles and photos. One of the articles was about Daisy Lane's hit-and-run accident."

"Why would Travis want to keep an article about her?"

"Not only her. The other two articles were about two other dead women. Both from Florida. One from Tallahassee and the other from Corlake."

"The dead women?"

"Yes. I don't get why Travis would keep the articles. It's really weird, Clayton. People read papers and toss them. They don't keep them unless they're important in some way. And there's something else. He also had photos of me."

"What do you mean, he had photos of you?" Clayton sounds panicked.

"We did a photo shoot a while ago, as Marcia and Travis wanted to have memories of the pregnancy, but my face was supposed to stay out of the shots. I only agreed to have my stomach taken."

"Right." Clayton says slowly.

"Travis asked me to smile, though. He said it would make me feel more comfortable. I never thought—"

"Are you telling me that he included your face without permission?"

"He did. And Clayton, there are other pictures of me there, too. He's been watching me, and taking photos," I say, running a shaking hand through my hair.

"Pictures of you? What the hell? This is not okay, you need to get out of there, and then we need to talk to the police. The offer still stands. Leave right now, come stay with us. We have a spare room."

I blink back tears. "That's so kind, Clayton. I can't believe you're inviting me to stay with you."

"With me and your other two biggest fans. It really wouldn't be a problem, Grace. I know you're due soon. If the baby decides to come later tonight, tomorrow, or the day after, I'll drive you to the hospital myself. If you don't want to stay here, that's fine too. I just want you out of that house."

He's right. Every bone in my body is telling me to leave right now. And I'd feel safer staying with Clayton than in a hotel room.

"I could pick you up, if you like," Clayton continues. "You only need to say the word."

"No. I don't want you coming to my rescue again in the middle of the night. I'll call a cab and will be with you very soon." I look at my watch. It's not midnight yet.

A sound outside the room stops me from saying more. Marigold must have heard it too because she turns her head to the door, ears perked.

"Clayton, hang on. I think someone is in the house." I get to my feet, my legs shaking.

"Do you think it's Travis?" The note of worry in his tone is clear on the line.

"I'm not sure. I'll call you back in a minute." I toss the phone onto the bed and approach the door. I'm not sure where I'm finding the courage or the strength to walk, with my chest squeezed tight and my knees weak.

"Grace, it's me," Marcia calls. "Can we talk?"

Relief gushes out of me and I leave the room to find her sitting on the living room couch, her face puce.

"Marcia, are you all right?" I ask nervously.

"You tell me." She stands up and paces the room, her hands clenched to fists. "Tell me if I should be fine or not."

"I don't understand what you're saying." I perch on the arm of the couch.

"I think you do, Grace. I'm not stupid. You were acting weird when I came over earlier, and you couldn't give me a real answer about what you were doing in our garden shed in the middle of the night. And what were you thinking, wandering around in the dark?"

I raise a hand to stop her. "Like I keep telling you and Travis, I'm a grown woman. I can take care of myself." My hand drops into my lap. "Actually, I think it's time for me to move out."

"Oh." She grabs the belt of her cardigan and wraps it around her hand. Then she looks up with a smile. "Why would you want to do that, Grace?"

"Because I need my space."

"But my mother isn't here anymore. I sent her away so you can have your space, and I told her she can't return until after the birth. So why would you want to leave?" Her voice is loaded and deep.

I chew the inside of my cheek as I search my mind for words. "Marcia, you and Travis are going through a lot right now. You know, after Beatrice's death... and everything. I think you also need to be alone to process what happened. I'll go stay with a friend, and when the baby is on the way, I'll call you."

"Wow. That sounds simple. How could I say no to that?" Her words drip with sarcasm.

"Yes, it *is* that simple. I've made a decision. I really think it would be good for all of us."

"Okay. If that's what you want, we have to respect your

decision." She's saying the right words, but her tone doesn't match.

"Thanks for understanding," I say.

"Sure. But before you go, let me show you the painting I did for the nursery. You won't see it if you're gone." She tugs tighter at the belt. "I just finished it."

I don't want to see the stupid painting. I want to get out of this house. But if that's what it will take to make her feel better about me leaving, it's a small price to pay.

"Okay," I say. "Let's go."

"Great." She lets go of the belt and I notice the pink mark it left on the back of her left hand. "Travis is still awake; I'll get him. I wanted to show it to both of you at the same time."

She leaves the guesthouse and returns five minutes later with a sleepy-looking Travis in tow. His tense expression tells me he was forced to come out.

On our way to the studio, Marcia grins at Travis over her shoulder. "Darling, you left the shed open earlier. Grace went to close it."

Travis stops walking and looks back at me, and I hope that my fear isn't showing in my eyes. I give him a thin smile, and we keep walking.

In front of the studio door, Marcia pushes the key into the lock and ushers us into the dark room, where the smell of paint and turpentine meets us.

Travis stays in the doorway.

"Ready?" Marcia asks.

"Yes," I mutter. I can still feel Travis's gaze on me.

"Surprise!" Marcia says, flicking on the lights.

My eyes land on the large painting covering one wall, and I choke back a scream, my hand clamped to my mouth.

# CHAPTER 34

A deep, strangled cry comes from behind me and I turn. Travis is backing out of the studio, his eyes wide with horror. I try to force my feet to move, to get me out of this place, but they refuse. My hand is still covering my mouth, holding back the bile inside my throat.

"I knew you'd both like it," Marcia says, her voice sweet and dripping with pride. "It's something, isn't it? I have to say it's probably my best work to date."

My hand falls to my side. I part my lips to speak, but I have no words.

"Grace, say something." Marcia comes to stand next to me. "Travis, what do you think?"

I don't respond to her or to the gagging sound Travis is making behind me. My eyes are transfixed on the painting, I can't seem to turn my head away. From a craft perspective, it's a true masterpiece, well-executed with powerful strokes and vibrant colors that breathe so much life into it the line between it and reality blurs into nothingness.

I knew Marcia was a talented artist. I saw her pieces of art displayed on the walls in the main house, and internet searches also led me to more art she's created and sold for top dollar. I just never thought she could create something so grotesque and disturbing.

A pregnant woman in white is lying in a pink satin-lined casket with a bullet hole in her chest, a naked baby curled up next to her. Both their eyes are closed.

The woman is me. She has captured my features to perfection.

"What is this?" I manage to croak, my arm around my abdomen.

Marcia approaches the painting. "It's you and the baby, of course." Her finger traces the lines of the baby's face before touching the scarlet blood on my white dress.

"What are you doing, Marcia?" Travis has found his voice, but he doesn't re-enter the studio. "What is that supposed to mean?"

"Oh, no, you don't like it?" Marcia turns to face him. "That hurts my feelings, Travis. I put so much sweat and blood into this piece of artwork."

"What has gotten into you? How could you create something so... so vile?"

"I think the word you're looking for is honest." She faces her art again, and I shift a few steps away from her.

Could I run back to the guesthouse and get to my phone before they catch me? I know I can't, not in my condition, but maybe I will have to try.

"This painting is a prediction of the future." She turns to look from me to Travis, eyes glinting with excitement.

"What the hell are you talking about, Marcia?" Travis shouts, stepping toward us.

"Sweetheart," Marcia says. "I know you're not ready for this. I wasn't either. I didn't plan for the reveal to happen tonight, but there are things in life we can't plan.

And since we're here now, we might as well lay the cards on the table."

She reaches into one large pocket of her cardigan. Her hand comes out holding a bunch of glossy photos. They're the photos of me from the shed. She studies the first photo for a while, then looks back at her husband.

Travis has gone pale and his hands are buried in his armpits. "Marcia, it's not—"

"Not what I think?" She nails Travis with a look. "Tell me, what exactly should I be thinking right now?"

While I try to inch further toward the door, Marcia continues in an eerily calm voice, "I'm confused, Travis. I thought we agreed that Grace's face was not going to be photographed. And what are you doing with all these photos of her?"

"Yes, but..." Travis's voice drifts off, then he clears his throat. "I thought it would be nice to have the complete picture. And I just wanted a record of this... this precious time, our baby developing."

"Don't you dare lie to me!" She tosses the photos to the floor, where they fan out. "The truth is, you wanted to see her face, her body, for the rest of your life. You wanted to look at your child and see the mother who gave birth to it."

"I'm not... I'm not the baby's mother, Marcia. You are," I say, wondering if, somehow, I can diffuse the situation for long enough to escape.

My comment is met with laughter. "Grace, I want that baby so much it hurts. But I've realized that if you're still around, it will never truly be mine." Her face hardens again, and she studies my face. "Poor Grace. You must be so confused. I guess I should fill you in on a few little truths."

"Don't do this," Travis begs, but she ignores him.

"Like I told you before, it was Travis's idea to get a

surrogate. I couldn't give him the child he so desperately wanted, so he decided that another woman should do it. It hurt at first, but I loved my husband and wanted him to be happy. And I wanted a baby, too. So, in the days that followed, I started liking the idea more and more and went along with it."

"I..." Travis starts but doesn't finish. His words transform into sobs. "I did it for you. You were suicidal, Marcia. I wanted to give you a baby, and you didn't want to adopt."

"Oops, I forgot to tell you something important," Marcia continues as if he hasn't said anything, her voice light and casual. "I had a perfectly healthy pregnancy once. It was shortly after Travis and I met. But Travis didn't want the child. He was at the height of his career and didn't want to be distracted."

"That's not what I said. I said—"

"You told me to get rid of it. You said we'd have more kids." Marcia is speaking to him, but her eyes are still on me. "I believed him. I was so naïve and in love that I did what he asked. I ended my pregnancy." Her voice is thick with tears now and that triggers the tears in my own eyes.

"I'm sorry," I say, because that's what she wants to hear. I sense she has so much more to say and a part of me is desperate to hear it.

"Two years later we got married, and Travis immediately wanted to try for a baby. You know why, Grace? Because according to our prenuptial agreement, in the event we got divorced, Travis would get a substantial amount of money—but only if we shared a child. It didn't matter whether that child was biologically ours or not. See, I never expected us to get divorced. At the time, I thought my husband loved me, not just my money." She pauses. "He only found out about my family's fortune after he asked me to marry him." She turns to Travis. "Darling, if you had known before then, would you still have asked me to get rid of our child?"

"Baby, please." Travis shakes his head, tears streaming down his face now. "I love you. Don't destroy what we have. We're expecting a baby." He takes a step toward her, then changes his mind.

"I'm not the one who has destroyed everything." Her voice is deep and dark. "You're incapable of keeping it in your pants, aren't you, Travis? You promised me that we'd be a happy little family. But all this time—"

"Marcia, I never cheated on you," Travis murmurs. "I'd never do that to us."

"You know what hurts the most?" Marcia continues. "It hurts my feelings that you think I'm stupid." She pulls out another batch of photos from her pocket and throws them at his feet. "Pictures don't lie, Travis."

Travis bends down and picks one of them up, but it slips from his shaking fingers and flutters back down.

"That's right, Travis. I hired someone to watch you. I know all about the women you betrayed me with."

I inhale sharply. "I should go." I head for the door, but Marcia shoots out a hand and sends it crashing into my chest, stopping me in my tracks.

"Where do you think you're going?"

I back away from her, my eyes pleading. "This has nothing to do with me, Marcia. It's between you and Travis."

"Well, you should have thought about that before having an affair with my husband."

# CHAPTER 35

## MONDAY, 13 MARCH 2017

Peter kept his promise to haunt me. Last year, on the anniversary of Rachel and the baby's deaths, he showed up at my house. Today is the second year, and it has been a particularly tough day for me. It was hard to get out of bed in the morning, to go on living my life knowing that my sister lost hers because of me. A couple of Xanax pills took off the edge, but not enough.

Expecting that Peter might show up at any moment makes it worse. I stand by the window, my arms around my body as I wait for his car to slide into the driveway. Last time, he showed up at exactly 7 p.m., the hour the doctors confirmed Rachel had died. I glance at my watch. One minute to go. One. Two. Three...

I count to forty-five and stop when I spot his car emerging from the darkness and sliding into the spot next to my Toyota. He doesn't exit the car, but simply sits in there, staring up at the house, the engine running. I know he won't speak to me either. His only goal is to remind me that I destroyed his life, and seeing him is enough. I haven't heard his voice for two years and I wish I could talk to him, but if I go out there, I know he'll drive off before I get a chance to speak. I'm tempted to try again tonight, to try and mend the bridge between us, but I fear it's already burned to ashes.

It's hard for me to remember Peter the way he used to be, happy and funny, with an optimistic outlook on life. He worked as a music teacher at Montern Hill, a Montessori high school, and his cheerful, bubbly nature fit the role perfectly. But that Peter is long gone, buried with his dead family.

The first time I met him, we hit it off instantly. I loved that he adored my sister, and she loved him the same way. Most couples don't love each other equally: all too often, one partner invests more than the other in the relationship. But not Rachel and Peter.

A part of me doesn't want to go out there, to end up disappointed again. I want to stay inside where it's safe, to protect myself from Peter's accusations.

*But it's your fault, you did this. Make it right.*

I put on a pair of overalls and rush out of my bedroom before he drives away. On my way down the stairs, as my knees turn to water, I mumble a silent prayer for strength. My hand shakes as I place it on the door handle and push it down, stepping out into the fresh, early spring air.

When I'm halfway to his car, I stop walking and frown. Something is different. Usually, as soon as I walk out the front door, he leaves, but not this time. Perhaps he's ready to talk? If so, I can't mess it up. But what will I say?

But I need to act; there's no time for me to think. I start walking again and don't stop until I reach the car, then I wait for him to roll down the window. He doesn't, just continues to stare at me through the glass. A faint smile curls one corner of his lips, then he lifts something to his head. I don't realize what it is until a loud bang rips through my eardrums.

A pistol.

I watch as his hand drops from his head to his side, and the gun falls from his hand and lands in the space between the driver and passenger seats.

Peter has just shot himself in front of me.

The world goes silent, and shock tears through me like a tornado. Scream after scream come pouring out of me, and I clutch the window as I try to push down the glass to get to him. "Oh, my God! Oh, my God! No, Peter!"

On the other side, I watch his body slump forward, his head hitting the steering wheel, smearing it with blood, so much blood. The car honks without stopping, but the sound is distant in my ringing ears. Suddenly, there's movement around me, people appearing from nowhere—neighbors, night-time dog walkers, strangers.

If I had been one of them, the sound of a gunshot would have kept me indoors with my doors and windows locked.

Someone grabs me by the shoulders and pulls me away from the car. People are screaming and gasping in horror.

"What happened?" a man asks me. "Are you all right?"

I ignore their questions as I beg for someone, anyone, to call 911. My phone is inside the house, and I don't want to waste any time.

When one of my neighbors informs me that the ambulance is on its way, my body goes suddenly limp and I start to fall. My knees give way, and she's not able to catch me in time. I go down fast and hit the concrete hard.

When I awake, I'm in a hospital bed and Sydney is at my side.

She had been on her way to my place, knowing it would be a difficult day for me, and she found only chaos. The neighbors told her what had happened, and she rushed to the hospital.

"He shot himself," I say, remembering everything that happened. "Peter shot himself."

"I know, honey. I know." Her words are smothered in tears.

"Is he... is he all right?"

Sydney looks away, giving me my answer. I don't stop crying until a nurse comes into the room and assures me I will be okay, that I only suffered a minor concussion.

When the nurse leaves, a police officer enters my room to ask me questions.

"I don't know what happened," I say, my voice trembling. Everything happened so fast. "I just wanted to talk to him..." My words dissolve into uncontrollable sobs.

The police officer waits until I calm down enough to speak again.

"I wanted to speak to him, but he put a gun to his head." I shake my head, awakening a headache. "I can't do this."

The officer promises he only has a few more questions.

"Mr. Collins was your brother-in-law, am I right?"

"He was." I choke back tears. "My late sister's husband."

*Was.*

I watch Sydney standing by the door, shifting from one foot to the other. I know she wants to come and comfort me, but there's nothing she can do to pull me out of the darkness, nothing anyone can do.

"Your sister died two years ago?" He glances at Sydney. She must have filled him in.

I lick my dry lips. "Yes. Rachel. Her name was Rachel Collins."

Tears blind my eyes and I look away.

"I'm almost done," the officer says. "Just give me a quick summary of what happened tonight. Did Mr. Collins say anything to you before he shot himself?"

"No," I reply. "He never did. He showed up this time last year as well, but we never spoke." I gasp for air, but it feels like holes have been punched into my lungs, causing oxygen to escape before it does me any good.

"He visited you two years in a row but never spoke to you? I don't understand."

"He blamed me for my sister's death... and their baby's."

As confusion deepens the lines on the officer's face, I explain, my voice low and weak. I tell him about Peter and Rachel wanting me to be their surrogate. I tell him how I agreed, then turned them down. I tell him how she became pregnant naturally again and paid the price with her life. He writes everything down in his little black notebook.

"So, your brother-in-law thought if you had agreed to be their surrogate, his wife would still be alive?"

I swallow hard. "He wasn't the only one who thought so." I turn away from him, not wanting to talk anymore, to remember. A sob catches in my throat. "I'm tired."

The officer continues to ask a few more questions, but I can't give him any more answers. The most important thing is that Peter, Rachel, and their little girl are all dead, and it's my fault. What more is there to say?

Two days after Peter died, Sydney moves in with me for a few days. She begs me to get out of bed every morning and fails on most days.

"I'm so sorry," she says one morning, gripping my hand tight. "But you need to know this is not your fault; Peter made the decision to end his life. You have nothing to do with it."

"How can you say that?" I blink away tears, but they

won't stop. "He killed himself because he was depressed. He lost his wife and his child. And I—"

"Did nothing wrong. You did nothing wrong." Sydney brings her face close to mine. "What happened to your sister could have happened to anyone. You are not responsible for all that happened. Do you understand me, Grace?"

"No," I say. We have to agree to disagree. "I'll never forgive myself."

When my sister died, half of me died with her. And now that Peter is also dead because of a choice I made, the half of me that had survived is fading into nothingness.

I don't deserve to live, to be happy.

"I'll go make you something to eat." Sydney taps my hand. "How about fish filets and veggies?"

"I'm not hungry," I whisper. "I feel like... like I want to die."

"Don't say that. Rachel would not have wanted you to blame yourself for this. You need to live, Grace. Enough lives have been lost."

"How can I live with this much pain?"

"It's going to be tough, but you're not alone. I'm here with you. We'll get through it together." Sydney slides into bed next to me and holds me like a mother would hold her baby, rocking me back and forth as I cry. She eventually leaves to go to the kitchen, and I get out of bed and tiptoe to the bathroom, where I open the medicine cabinet. There's quite a collection of pills inside, some prescribed to me when I was discharged from hospital and some from before. Pain meds, anxiety meds, sleeping pills. I pick up the white bottle of sleeping pills and pour the little balls into the palm of my hand. A teardrop drips from my eye and plops onto one of them, turning it a few shades darker.

I tip my head back, toss the chalky pills into my mouth,

and pour myself a glass of water. After swallowing a bunch of the pills, I sit cross-legged on the bathroom floor and wait for them to work, to take me away to a place where it won't hurt so much. It feels like hours until something happens, then the pills start to do what they are supposed to do. I close my eyes, hoping it will be for the last time.

But my wish doesn't come true.

I wake up in the hospital, getting my stomach pumped. Sydney had come looking for me and managed to unlock the bathroom door. She immediately called 911, and the paramedics saved my life—a life I don't want to live.

# CHAPTER 36
## ONE YEAR AGO

Before Peter committed suicide, even though I was mourning my sister and I lost my high-paying job, I managed to hold on to some small pieces of my life, living on nothing but my savings. But when Peter died, what was left of my life went up in smoke. Within eight months, I lost my house, my car, and myself.

Finding a job at another big magazine was impossible. Roman had been so bitter that he'd dragged my name through the mud. I did manage to get a crappy, low-paying job at a weekly newspaper, but I just couldn't hold on to it. My savings were dwindling, and if it hadn't been for Sydney begging her sister to give me a part-time job at Dear Blooms, I'd have no source of income now.

In addition to finding me a job, Sydney also convinced me to move in with her and her family while I search for a new place. I know she wants to keep an eye on me, to make sure I don't do something stupid again.

What she doesn't know is that I'm making a different plan to change the emotional wreckage I am in. She has no idea what I do when I'm home alone with my laptop. Working at the flower shop three days a week means I have a lot of time on my hands, and I'm searching for a way to ease the pain.

A little over four months after moving in with Sydney and her family, I'm sitting at their kitchen table early in the morning, my laptop in front of me. Her husband, Jeff, a fire-fighter, and their two daughters have already left the house for school and work, and Sydney will also step out any minute.

"What are you up to?" she asks when she walks into the kitchen. Dressed in an ivory sheath dress and cropped jacket, she looks elegant and powerful, ready to sell homes as one of the top real estate agents in Miami. I feel a sting when I remember the days I dressed up to go to a high-powered job.

"Looking for a job." My computer is turned away from her, so she can't see what I was up to.

Working at Dear Blooms was only supposed to be temporary, but the thought of going back to being a maga-zine editor makes me feel exhausted. I don't have the energy or the mental space to do any type of work, let alone one that requires so much responsibility. I'm well aware that Camille complains about me to Sydney. I eavesdropped on one of their phone conversations and heard her tell Sydney that I'm lazy and disengaged. I know she only gave me the job as a favor to her sister.

There's really no point in me looking for another job right now. In the state I'm in, no one would give me one. I did go for a job interview at a small magazine last month, and halfway through the interview, I burst out crying. How would I ever hold down a job when I can't even control my emotions?

"Are you scheduled for therapy this week?" Sydney takes a sip of hot coffee, the steam rising up to her face.

"Sorry, what did you say?"

I heard exactly what she said, but I need a moment to come up with a convincing response. There's no way I'm going to tell her that I stopped going to a therapist a month ago. All he did was dig up the past by making me repeat the painful moments of my life. I hate sharing my pain with a complete stranger who cares more about the money than my well-being, and that reserve of money gets smaller every day.

"He's on vacation this week," I lie, "but we have an appointment for next Wednesday."

"Great," Sydney says, smiling.

*Please leave,* I think, and guilt gnaws at me. I shouldn't be thinking like this, wishing her out of her own home, but when we're together, I feel like I'm in a room with my mother, not my friend. I will be moving into my own place in a week, and I can't wait to have my own space again. The small studio apartment will be a downgrade from my town-house, but it's all I can afford at the moment.

Sydney finally leaves, and I'm free to torment myself in peace without anyone looking over my shoulder. I don't even eat the breakfast I made for everyone—omelets, toast, breakfast sausages, and freshly pressed grapefruit juice. I'm responsible for breakfast every morning; it's the least I can do.

I pick up the untouched meal and push it to the back of the fridge to have for lunch. I'll force myself to eat it later. Heading into the living room, I settle on the couch with a multi-colored quilt covering my legs and my laptop on my lap, its warmth heating my thighs. I click on one of the twenty articles I saved last night for reading in the morning.

Before I know it, it's midday and I've been on the computer for three straight hours. I need to get off the couch, eat something, and take a shower, one more thing I force myself to do on a daily basis. Everything that has to do with taking care of myself is a struggle.

I manage to make it to the shower, and the moment I stand under the water, I begin to feel calmer. But afterwards, as I stand in front of the bathroom mirror, I can't even recognize myself. I have lost so much weight; my large eyes are sunken, and my hip bones jut out. I have never been a thin person, and the look doesn't suit me. My once thick hair has started to thin and the bags under my red, swollen eyes no longer go away; not even makeup can cover them up anymore. I throw on an oversized t-shirt and leggings. Since I don't work on Wednesdays, I have nowhere to go except to the grocery store for dinner ingredients. I hate being out of the house. Watching mothers on the street pushing strollers and holding their kids' hands reminds me of what my sister had so desperately wanted and was denied.

After getting dressed, I return to the couch. Sydney has called me; she's always checking in on me in between her showings. I text to let her know I'm okay, and she doesn't have to worry. At least I had a shower; that's something. I'll make sure to eat something before she comes home.

After reading three more stories about surrogacy, I go to a website covered in pictures of couples and babies—surrogacynext.com. When I read the first paragraph on the website, something inside me shifts, and just like that, everything changes. I've been thinking about this and researching it for a while, but now I'm certain. I'm going to do it.

In the days that follow, I scour the web for more information and read everything I can find on the topic of surrogacy. I even go as far as joining forums where childless mothers hang out, reading endless threads full of pain. Pain that I can do something about. Therapy could not help me, but maybe giving someone the gift of a human life will.

Unfortunately, it isn't as easy as I thought it would be.

Signing up with agencies is out of the question. One of the requirements is that the applicant should have had at least one healthy pregnancy, and I have never been pregnant. I don't qualify. But now that it's in my head, my obsession will not release me. There must be another way.

I come up with another strategy, which involves following childless mothers online after getting their social media handles from the forums. I study them and their lives, learning everything I can about them, offering words of support when they share their pain with the world.

I soon become friends with one of them—Marcia Thorpe. We write back and forth and even end up speaking on the phone. She and her husband, Travis, have the perfect life, and the only thing missing is a baby. During our frequent conversations, I listen as she cries about the babies she has lost. She even reveals that her husband proposed surrogacy and they did approach some agencies, but they had not been able to find someone they connected with. I understand, because asking someone to have a baby for you is a very personal thing. That's why Rachel asked me to do it for her, instead of a stranger.

I did my research online and have a file on Marcia and her husband, who, unlike her, didn't come from a rich family but made a name for himself as a self-taught photographer. They both seem perfect, and I can tell how much love Marcia has to share. Soon, I decide that they will be the couple to receive my gift.

Five months after Marcia and I connect, I drive to

Wellice, pretending to be passing through town. The truth is, I wanted to meet her face to face, to connect with her on a personal level. The moment we see each other, we are like old friends, and our meeting goes better than I could have hoped for. Two days before I leave town, Marcia invites me to their home, and I get to meet Travis. When I return to Miami, we stay in touch, talking almost every day, and a month after we meet in person, I make Marcia an offer. I will carry their baby.

I never thought being a surrogate could lead to my death.

# CHAPTER 37

## PRESENT

I reel back, deeper into the studio, as if Marcia has slapped me across the face.

"What?" I can barely form the words. "What are you talking about?"

Marcia rolls her eyes. "You really thought I didn't know about your secret affair? When this whole thing started, I thought I liked you. You fooled me into believing that you were my friend. Honestly, when Travis invited you to stay, my instincts told me it was a bad idea, knowing what he's like, but I ignored them. Then I caught him watching you... all the time."

"Marcia, you're mistaken. Nothing ever happened between me and Travis, I can promise you that."

"She's right," Travis manages. "You're being paranoid."

"Paranoid?" she scoffs. "Then why would you have photos of her? Why would you hide them in the shed?"

"I told you. I just—"

"Don't," she warns, nostrils flaring. "Don't you dare lie to me again! From the moment she arrived in this house, you couldn't keep your hands off her." Her eyes pin me down again. "I kept telling myself that maybe I was imagining things. Then I caught you together that night when you, Grace, pretended to have had a nightmare."

Travis is right: she's clearly paranoid. I have no idea what he did with those other women, but how can she even think I had an affair with her husband?

"I never asked your husband to come to my room that night," I say, trying to keep my voice calm. "I woke up from a nightmare, and there he was."

"That's not how it looked to me. From what I recall, you were quite cozy together."

"You don't know what you're talking about," Travis says roughly.

"I wasn't the only one who knew something was going on, you know. Beatrice did too." She glares at her husband. "That's why she's dead isn't it, Travis? You didn't want her to get in the way of your plans. After the baby was born, you planned on waiting a year before leaving me and cashing in. Beatrice heard you talking to someone on the phone, telling them exactly how you planned to screw me over. And that you want to raise the child without me. You were going to take *my baby*. And I bet you wanted to go off and do it with Grace."

My eyes go to Travis, searching for a reaction. He's now standing slumped against the doorframe. I know that can't be true, though. Beatrice was a good person and she cared for Marcia. If she had suspected that Travis and I were betraying her, she would never have been kind to me.

Marcia puts a hand on Travis's cheek. "I know what you did to Beatrice. I followed you to her house, I saw you go in after her." She drops her hand again. "I could have gone to the police, but I have my own plans."

Panic rising in my chest again, I try to push past her

and, this time, she shoves me back with both hands, and I almost fall to the ground.

"I said you're not going anywhere," she spits, and her eyes are like ice. "I'm not finished."

"I didn't kill Beatrice. I just went to talk to her." Travis pushes himself away from the doorframe. "This is ridiculous. I won't listen to this nonsense." He starts to stumble away.

"Then I'll make you." I'm frozen in horror, watching the silver pistol emerge from Marcia's pocket. There's a brief silence, and then a loud crack pierces through my brain.

I'm instantly transported back to the night Peter killed himself, and as Travis cries out and falls to his knees, my body starts to shake, my teeth chattering.

"Ready to listen now?" Marcia asks, dropping the gun back into the pocket, and turning back to me calmly, like she hasn't just shot her husband in the leg.

"What do you want?" I ask her, my nails digging into my palms as I try to gain control of the situation. "Do you really want to hurt me and an innocent baby?"

"I never wanted to hurt the baby, Grace. Not until I realized you were never going to let me have it. And even with you gone, it will forever be tainted by your betrayal."

"Stop," Travis pleads with her. "Don't do it."

"Why not?" Marcia asks, a sadistic smile on her face. "I begged you to stop lying, cheating, and hurting me. But you kept right on going."

As Travis curls up in the dirt, clutching at his leg to stop the bleeding, Marcia reaches for a wooden chair and drops into it, pointing the gun at me. "Grace, it's not as if you haven't had any warnings. I couldn't help myself from lashing out at you sometimes, when I saw how my husband looked at you. And the entire time you thought it was my mother—exactly what I wanted you to think."

"It... it was you?" My voice is barely above a whisper.

"Mostly. That night you found your bathwater red, I couldn't exactly be in two places at one time, so I asked for a little help. I told Beatrice to make you a nice bath, where to find the bath bomb. The silly woman never realized what she was doing."

Shock and hurt ripple through me, heat flushing up my neck. "How could you, Marcia? What kind of sick person are you?"

"I guess you'll know by the end of tonight." She pauses. "That night when I saw the way you and Travis looked at each other, I just wanted to terrify you a little, maybe cause a panic attack, like the kind you've been experiencing since your brother-in-law shot himself in your driveway."

Blood drains from my face. "How do you—?"

"You think I'd let a stranger into my home without doing my research?" She taps her forefinger against her lips. "I was suspicious from the moment you made me that offer. I thought there had to be something wrong with a woman who would give a stranger a baby without any compensation. And it turned out I was right. You tried so hard to hide it, but I knew."

My knees grow weak, and I grab the nearby desk to stay upright. Marcia stands and closes the gap between us, resting a hand on my back.

"It's okay, Gracie," she whispers into my ear. "Hang in there a little longer. It will all be over soon." She sits back down and plays with the gun, smiling to herself.

This is it. She is going to kill us both; she's convinced we had an affair and there's no way I'll be able to talk her out of it. But then she puts her hand in her pocket, and pulls it out, holding what look like the three articles I saw in the shed earlier.

"Travis," she says, "have you ever stopped to wonder why your mistresses keep dropping dead like flies? I think you have, since you've been collecting these articles."

Travis lifts his head a few inches from the ground, then grunts with pain and drops it again into the dirt.

"My darling husband, I have a little secret I want to share with you."

# CHAPTER 38

Marcia tears the newspaper articles to shreds, sending the pieces falling to the floor like confetti. "I was so done with watching you and your mistresses destroying our marriage."

Horror cuts through me. I want to speak, to defend myself, to find a way out of here, but I can't think of anything that will help.

"There's only one more mistress left." Marcia points at me. "I was going to wait for the baby to be born, but now I don't want any part of her. I'll find another way to have my own child." She looks back at Travis. "Grace and the baby will die, and you will get to watch."

While panic ricochets through me, Travis writhes on the ground and tries to crawl away, but Marcia shoots him again, I'm not sure where. I scream as I watch him go limp. There's blood everywhere.

Marcia killed three women. And if I don't do anything, the baby and I are next. My breathing turning frantic, I pray that Clayton is on his way here, that he sensed something was wrong when I didn't call him back. But what if he's not coming? Or what if he's too late?

Bile rises in my throat as I watch Marcia turn the gun over in her hand. If it were just me, I'd probably have given up and allowed fate to take its course, but I'm not alone. I cannot let her kill my baby.

Fear coils itself around my heart, and instead of weakening me, it sends adrenaline surging through my entire body, giving me a strength I never would have expected. I scream as I lunge for her, knocking her off the chair and reaching for the gun in her hand. She's too strong for me, but I'm not ready to let go.

I tighten my fingers around her wrist and press my nails into her skin. She shrieks and curses, but doesn't let go of the weapon, and she soon disentangles herself from my grasp and scoots away.

Now the gun is pointed to my abdomen. I failed.

"I'm sorry it has to end this way, Grace," she says, again with that awful smile.

I close my eyes and wait for her to shoot.

As I wait for the sound of a gunshot, I wonder if it will be the last sound I'll hear before I die. Or will the bullet hit me before the sound rings out?

Then there's a click and Marcia curses. I open my eyes in time to see her cheeks smeared with tears and dark mascara, her eyes spitting fire. She must have run out of bullets, and I can't believe my luck. I wonder if Rachel is watching over me, my guardian angel.

Thinking of my sister gives me courage, and in an instant I know this is my chance to end this madness. I grit my teeth, and fight for my life. For my baby's life.

We both cry out when my punch lands in the center of her face. The pain spreads like ice from my knuckles, through my fingers, to the rest of my arm.

"You'll regret that," says Marcia, and she runs toward

me and grabs me by the shoulders before shoving me into a shelf lined with painting supplies. Brushes of various sizes, cans of paint, and easels clatter to the floor around me. I slide to the floor too, but I quickly get back on my hands and knees and crawl away. Marcia is bending down, looking for the gun among the mess, probably preparing to strike me with it. I need to get to my feet and act before she has a chance. But it's too late. Before I can take another swing at her, she runs to the door and leaves, slamming it shut.

Panic wells up inside my throat at the sound of the key turning in the lock.

I'm trapped.

As I search around for something to help me break down the door, I smell the smoke.

A liquid is glistening on the floor next to the door, and I jump back, seeing the fire lapping it up, spreading quickly toward me. Marcia must have shoved a lit match through the crack under the door.

Shivering with fear, I look around me at the cans and bottles that fell from the shelf when I went flying into it. She knows there are enough chemicals in the studio to cause the entire place to explode. She's out there getting what she wants, forcing Travis, if he's still alive, to watch me and his baby die.

As the smoke thickens around me, I grab a rag and press it to my nose. I wish I had water to wet it with. I hurry to the window, but it is too small for someone, let alone a pregnant woman, to squeeze through.

There must be another way.

*Think, Grace. Think.*

Coughing uncontrollably, my gaze lands on the couch leaning against one wall of the studio. There's a white knitted blanket draped over its back. Marcia probably throws it over her shoulders when she works late into the night. My eyes burning from the thick smoke, I look back at the fire, watch it grow large enough to block my way.

I could try to smother the flames, but they're spreading so fast, and I'd be in danger of getting burned sooner. And, even without the fire, I won't be able to get through a locked door, and I could end up dying from smoke poisoning.

Then it hits me.

As the flames lick the wooden door, I see that over on the coffee table there is a large stack of magazines and news-papers. After everything Marcia said, I'm not surprised that most of the magazines are *Living It* issues. She must have known that I used to work there. I grab the newspapers and send them flying in the direction of the flames framing the lower part of the door as they would burn faster than the glossy magazines.

I'm coughing and wheezing, and tears are streaming down my cheeks, but quitting is out of the question. I can already imagine the fire searing through my skin and flesh.

The fire is now eating faster through the door, and I drop the cloth and grab the wooden chair Marcia was sitting on. The heat of the fire warns me away, but I don't get close enough for it to scorch me. With all the strength I have left, I throw the chair at the door. I'm not able to see enough through the smoke anymore to tell if it left a dent, so I throw something else at it. Another chair, a metal one this time, belonging to the garden furniture set near the river.

The fire is growing angry, engulfing both chairs. I continue to throw objects at the door until I and the fire break it down.

What now?

Even though there's a way out, the doorway is

completely engulfed in flames. There's no way I can make it through without getting burned.

But if I do nothing and remain in the studio, I am certainly going to die, and my baby too.

Thinking fast, I glance at the couch again. One end is already burning up, the smell of the leather thick as it reaches my nose. I stumble toward it and snatch the blanket, shaking the flames off and stomping it with my feet until no sparks are left.

My chest is burning and my body is heating up. The baby gives me a sharp kick in the ribs.

*Please hang in there, little one. I'll get us out of here.*

There's only one way out for both of us.

I drape the blanket over my head and most of my body, and before I can lose my courage, I run through the burning doorway, stumbling over the chairs.

I make it outside, but the blanket is on fire and so are my hair and clothes. The pain is excruciating. I could run to the river, but I won't make it in time. I'm screaming as I throw off the burning blanket and fall to the ground and roll, doing my best to stifle the flames. The strong sulfuric smell of my hair sears its way up my nostrils. The only part of my body that's not burning is the part covered by the bathrobe. My feet are on fire. My hair is on fire. My hands are on fire.

I can't shake it off, and I'm on the verge of giving up. Then something large falls on top of me, soft like a quilt. And it feels like someone is holding me in an embrace.

I hear my name, but I don't recognize the voice. I'm too focused on the searing pain on my skin.

Then my cover is lifted, and I only see her face for a few seconds before my eyes close.

# CHAPTER 39

Clayton walks through the door of my hospital room and smiles down at me. "How are you feeling?"

"I don't know," I say truthfully. "It will take a while to process."

"That's understandable. You went through hell. I'm so sorry I didn't get there in time, Grace."

Clayton had been minutes behind the ambulance, and he had rushed to the hospital after them. When I was transferred to a larger, better equipped one in Tallahassee, he'd taken the short drive up from Wellice every day to see me.

My eyes well up as I look at him. "You're here now, and it isn't your fault. I can't believe Agnes saved my life," I say.

That night, she stayed with me as I drifted in and out of consciousness and rode with me in the ambulance. She looked down at me with tearful eyes and squeezed my hand as I was wheeled into surgery for the emergency C-section. The woman I thought hated me and wanted me gone called the cops on her own daughter, and she put out the fire that was threatening to burn me alive.

When I came out of surgery, she was gone. I never got

to talk to her, to ask why she did it, or how she happened to be there at the right time.

A nurse enters and smiles down at me. "How's the pain?"

"It comes and goes," I murmur.

My eyes travel down the length of my body, taking in the bandages on my hands, legs, and feet. I can't see the one around my head, but I feel it pressing against my sore scalp.

"You're so brave. I'm going to give you another dose of painkillers to make you comfortable. You'll be up and running before you know it."

Doctors told me I'm lucky to have only suffered second-degree burns. A full recovery is expected, and the hair-producing follicles on my scalp should heal and allow for hair regrowth.

But the burns on my body are the last thing on my mind.

Clayton waits until the nurse leaves and shifts closer to the bed. "Have you thought yet about what you want to do about the baby?"

"I'm keeping her," I say without hesitation.

The idea of giving my baby away to someone else now, especially after everything we've both been through, terrifies me. Marcia is probably going to prison for the rest of her life, and Travis didn't survive that night of horrors. The paramedics were able to revive him on the scene, but he died at the hospital after a cardiac arrest during surgery.

I know I'm alive because of my child. I tried killing myself before, and I failed. If the idea of surrogacy hadn't come to me, giving me something to live for, I'd probably have tried again. And, three days ago, my baby gave me the courage to run through fire in order to save us both. She went through so much and still lived. We both did.

"Are you sure?" Clayton grins. "If that's what you really want to do, I think it's great."

"I've never been surer about anything in my life. She's mine." Tears well up in my eyes and Clayton pulls a tissue from his pocket and dabs them away.

"You'll be one hell of a great mom," he says, his own eyes moist.

"Thank you." I pause. "I'll try my best."

Becoming a surrogate was a chance for me to wipe the slate clean. At the end of the journey, I had hoped for a fresh start. And that's what I got, just not in the way I thought.

A nurse brought my baby to me an hour ago, and when I looked into her face, for the first time in years I felt a flicker of joy. She will be brought to me again before lunch.

"Have you heard anything about Marcia?" I ask Clayton. "Has she spoken yet?"

"According to the papers and the gossip in town, no. She just stares into space all day." He pushes a hand through his hair. "But enough evidence was found among the remains of her art studio, and in the basement of their house, to prove she committed those three murders, besides killing her husband and trying to kill you."

"She really killed those women?"

"Looks like it. She killed Daisy herself, but she hired someone to kill the others."

I close my eyes, thinking about the woman I thought I knew, who I thought was my friend. "I almost feel sorry for her. She was clearly very unwell."

"Yeah. Folks around town are saying that she was a jealous woman, and she accused most women in Wellice of sleeping with her husband, especially the female employees at MereLux, Inc. That's why she was on an extended leave."

Marcia told me she took a step back from the family business so she could be more present during the pregnancy. She lied, like she did about so much else.

"Could she have made up the affairs?"

"Maybe, maybe not. But to tell you the truth, I don't much care at this point. I'm just happy you and the baby are safe." Clayton puts his hand on mine, and even with a bandage between us, an electric current flows from him to me.

"Have you heard anything more about what really happened to Beatrice?" I ask.

"Yeah. As it turns out, she did fall down the stairs. Police believe she tripped on a throw rug near the top of the stairs and fell backward."

I nod and say nothing. Travis admitted that he followed Beatrice home that night, wanting to speak with her. They may have had another argument, and she ran up the stairs to escape him, tripping in the process.

Whether Beatrice was murdered or died by accident, the outcome is the same. She's gone, and the thought fills me with sadness.

We don't speak anymore. We just sit in silence until a neonatal nurse walks in with the baby in her arms. My baby.

The moment she places her in the bassinet next to my bed, I smile and say her name for the first time.

Rachel.

# EPILOGUE
## THURSDAY, 16 SEPTEMBER 2021

I spin the cake around, making sure the white icing is covering every inch. Satisfied, I pick up the candle, shaped like the number two, and press it into the center of the chocolate sponge cake. I'm about to put sprinkles and butterflies on the edges and sides when the doorbell rings. I rush out of the kitchen to the living room, where Clayton is sitting on the floor, building Lego towers with Rachel and Heidi. The room is decorated with a birthday banner, streamers, pom-poms, and gray and pastel pink balloons.

"Isn't the party starting in two hours?" Clayton asks.

"It's supposed to," I say. "Sydney has a habit of coming early. Let me see if it's her."

Three months ago, Sydney did make her dream of visiting Africa come true, and she and Jeff renewed their vows in the Namib desert of Namibia. The two of us are heading on our girls' trip to Austria in four months.

On my way to the front door, I rub my hands up and down the flour-covered kitchen apron, but when I open the door, I gasp.

"Agnes?" I whisper.

She's standing in front of me, holding a box draped with a white cloth.

I haven't seen her since Marcia's trial, when I sat on the witness stand, recounting the events of the night she tried to murder me and the days that led up to it.

"I'm sorry to come unannounced," she says. Her voice is different, deflated. "I thought you might not want to see me."

I stare at her, my tongue too thick to let any words out. Finally, I say, "Do you want to come in?"

"No, thank you," she says. "You're probably busy with your daughter's birthday. I don't want to get in the way."

"You came all the way to Miami. You might as well come in for a few minutes."

She hesitates before stepping over the threshold.

We stand opposite each other, awkwardly. So much has changed since we last saw each other. She certainly has. She's wearing a plain beige t-shirt and jeans, and her graying hair is tied back in a ponytail. With no makeup on, I can see how tired she is, the lines criss-crossing her paper-thin skin.

"I'm sorry," she says. "That's what I came to tell you."

She's waited this long to come and speak to me. Even in court, she avoided me, and I understood. It must have been so painful, to know what her daughter was capable of.

"Thank you," I say. "Thank you for saving my life that night."

She blinks several times. "It's the least I could do." Her voice is shaking. "I didn't hate you, Grace. I just didn't understand the situation, and I had a feeling that something was going to go wrong somehow. I wanted to stop it. That's why I offered you the money to leave."

"I don't hold anything against you, Agnes," I reply. "And your instincts were right."

From the corner of my eye, I notice a movement, and I know it's Clayton, checking to see I'm okay.

Unfazed, Agnes continues, "I apologize for the things I said and did to you, and most of all, I'm sorry for what Marcia put you through. She was not herself, not while she was in that marriage. I always knew that Travis was not good for her." Her gaze leaves mine and drifts to the box in her arms. "She had an unhealthy obsession with him, but I had no idea it was, well, deadly." She looks up again. "Your hair is nice. The short cut suits you."

"Thank you." I run a hand through my hair, my fingers passing over the coin-sized scar at the back of my head, left over from my burns. "Agnes, you don't have to apologize," I say. "Time heals not all, but most wounds."

She gives me a sad smile. "How's your daughter?"

"Rachel," I say. "Her name is Rachel, and she's fine."

"You named her after your sister?" she asks, and I nod.

I never wanted my story to come out in public, but during Marcia's trial, the press was able to uncover the reason why I became a surrogate in the first place.

"Marcia spoke to me last week," she says, lowering her eyes to the box in her hands.

I raise an eyebrow. "She did?"

Until now, Marcia, who's serving her sentence in a prison in downtown Tallahassee, hasn't said one word to anyone since the night she tried to murder me. No one was able to make her speak, not the police, not the press, not her own mother.

"What did she say?"

"She told me to give you this." She puts the covered box in my arms.

"What is it?"

Agnes slides the cloth off to reveal what's inside.

*Meow.*

Marigold appears, and tears spring to my eyes. I've really missed her and never thought I'd see her again.

"She wants you to have her," Agnes says. "You and this cat must have formed quite the bond."

"We did," I whisper.

I guess Agnes is not the only one apologizing. In her own way, Marcia is too.

When I put a hand on the pet carrier box, Agnes notices my ring. "You're engaged!" she says.

I turn to look at my fiancé, then back at her. "Yes, we're getting married next year."

"Congratulations," she says, with a genuine smile, and I thank her.

Clayton and I grew closer while I was in the hospital and, when I was discharged, our relationship progressed at a speed that took both of us by surprise. A year after I left Wellice, he moved to Miami, landing a job with one of the most prestigious law firms in the city. As for me, I started a nonprofit magazine that features articles of authentic, raw stories from real women who want to be heard. No glamor, no cosmetics. I run the magazine part-time with a small team while working as a senior editor for a publishing company.

All in all, life is good, and my daughter has everything to do with it.

An hour after Agnes leaves, I find an envelope taped to the underside of the carrier box. With Marigold in my lap purring contentedly, I read the letter inside.

*Dear Grace,*

*I hope you'll take a moment to read this letter.*

*Let me start by saying I'm sorry. I've had enough time to think, and I realize that I punished you for a crime you did not commit.*

*If you think I'll try to talk myself out of the other crimes I committed, I won't. Yes, I was involved in the murders of Lorie Dawn, Julia Williams, and Daisy Lane. I'm guilty as charged, and I belong behind bars.*

*Do I regret what I did? I wish I could say no, but I'd be lying. You will be shocked to hear that those women did not sleep with my husband. The affairs did not happen because I did something about it. My mother always told me that prevention is better than cure.*

*What my mother also taught me was that if I want something, I should be willing to do everything it takes not only to get it but also to keep it.*

*That's what I did. The moment I laid eyes on Travis, I knew he was the one I wanted to keep. Most people don't really mean it when they say "I do, till death do us part," but I did.*

*My husband appreciated beautiful women, and he loved to photograph them. I knew about this long before I married him, but after the wedding, I wanted to be the only woman he looked at.*

*My jealousy almost destroyed our marriage. In the end, he quit photographing other women; it was his gift to me, and I thought that would be the end of it.*

*But Lorie, Julia, and Daisy all had their eyes on my man. They each went on a first date with him. So I killed them before the affairs began, and I do not regret it. If I had not done it, my husband would have left me for one of* them. I knew he was capable of it because, when we met, he was in a serious relationship with someone else. I was the other woman... until I wasn't.

I thought you were one of the women who lusted after my husband, that you were out to betray me, but after hearing about your sister and watching you on the stand, I knew you were innocent.

You were my friend, and you genuinely wanted to help me, while also helping yourself heal in the process. Maybe Travis had his eye on you, but you didn't encourage him.

I'm sorry for misjudging you. I'm sorry for making your life hell, and I'm sorry for pushing you to the brink of death. Maybe one day you'll forgive me. Maybe you won't. I don't know if I care at this point... about anything.

You probably don't care how I'm doing, but I'm glad to say that I've never been more at peace. The day they told me that Travis was dead, I had the best sleep I had in years. Our marriage lasted "till death do us part" and now that he's gone, so is the fear and constant anxiety of losing him. The war is over, and I can rest in my little cell and wait until we meet again on the other side.

Grace, this letter is not an invitation asking you to visit me. I never want to see you again; it will be too hard for both of us.

It's difficult for me to live with the knowledge that you're the mother of my husband's child, but some stories don't end the way we want them to. You got the better end of the deal and I don't begrudge you for it. You were my only real friend, Grace, and after what fate and I have put you through, you deserve a break.

I've asked my mother to bring Marigold to you

---

*because, in the end, she liked you more than me. Now you get to keep her, and the baby.*

*In this envelope, you should also find a check for fifty thousand dollars. Please take the money. I owe you more than that for the pain I caused you and your baby.*

*Have a good life, Grace.*

*Goodbye forever,*

*Marcia*

I wipe my eyes and look up to find Nina standing in the bedroom doorway.

Still reeling from what I just read, I go and hug my future mother-in-law. "I had no idea you were coming."

"I wanted to surprise you. I didn't want to miss my new granddaughter's second birthday."

"Thank you," I say. That's all that's left to say: thank you.

I'm grateful for the things that happened, and I'm grateful for the things that didn't.

For two years, I tried to understand why Marcia did the things she did. Even though I'm shocked that she killed innocent people with no remorse, her letter is the key I need to lock the door to the past forever and start again.

I'll donate some of the money to the recycled goods shop in Wellice, where I'd bought Sydney's handbag, and the rest will go toward Rachel's education fund.

"No," Nina says. "I'm the one who's thankful. You gave my son a brand-new life."

She takes my hand and together we stand on the landing, watching Clayton tickling the girls on the shaggy living room carpet.

He pauses to gaze up at us and winks.

If I had the power to go back and change anything in my life, I'm not sure I'd want to, except of course for my sister dying. But if it wasn't for what happened, I wouldn't be here, where I belong. And now, finally, I'm free from my past, and I am safe.

Later, when I'm clearing up after the party, I find an envelope among a pile of cards for Rachel, but it's addressed to me.

I open it and shake out the contents, and a diamond engagement ring falls out.

It's an exact replica of the one Chad gave me, when he proposed a lifetime ago.

There's a single note inside the envelope, two short sentences that cause my throat to tighten with dread.

Peering through the window, my eyes search the street for any sign of him, but he's nowhere in sight. The last time I heard about Chad was when he showed up at Sydney's house. Now this. How did he even get my address, and when will he ever stop?

My eyes land on the note in my hand and I get my answer. He's never going to.

*It's not over, Grace. I won't let him have you. I'm going to get you back.*

# A LETTER FROM L.G. DAVIS

Dear reader,

I appreciate you taking the time to read *Perfect Parents*. If you would like to be notified when my next book comes out, please use the link below to sign up for my mailing list. Your email address will never be shared with anyone, and you can unsubscribe at any time.

*www.bookouture.com/l-g-davis*

Of all the books I've written, this was the most fun to write, and I couldn't wait to share it with the world.

While it was sometimes hard to see Grace go through so much, she was a character that really came from my heart and I loved writing her story.

I hope you enjoyed walking through the streets of the fictional town, Wellice, and hanging out at Clayton's Coffee Lounge.

If you enjoyed reading *Perfect Parents*, it would mean a lot if you left a review. This will enable other readers to decide if they want to read this book or some of my other novels.

Connecting with my readers brings me a lot of joy. If you would like to get in touch with me, you can reach me on my Facebook page, Instagram, Twitter, or my website. Feel free to contact me at any time.

Thank you again for reading.

Much love,

Liz xxx

http://www.author-lgdavis.com

facebook.com/LGDavisBooks

twitter.com/lgdavisauthor

instagram.com/lgdavisauthor

# ACKNOWLEDGMENTS

Thank you so much for purchasing a copy of *Perfect Parents*. It really means the world to me. I can honestly say that this book was the most rewarding to write.

Even though writing is often a solitary endeavor, I owe a lot of gratitude to the people who were always there for me. Firstly, I want to thank my wonderful husband and children for always supporting me and inspiring me. Thank you for putting up with my long days on the computer when I had tight deadlines. I love you so much.

I would also like to thank the people behind the scenes who made this book shine. My editor, Rhianna Louise, deserves a special mention. The editing process for this book was not easy, but you've been there for me through the ups and downs. I'm not sure I can ever write another book without you by my side. Thank you so much for your insight and support. You are simply the best.

I also want to thank the wonderful people at Bookouture for giving me this opportunity to give this book its wings. The editors, publicity and marketing teams, the cover designers, the audiobook narrators, and everyone else who made this happen, you all deserve a big thank you. The experience of working with you all has been wonderful, and I am grateful and proud to be a member of the Bookouture family.

Last but not least, I want to thank all my readers who

have been with me from the start. I've said it before, but I'll keep saying it again: I couldn't have done this without you. If it weren't for you, I wouldn't be able to do what I love for a living. You are the reason I write.

Love you all.

Made in the USA
Monee, IL
09 September 2022

13687124R00173